核心素養
108課綱

英文閱讀素養訓練課

Super Reading
Story Training Book

經典文學故事

108 課綱閱讀素養培植書！

以名著閱讀法，打造閱讀原文書的實力
不用頻查字典就能品嚐最原味的感動

Michael A. Putlack & e-Creative Contents・著   陳怡靜／彭尊聖・譯

108課綱閱讀素養培植書！以名著閱讀法，打造閱讀原文書的實力！

一旦掌握英語閱讀的技能，就能藉由閱讀拓展國際視野，因此閱讀訓練非常重要，是一定要打好基礎的入門功夫，本套書要把閱讀訓練法中最有效的「**名著閱讀法**」傳授給你，幫助讀者**培養閱讀原文書的實力**，體驗不用頻查字典就能品味原文小說的感動。

1 本套書精選**15篇世界經典文學名著及改編童話故事**，如丹麥安徒生童話之中的《小美人魚》、英國大文豪狄更斯的《聖誕頌歌》、俄國寫實作家托爾斯泰的《人靠什麼活著》等大作，帶你品味文學芬芳，提升人文素養；搭配彩繪插圖，賞心悅目，增添學習樂趣。

2 本套書共有六個學習階段（6 steps），依文章難易度分為兩冊：

《童話寓言故事》 包含Step 1~Step 3，適合**初學**者
《經典文學故事》 包含Step 4~Step 6，適合**進階**學習者

3 每一冊各分兩大部分，精心設計各種實用學習幫手，讓你更有效率、更輕鬆地學會閱讀原文書：

課本 Main Book：全英語呈現，藉由學習幫手不需字典也能讀懂
訓練書 Training Book：英文語句、文法結構大解密

4 讀完一段課文後，隨即有**Stop & Think**測驗掌握**主旨**及**細節**的能力，以及有**Check Up**練習各種**常見的閱讀測驗題型**，如字彙選填、是非題及配合題等5種題型變化，不僅驗收閱讀理解成效，也為日後參加英語檢定考試作準備。

強力推薦給這些人！

- 準備會考和大考學測的學生。
- 想把英語根基扎得又深又牢的人。
- 想順暢閱讀《時代》雜誌推薦小說原著的人。
- 想在多益、托福等各種英文考試中得高分的人。
- 想上全英語教學或雙語教學課程的人。
- 正準備出國留學的人。

培養不用字典就能讀原文小說的實力，現在，就讓它變成你的競爭力吧。

How to Use This Book

本書的使用步驟

本套書共兩冊,每冊各分兩大部分,第一部分為**全英文的課本**,第二部分為**拆解英文語句的訓練書**,訓練書是為提升「即讀即解」的能力和「理解英語句子結構」的能力而編寫的。

Main Book 課本 | 六個學習階段(6 steps),共15篇故事。

1 **讀課文(Main Text)**
首先,只看全英文的課文,不懂的單字或用語,可以透過精心設計的學習幫手了解字義,因此不需字典也能讀懂課文:

- **彩圖字彙解說**,圖像學習超easy。
- **英英單字注釋**(Key Words),快速擴充字彙量。
- **課文中附註英文釋義**(English Definition),搭配上下文,熟練字彙運用。
- **文法解析**(Grammar Point)學習常見句型。

2 **試做練習題(Stop & Think / Check Up)**
讀完課文後,立即透過5種測驗題型,檢核字彙能力及文章理解程度。

Stop & Think ➡ 引導式問題,訓練你**抓出文章主旨**(main idea)及**細節**(details),以及培養獨立思考的能力。

Check Up ➡ 英語檢定常見題型,**是非題、字彙選填、選擇題**及**配合題**,為參加考試作準備。

Training Book　訓練書

訓練書提供了即讀即解的課文，以意義為單位來斷句，以斜線（/）標示句子的結構，還設計了**用法特寫**（Close Up）和**文法解析**（Grammar Point），加強英文句型及文法能力。書末附有課本的正確答案和翻譯。

Main Text
• **Chunking**
  for Speed Reading
• **Listen & Read Aloud**

Words to Know
Close Up

Translations and Expressions

Grammar Point

3　查看訓練書

首先將**單字學習**（Words to Know）裡重要關鍵英單的中文釋義瀏覽一遍，接著讀**斷句課文**（Chunking），藉由清楚劃分句子的結構，可達到「即讀即解」的成效。再對照**中文翻譯**與**重要片語中英對照**（Translations and Expressions），以意義為單位來理解英文課文，同時亦作為中英翻譯練習參考，還可透過學習幫手Close Up，和Grammar Point學習片語、句型及文法。

4　挑戰看斷句課文自行翻譯

現在不看翻譯，參考活用斷句標示（/），試著**自己翻譯英文課文**。若有不明之處，就再確認中文釋義和英文用法，反覆查看，直到完全理解為止。

5　聽MP3朗讀並複誦

背英文時，**一面看一面讀出聲音**，記得更牢。本書隨書附贈MP3，課文皆由英語母語人士以正確、清晰的發音朗讀。聽課文時，要注意斜線（/）斷句的地方，並注意聽母語人士的**發音、語調及連音**等。最好自己在課文上把語調和連音標示出來，然後大聲地跟著MP3朗誦，盡量跟上英語母語人士的速度。

6　不聽MP3，自己朗讀課文

接著，不聽MP3，自己唸課文，並盡量唸得與母語人士一樣。若有發音或語調不順的地方，就再聽一次MP3，反覆練習。

7　重新閱讀英文課文

現在再回來看課本，再讀一次英文課文，並試著解題，如果讀得很順，練習題也都答對，訓練就成功了。

★ 正確答案請見訓練書書末的〈Answers & Translations〉。

The Introduction of Training Book

訓練書特色說明

透過「斷句」掌握「即讀即解」的竅門

　　為了能更快、更正確地閱讀英文，就需要能夠掌握英文的句子結構。而要培養英文句子結構的敏銳度，最好的方法就是以各「**意義單元組**」來理解句子，也就是將英文句子的「意義單元組」（具一個完整意義的片語或詞組），用**斷句**（chunk）的方式分開，然後再來理解句子。只要能理解各個「意義單元組」，那麼再長的句子，都能被拆解與理解。

　　聽力也是一樣，要區分「意義單元組」，這樣能幫助很快聽懂英文。例如下面這個句子可以拆解成兩個部分：

I am angry / at you.
我生氣　　　對你

　　我們會發現，這個句子由兩個「意義單元組」所組成。不管句子多長多複雜，都是由最簡單的**基本句型（主詞＋動詞）**發展而成，然後再在這個主要句子上，依照需求，添加上許多片語，以表現各式各樣的句意。

　　在面對英文時，腦子裡能立刻自動快速分離基本句型和片語，就能迅速讀懂或聽懂英文。在讀誦英文時，從一個人的斷句，大致就能看出個人的英文能力。現在再來看稍微長一點的句子。經過斷句以後，整個句子變得更清楚易懂，閱讀理解就沒問題了：

Beauty was not only pretty / but also kind and smart.
美麗不僅漂亮　　　　　　　還很善良、聰明

一個句子有幾個斷句？

一個句子有幾個斷句？有幾個「意義單元組」？這是依句子的情況和個人的英語能力，而有不同的。一般來說，以下這些地方通常就是**斷句的地方**：

★ 在「主詞＋動詞」之後
★ 在 and、but、or 等連接詞之前
★ 在 that、who 等關係詞之前
★ 在副詞、不定詞 to 等的前後

另外，**主詞很長**時，時常為了要區分出主詞，在**主詞後也會斷句**。例如：

A man / who wants to learn / can learn anything.
人　　　願意學習　　　　　　就能學會任何事

對初學者來說，一個句子裡可能會有很多斷句的斜線，而當閱讀能力越來越強之後，你需要斷句的地方就會越來越少，到後來甚至能一眼就看懂句子，不需要用斷句的方式來幫助理解。

本訓練書因為考慮到初學者，所以盡可能細分可斷句處，只要是能分為一個「意義單元組」的地方，訓練書上就標示出斷句。等你的英文實力逐漸提升，到了覺得斷句變成是一種累贅，能夠不用再做任何標記就能讀懂課文時，就是你的英文能力更進一階的時候了。透過斷句的練習，熟悉英語的排列順序和結構，你會驚訝地發現到，自己的閱讀能力突飛猛進！

Table of
Contents

《 經典文學故事 》

《童話寓言故事》

Step 1

Step 2

Step 3

Super
Reading
Story
Training
Book

MAIN
BOOK

Step

4

What Men Live By

— Leo Tolstoy

•

How Much Land Does a Man Need?

— Leo Tolstoy

What Men Live By

♪ 01

shoemaker

hut

fret

naked

There was once a poor shoemaker named Simon. He had no house or land. He lived in a hut with his wife *---> small house, cottage* and children. One morning, he went to the village to buy some sheepskins for a winter coat. He had only three rubles, but he planned to visit some of his *---> was going to* customers on the way. They owed him five rubles for *while going there <---* *---> had to pay* work he had already done.

Simon visited several customers' houses, but he could not collect any money. He went to the store and *---> gather, receive* asked if he could buy the sheepskins on credit. But the *---> whether* *---> without cash* shopkeeper refused to give them to Simon. *---> turned down ≠ accepted*

Simon felt downhearted and started walking *---> was sad* homeward. "Though I have no sheepskin coat, I don't care. I can live without a coat. Yet my wife will surely *---> Still, Nevertheless* fret," he thought. *---> get upset*

While he was walking home, he passed by a church *---> went by*

Stop & Think

Why couldn't Simon pay for the sheepskins?

KEY WORDS

- **on the way** while going somewhere
- **refuse** to turn down; to reject
- **homeward** toward home
- **robber** a thief
- **look back** to look behind oneself

- **owe** to have to pay money to
- **feel downhearted** to be sad; to be depressed
- **naked** having no clothes on
- **interfere** to get involved
- **frightened** scared

at the bend in the road. Simon saw something white behind the church. He did not know what it was. He came closer, and, to his surprise, it was a naked man. He was sitting against the church without any clothes on.

→ not wearing any clothes

Suddenly, Simon felt afraid. "Robbers must have killed him and stolen his clothes. If I interfere, I will have a big problem," Simon thought.

Thieves ←

steal–stole–stolen ←

→ get involved

Simon continued walking, but when he looked back, he saw the man was moving. Simon felt more frightened.

→ scared

"If I go there, he might kill me for my clothes. Even if he doesn't attack me, what can I do for him?" thought Simon.

Even though ←

→ ≠ defend

He ran down the road. But he suddenly stopped.

robber

Stop & Think

What did Simon see behind the church?

CHECK UP True or false?

1 Simon had five rubles. _____
2 Simon wanted to buy some sheepskins. _____
3 There was a robber next to the church. _____
4 Simon was afraid of the naked man. _____

GRAMMAR POINT

though / if / even if

- **Though** I have no sheepskin coat, I don't care.
- **If** I interfere, I will have a big problem.
- **Even if** he doesn't attack me, what can I do for him? (**even if = even though**)

stick

surprised

felt boots

"What am I doing? The man could be dying!" He felt guilty, so he turned around and went back to the church. `--> felt bad`   `--> turned back`

When Simon went behind the church, he saw that the stranger was a young man. He was freezing and frightened. `--> very cold` Simon immediately took off his coat and put it around the man. `--> removed ≠ put on` Then, he put boots on the man. `--> ≠ took off` Simon had an extra pair of boots. `--> additional`

"Can you walk?" asked Simon. "It's too cold to stay here. I will take you to my home. Here is a stick for you to lean on while you walk." `--> rest on`

The man stood up and looked kindly at Simon. But `--> got up *stand-stood-stood` he did not speak. As they walked to Simon's home, Simon asked him where he was from and how he got to the church. The man replied with a calm voice, "I'm not from around here. God has punished me." `--> quiet`

Simon was surprised by the response. But he said, "Well, God rules all men. Come home with me and at `--> controls`

Stop & Think
What did Simon give the man?

KEY WORDS

- **feel guilty** to feel bad
- **freezing** very cold
- **punish** to penalize a person for doing something wrong
- **disappointment** the state of being disappointed; displeasure
- **drunk** a person who is drunk
- **drunkard** a drunk
- **go back** to return
- **lean on** to lean against; to rest on
- **supper** a light dinner

least make yourself warm." As Simon walked with the stranger, he felt glad to help another person.

Simon's wife was preparing dinner when Simon and the man came into the house. Matryna noticed that the man had no hat and was wearing felt boots. And he was wearing her husband's coat. Simon had no sheepskins. Her heart was ready to break with disappointment. "He has been out drinking, and now he has brought another drunk home with him," she thought.

drunk = drunkard

bench

vodka

saw, became aware ←
was about to →
≠ satisfaction →
bring–brought–brought

Simon took off his hat and sat down on the bench as if things were all right. Then, he said, "Have a seat, my friend, and let us have some dinner."

Matryna became very angry and said, "I cooked dinner, but not for you. You went out to buy some sheepskins but bring a strange man home instead. He doesn't even have any clothes of his own. You must have spent all our money on vodka. I have no supper for drunkards like you."

drunks →

Stop & Think
What did Simon's wife think about her husband?

CHECK UP Finish the sentences.

1 The man said that
2 Simon felt glad
3 Matryna was
4 Matryna thought that Simon

a. very disappointed with Simon.
b. to help another person.
c. was a drunkard.
d. God had punished him.

GRAMMAR POINT

what/where/how . . . + S + V (indirect question)
• Simon asked him **where he was** from and **how he got** to the church.

curious

anger

be folded

in pain

Simon tried to explain to his wife how he had met the man, but she did not listen. She angrily walked out the door, but then she stopped undecidedly; she wanted ⤳ *not decided, not determined*
to work off her anger, but she also wanted to learn what ⤳ *release*
sort of a man the stranger was. She was curious about the man.

"If he were a good man, he would not be naked. Where is he from?" she asked.

"That's just what I'm trying to tell you," answered Simon. "When I passed the church, I saw him sitting ⤳ *went by*
there naked and frozen. God made me go to help him, *ice cold* ⤶
or he would have died. What should I have done? So I helped him get up, gave him my coat, and brought him here. Don't be so angry with me. Anger is a sin."
⤳ *Being mad or angry*

As Matryna listened to her husband, she looked closely at the man. He sat on the bench without moving. His hands were folded on his knees, and he looked down at the floor. His eyes were closed as if he ⤳ *fold–folded–folded*
were in pain.
⤳ *hurting, pained*

Stop & Think

What did Simon say to make Matryna calm down?

KEY WORDS

- **undecidedly** unable to make up one's mind
- **sin** something one does that is against the laws of God
- **be in pain** to hurt   • **soften** to become less hard (≠ harden)
- **feel pity for** to feel bad for someone (= take pity on)   • **feed** to give food to someone
- **reward** to give something to someone for doing a good deed

"Matryna, don't you love God?" asked Simon.

Suddenly, her heart softened toward the stranger. She
became soft
went back into the kitchen. She set the table and served

set the table

dinner. While they were eating, Matryna felt pity for
felt sorry
the stranger. She did not feel angry anymore. She even

began to like him. At that moment, the man looked

at Matryna and smiled at her. A light seemed to come
appeared to
from his face.

When they had finished supper, she asked the man

where he was from. But the man said he did not know.

All he said was, "God punished
me. I was naked and freezing
cold. Then, Simon saw
felt pity for, pitied
me, took pity on me, and
brought me here. You have
feed–fed–fed
fed me and pitied me, too.
pity–pitied–pitied
God will reward you."
repay ≠ punish

CHECK UP Answer the questions.

1 What did Matryna feel for the stranger?
   a. concern   **b.** love   **c.** pity

2 What happened after the man smiled?
   a. A light came from his face.   **b.** Simon felt pity for him.   **c.** Matryna's heart softened.

GRAMMAR POINT

if . . . (subjunctive)

• If he **were** a good man, he **would** not **be** naked.
• God made me go to help him, or he **would have died**.
  (= **If** God **had** not **made** me go to help him, he **would have died**.)

grieved

wake up

Matryna gave the man some clothes, and he went to get some sleep. Then, she and Simon went to bed, too, but Matryna could not sleep. She could not get the stranger out of her mind. Then, she suddenly remembered that they had eaten their last piece of bread, so there was nothing left for tomorrow. She felt grieved. → *felt sad, felt very bad*

forgot

"Simon, what will we do tomorrow?"

"As long as we are alive, we will find something to eat," Simon answered.

The next morning, Simon and Matryna woke up and saw that the stranger was already awake. He looked much better than the day before. *not sleeping ≠ asleep*

Simon said, "Well, friend, we have to work for a living. What work do you know?"

"I do not know anything," answered the man.

Surprised, Simon said, "A man who wants to learn can learn anything." *Shocked*

"Then I will learn how to work."

"What is your name?" asked Simon.

Stop & Think

What work did Michael know?

KEY WORDS

- **get . . . out of one's mind** to forget about something   • **feel grieved** to feel very bad
- **wake up** ≠ fall asleep   • **awake** ≠ asleep
- **carriage** a wagon drawn by horses   • **servant** a person who works for another
- **stride into** to walk into *stride–strode–stridden   • **master** a skilled person; a person in charge

"Michael."

"Well, Michael, if you work with me, I will give you food and shelter," offered Simon.

carriage

"May God reward you," answered Michael. "Show me what to do."

→ *a safe place, a home*

Simon showed Michael how to make boots. Michael learned quickly and was very skilled. He ate little food and almost never went anywhere.

→ *skillful*

servant

He made boots so well that many people came to Simon's shop. Soon, Simon began to make a lot of money.

→ *earn money*

A year passed. Michael lived and worked with Simon. One day, Simon and Michael were working hard when a carriage drawn by three horses drove up to the hut. A servant opened the door, and a gentleman wearing a fur coat got out. He strode into the hut and asked, "Which of you is the master bootmaker?"

→ *pulled by *draw–drew–drawn*

→ *went up to *drive–drove–driven*

→ *got off ≠ got on*

→ *walked into*

→ *shoemaker*

fur coat

Stop & Think

Who was in the carriage?

CHECK UP Put the right words.

| Michael | skilled | bread | shelter |

1 Simon and Matryna had no more of _____ .
2 The stranger's name was _____ .
3 Simon offered Michael food and _____ in return for work.
4 Michael became a very _____ bootmaker.

GRAMMAR POINT

"–ing" form (present participle) / "–ed" form (past participle)

• *A gentleman **wearing** a fur coat got out.* (**active meaning**)

• *A carriage **drawn** by three horses drove up to the hut.* (**passive meaning**)

leather

lose one's shape

"I am, sir," Simon answered.

Then the gentleman said, "Do you see this leather here?"

"Yes, it is good leather, sir."

"You fool," laughed the gentleman. "It is the finest [best, nicest] leather. It comes from Germany and is extremely [very, really] expensive. I want you to make me a pair of boots that will last [remain in a good condition] for years. If they lose their shape [change shape] or fall apart [break], I will throw [send] you into prison [jail]. After one year, if the boots are still good, I will pay you ten rubles for them," said the rich man.

Simon was terrified [very scared], but Michael advised him to make the boots. So Simon agreed, and then he measured the gentleman's feet. While he was doing that, Simon saw Michael was gazing behind the rich man as if someone were there. [looking, staring]

Suddenly, Michael smiled, and his face turned bright. → became

"What are you grinning at, you fool?" shouted the → smiling at
man. "You had better make these boots on time. I will
come back in two days." → not late

prison

"They will be ready," answered Michael.

After he left, Simon looked at Michael and said,
"Michael, we must be cautious with this expensive → careful
leather. We cannot make a single mistake."

measure

Michael started cutting the leather, but he did not
cut it for boots. Instead, he started to make soft slippers.
Simon saw what Michael was doing, and he was
shocked. → surprised

slippers

"What are you doing, Michael? The gentleman
ordered boots, not slippers. You've ruined that leather. → spoiled, destroyed
What's going to happen to me now?"

Stop & Think

What did Michael do when he looked behind the gentleman?

CHECK UP   Choose the right words.

1 The gentleman showed Simon some _____ leather. (expensive | cheap)
2 The gentleman _____ Simon. (angered | terrified)
3 The gentleman wanted his boots in _____. (two weeks | two days)
4 Michael made _____ for the gentleman. (boots | slippers)

GRAMMAR POINT

as if . . . (subjunctive)

• Michael was gazing behind the rich man **as if** someone **were** there.

rush

corpse

crippled

At that very moment, the gentleman's servant rushed into the hut. *hurried into, ran into* ←

"My master does not need boots anymore," he announced. "He is dead. He did not even make it home alive as he died in the carriage. My master's wife sent me here to cancel the order for boots. Instead, she wants you to quickly make a pair of soft slippers for his corpse." *dead body*

stated, said →

because, since →

stop →

shocked, stunned →

Simon was amazed. Michael took the pair of soft slippers he made and handed them to the servant. *gave to* →

More time passed, and Michael had now lived with Simon for six years. He never went anywhere, and he was always quiet. He had only smiled two times in six years: once when Matryna gave him food and a second time when the rich man was in their hut. Simon adored Michael and was afraid that Michael would leave him. *didn't go anywhere* → *for* → *liked very much, loved* ←

One day, one of Simon's sons came running to Michael. "Uncle Michael," he cried, "Look! A lady with two little girls is coming, and one of the girls is lame." *unable to walk properly* ←

Stop & Think

What happened to the gentleman?

KEY WORDS

- **corpse** a dead body
- **hand . . . to** to give something to someone
- **lame** unable to walk properly
- **be a master at** to be very skilled at doing something
- **confused** puzzled; not understanding
- **give birth to** to bear; to produce a baby
- **amazed** shocked; stunned
- **adore** to like very much (≠ hate)
- **crippled** disabled
- **crush one's leg** to break one's leg

Michael immediately stopped work and looked out the window. Simon was surprised since Michael never looked outside. Simon also looked out and saw that a well–dressed woman with two little girls was coming to his hut. One of the girls was crippled in her left leg.
  --→ disabled

The woman came in and said, "I want leather shoes for these two girls for spring."

Simon answered, "I have never made such small shoes, but my assistant Michael is a master at making shoes, so he can do it."
   --→ helper   --→ is very skilled at

Michael was staring at the girls as if he had known
looking at, gazing at ←----   --→ like
them before. Simon was confused, but he began to
   --→ puzzled
measure the girls' feet. The woman mentioned that the girls were twins.
   --→ said, told

Simon asked, "How did it happen to her? Was she born this way?"
   broke, squashed ←---
"No," the woman answered. "Her mother crushed her leg. Their father died one week before they were
  --→ die–died–died
born. And their mother died right after she gave birth to them."
   bore ←--

twins

give birth to

CHECK UP True or false?

1 Michael smiled two times in six years.   _____
2 A woman with two girls came to Simon's hut.   _____
3 The two girls were cousins.   _____
4 The woman was the girls' mother.   _____

GRAMMAR POINT

tense agreement

• Simon **was** afraid that Michael **would** leave him.

nurse

sigh

wipe tears

She continued, "My husband and I were their neighbors. When I visited their hut, I found that the mother, when dying, had rolled on this child and crushed her leg. The babies were left alone. What could I do? I was the only woman in the village with a baby, so I took both girls and nursed them as well.

people who live near another

rolled over onto

broke

"I thought the crippled one would die, so I did not feed her at first. But I had so much milk that I could feed my son and both girls. Then, my own son died when he was two." She sighed.

"I thank God for giving me these two girls. I would be very lonely without them. They are precious to me."

lonesome, feeling alone

very dear, valuable

She wiped some tears from her face as she told the story.

wipe–wiped–wiped

a wise saying

Then, Matryna said, "The old proverb is true. 'One may live without father or mother, but one cannot live without God.'"

Stop & Think

How did the girl's leg get injured?

KEY WORDS

- **roll on** to roll over onto
- **nurse** to provide milk for a baby; to feed
- **lonely** feeling alone
- **proverb** a wise saying
- **forgive** to pardon *forgive–forgave–forgiven

- **crush** to break; to squash
- **sigh** to exhale loudly
- **precious** dear; valuable
- **bow** to bend over in a sign of respect
- **gloomy** sad; depressing

As they talked, suddenly a bright light filled the room. They looked at Michael, who was the source of this light. He was smiling and looking up at the heavens.

origin ←

the sky →

heavens

After the woman left with the girls, Michael bowed low to Simon and Matryna. "Farewell," he said. "God has forgiven me. I ask your forgiveness, too, for anything I have done wrong."

Goodbye →

pardoned →

beg forgiveness →

bow

They saw a light was shining from Michael. Simon bowed to Michael and said, "I see that you are not an ordinary man. But please tell me. When I first met you and brought you home, you were quite gloomy. But you smiled at my wife after she gave you some food. Then, when the rich man came and ordered boots, you smiled again. Finally, when the woman brought the girls, you smiled a third time. And now you have become as bright as day. Why is your face shining like that, and why did you smile those three times?"

normal →

sad, depressing →

shine

Stop & Think

What happened as everyone was talking?

CHECK UP Finish the sentences.

1 The woman said the girls
2 Michael asked Simon and Matryna
3 Simon realized that Michael

a. was not an ordinary man.
b. were precious to her.
c. to forgive him.

GRAMMAR POINT

may

• One **may** live without father or mother. (**possibility**)

Michael answered, "Light is shining from me because I was punished, but now God has forgiven me. I smiled three times because God sent me here to learn three truths, and I have learned them. I learned the first
----> facts
when your wife pitied me, so I smiled then. I learned
----> at that time
the second when the rich man ordered the boots, so I smiled again. And I learned the third when I saw the little girls, so I smiled for the third time."

Simon asked, "Michael, why did God punish you? And what are the three truths? I would like to learn them for myself."

Michael answered, "God punished me because I disobeyed him. I was an angel in Heaven, but I
----> ≠ obey
disobeyed God. God sent me to take the soul of a
make the person die <----
woman. I came down to Earth and saw a sick woman lying alone. She had just given birth to twin girls. The woman saw me and said, 'Angel of God, my husband has just died, and there is no one to look after my girls.
----> nurse, take care of

angel

breast

pray

Stop & Think

Why did God punish Michael?

KEY WORDS

- **disobey** to not follow a command or order
- **care for** to take care of
- **pray** to make a prayer
- **dwell** to live

- **lie alone** to be by oneself
- **breast** a woman's chest
- **stay alive** to not die
- **live by** to be supported by

Do not take my soul. Let me live to care for my babies. Children cannot live without father or mother.'"

→ take care of

Michael continued, "I put one child at her breast and put the other in her arms. Then, I returned to Heaven. I told God, 'I could not take the mother's soul. Her husband died, and the woman has twins and prays to stay alive.'"

→ live, not to die

"But God said, 'Go back and take the woman's soul, and learn three truths: Learn what dwells in man. **Learn what is not given to man.** And learn what men live by. When you learn all three things, you may return to Heaven.'"

→ lives

→ be supported by

What did God order Michael to learn about?

CHECK UP Answer the questions.

1 Why did Michael smile three times?
   a. He learned three truths.   **b.** He saw God.   **c.** He knew the little girls.

2 Whose soul was Michael supposed to take?
   a. Simon's soul   **b.** the mother's soul   **c.** the girls' souls

GRAMMAR POINT

be + p.p. (passive)

- I **was punished** (by God), but now God has forgiven me.
- Learn what **is** not **given** to man.

wings

crawl

frown

→ returned *fly–flew–flown

"So I <u>flew</u> back to Earth and took the mother's soul. The babies <u>fell</u> from her breast. Her body rolled over on the bed and <u>crushed</u> one of the baby's legs. I tried to fly up to Heaven with the mother's soul, but my wings suddenly <u>dropped off</u>. Then, I fell to Earth. That is how you found me, Simon."

→ fall–fell–fallen

→ fell off

Simon and Matryna now understood who had been living with them, so they began to cry for <u>joy</u>.

→ happiness

The angel Michael said, "I was alone in the field and naked. I had never known cold or hunger until I became a man. I crawled to a church. Then, I saw a man coming down the road.

"He frowned as he passed me, but he came back a few minutes later. He gave me some clothes and brought me to his house. When I entered the house, his wife <u>seemed</u> very angry. She wanted to send me back into the cold, but her husband mentioned God to her. The woman changed <u>at once</u>. When she brought me some

looked ←

→ instantly

Stop & Think

What did Michael do when he returned to Earth?

KEY WORDS

- **drop off** to fall off
- **frown** ≠ smile
- **mention** to say about something
- **crawl** to walk on one's hands and feet
- **stand** ≠ sit
- **last** to continue in time; to remain in useful condition

food, I looked at her. I noticed she had changed. She had become alive, and God was in her." →teaching

"Then, I remembered the first lesson God had sent me. God told me, 'Learn what dwells in man.' I understood. It was love. Love lives in men. God had shown me the first truth, so I smiled." ⇢ show–showed–shown

"After a year, a rich gentleman came to order some boots. I looked at him and saw the Angel of Death standing behind him. Only I could see the Angel of Death, so I knew that he would die soon. The man was about to die, yet he wanted boots that would last for years." → was going to

command

"Then, I remembered God's second order: 'Learn what is not given to man.' I learned that men are not given the knowledge to know what they need. So I smiled for a second time."

Stop & Think

What was the second truth?

CHECK UP   Choose the right words.

1   Michael could return to _____ after he learned all three truths. (Heaven | Earth)
2   Michael learned the _____ truth from Matryna. (first | second)
3   Michael learned another truth from the _____. (rich man | poor man)

GRAMMAR POINT

not/never . . . until . . .

• I had **never** known cold or hunger **until** I became a man.

roof

ray of light

"I still did not know the third truth, so I have waited for God to reveal it.
→ show ≠ hide

"In my sixth year here, the woman and the two girls came. I recognized the girls and listened to how the
→ knew
woman had kept them alive. After she told the story, I
→ living ≠ dead
realized that the woman had loved two children who were not her own. I saw the living God in her, and then I learned the last lesson: I learned what men live by. I knew God had revealed it to me and had forgiven me, so I smiled for a third time."

→ was enclosed by
Just then, Michael's body was surrounded by a bright light. He said, "I have learned that all men live not by care for themselves but by love. I did not die because a man and his wife took pity on me and loved me. The

Stop & Think
What was the third truth?

KEY WORDS

- **reveal** to show (≠ hide)
- **recognize** to know who a person is
- **be surrounded by** to be enclosed by; to be encircled by
- **orphan** a child with no parents
- **ray of light** a sunbeam; sunlight
- **spread** to extend
- **remain** to be left

children with no parents

orphans stayed alive because of the love of a woman who was not their mother. And **all men live because love is in them.** A person who has love is in God, and God is in that person because God is love."

Then, the roof opened, and a ray of light fell down from Heaven. Michael spread his
spread–spread–spread
wings and flew up in the light.
went up
Simon stood there, gazing after him. After a while, the roof was closed. No one but Simon and his family remained.
were left

CHECK UP Choose the right words.

1 Michael learned the _____ truth from the woman. (third | second)
2 A _____ light surrounded Michael's body. (dim | bright)
3 Did Michael fly away from Simon's house? (Yes | No)

GRAMMAR POINT

because+S+V / because of+noun

- I did not die **because** a man and his wife took pity on me and loved me.
- The orphans stayed alive **because of** the love of a woman.
- All men live **because** love is in them.

How Much Land Does a Man Need?

An elder sister went to visit her younger sister in the country. The elder sister was married to a tradesman in town and the younger sister to a peasant in the village.

peasant

As the sisters sat over their tea talking, the elder began *[poor farmer]* *[talking over a cup of tea]* to boast about the advantages of town life. She talked *[brag]* *[benefit ≠ disadvantages]* about how comfortably they lived there, how well *[easily]* they dressed, what good things they ate and drank, and how she went to the theater and other types of entertainment. *[something fun]*

theater

The younger sister was annoyed and in turn mocked *[bothered]* *[laughed at]* the life of a tradesman. She stood up for the life of a peasant. *[defended]*

"I would not change my way of life for yours," she said. "We may live roughly, but at least we are free *[toughly]* from anxiety. You live in a better style than we do, but *[worry]* though you often earn more than you need, you are very likely to lose all you have." *[seem to, look like]*

Stop & Think

Why was the younger sister annoyed?

KEY WORDS

- **peasant** a poor farmer
- **in turn** one after another; as a result of something
- **stand up for** to defend
- **chatter** talking; gossip

- **annoyed** bothered
- **mock** to make fun of; to laugh at
- **lie on** to recline on
- **the Devil** Satan; Lucifer

She continued, "We know the proverb 'Loss and gain are brothers twain.' It often happens that people who are wealthy one day are begging for their bread the next. Our way is safer. Though a peasant's life is not a fat one, it is long."

> saying
> two
> asking for
> not a rich life
> the head of the household

beg

Pahom, the master of the house, was lying on the top of the stove, and he listened to the women's chatter.

"It is perfectly true," he said. "Busy as we are from childhood farming Mother Earth, we peasants have no time to let any nonsense settle in our heads. Our only trouble is that we haven't got enough land. If I had plenty of land, I wouldn't fear the Devil himself!"

> talking, gossip
> the earth
> live in
> be afraid of

The women finished their tea, chatted a while about dresses, and then cleared away the tea things and lay down to sleep. But the Devil had been sitting behind the stove and had heard all that was said.

> cleaned up

Stop & Think
How would Pahom feel if he had plenty of land?

CHECK UP   Answer the questions.

1   How did the younger sister feel about her way of life?
   a. She felt anxious.   **b.** She liked it.   **c.** She wanted to change it.

2   Where was the Devil sitting?
   a. on the stove   **b.** behind the stove   **c.** under the stove

GRAMMAR POINT

that + S + V (that−clause)

- **It** often happens **that** people who are wealthy one day are begging for their bread the next.
- Our only trouble is **that** we haven't got enough land.

seed

sow

harvest

plow

He was pleased to hear that the man had boasted that if he had plenty of land, he would not fear the Devil himself.

"All right," thought the Devil. "We will have a contest. I'll give you enough land, and by means of that land, I will get you into my power."

compete, bet

through

One day, Pahom heard that a neighbor was going to buy fifty acres of land, so he felt envious. Pahom and his wife sold some of their property and borrowed some money. Then, they bought a farm of forty acres.

sell–sold–sold

was jealous

≠ lent

So now Pahom had land of his own. He borrowed seed and sowed it on the land he had bought. The harvest was a good one, and within a year, he had managed to pay off his debts. So he became a landowner. When he went out to plow his fields or to look at his growing corn, his heart would fill with joy.

planted

pay back the money

be filled with

KEY WORDS

- **property** land or buildings
- **trespass** to go onto land that is not one's own
- **district court** regional court
- **be taught a lesson** to be punished
- **sneak onto** to go somewhere without being seen

- **manage to** to be able to do; to deal with
- **lose patience** to become impatient
- **overlook** to ignore; to forget about
- **upset with** angry at
- **take someone to court** to sue a person

However, over time, some of the peasants in the neighborhood began to trespass across Pahom's land with their cows and horses. For a long time, Pahom forgave the owners. But at last he lost patience and complained to the district court. He thought, "I cannot go on overlooking it, or they will destroy all I have. They must be taught a lesson."

> as time goes by

became impatient ←

> forgiving

> be punished *teach–taught–taught

sneak

Pahom began to fine his neighbors for trespassing on his land. This made them very upset with him, so they started to trespass on his land on purpose. Sometimes, they even sneaked onto his land at night and chopped down his trees. Pahom was furious.

> charge money

> angry at

intentionally ←

cut down

> very angry

furious

He tried to figure out who was doing it, and he decided that it was probably Simon. He took Simon to court, but Pahom had no evidence against Simon. The judges let Simon go, so Pahom got angry at them and quarreled with the judges and with his neighbors. Threats to burn his building began to be uttered.

> find out

> sued

> proof

> Warnings

said ←

judge

Stop & Think

Why did Pahom fine his neighbors?

CHECK UP Finish the sentences.

1 The Devil decided to
2 Pahom bought a farm
3 Pahom's neighbors began to
4 Pahom took Simon

a. and became a landowner.
b. trespass on his land on purpose.
c. have a contest with Pahom.
d. to court for trespassing.

GRAMMAR POINT

if . . . (subjunctive)

• If he **had** plenty of land, he **would** not **fear** the Devil himself.

rumor

estate

About this time, there was a rumor that many people were moving to a new place. "There's no need for me to leave my land," thought Pahom. "But some of the others might leave our village, and then there would be more room for us. I would take over their land myself and make my estate a bit bigger."

gossip

space

land

get control of

One day, Pahom was sitting at home when a peasant passing through the village happened to call on him. The peasant was allowed to stay the night, and supper was given to him. Pahom had a talk with this peasant and asked him where he had come from. The stranger answered that he had come from beyond the Volga River, where he had been working. He said that many people were moving there. Anyone who moved to the village was given twenty–five acres of land for free.

going through

visit

past

for nothing

"The land there is very good," said the peasant. "One peasant moved to the village with nothing at all, but now he is very wealthy."

Pahom's heart was filled with desire. He thought, "Why should I suffer in this narrow hole if one can live

experience pain

Stop & Think

What did the stranger tell Pahom about the village?

KEY WORDS

- **rumor** gossip or information which may not be true
- **pass through** to go through
- **for free** without having to pay money for
- **find out** to learn about
- **grow tired of** to get tired of; to dislike

- **estate** a large amount of land
- **call on** to visit a person
- **suffer** to experience pain
- **better off** richer; wealthier
- **rush for** to hurry after; to run to

so well elsewhere? I will sell my land here, and with the money I get, I will start all over again with more land. But I must first go and find out all about it myself."

> once again, from beginning

ten times

So Pahom went down to the land beyond the Volga. It was just as the stranger had said. The peasants owned plenty of land. The village gave each person twenty–five acres of land, and people could also buy as much land as they could afford. Pahom moved with his family to the new settlement.

> had

> be able to pay

> place to live

argue

Pahom had much more land than before. In fact, he was ten times better off than he had been. This made Pahom very happy. But after he got used to it, he began to think that even here he did not have enough land. He grew tired of having to rent other people's land every year. Wherever there was good land to be had, the peasants would rush for it and argue about the land.

> richer, wealthier

> was adapted to

> got tired of

> lease

> run to

Stop & Think

Why was Pahom not happy in the village?

CHECK UP True or false?

1 The peasant came from a land beyond the Volga River. _____
2 The village beyond the Volga gave everyone 250 acres of land for free. _____
3 Pahom visited the village to find out about the land. _____
4 Pahom was ten times better off than before. _____

GRAMMAR POINT

where / wherever (relative adverb)

- He went to *a place* **where** they had pitched their tents.

- He had come from *beyond the Volga River*, **where** he had been working.

- **Wherever** there was good land to be had, the peasants would rush for it.

chief

prairie

gift

"If it were my own land," thought Pahom, "I would be <u>independent</u>, and there would not be all this unpleasantness."

> *free ≠ dependent*

So Pahom began <u>looking out for</u> land which he could buy. One day, a <u>peddler</u> went by his house. He said that he was just returning from the land of the Bashkirs, which was far away. There, he had bought thirteen thousand acres of land for one thousand rubles.

> *searching for, hunting for*
> *tradesman, merchant*

"That area has so much land that you could walk for a year and still be in the land of the Bashkirs. They sell their land for very cheap prices. All one has to do is make friends with the chief. The land lies near a river, and the whole prairie is <u>virgin soil</u>."

> *undeveloped land*

Pahom was curious, so he <u>made up his mind</u> to visit the land of the Bashkirs. Before he went there, he bought some gifts. The peddler had told him that it was their <u>custom</u> to give gifts.

> *decided*

traditional habit ←

On the seventh day of his travels, he came to a place where the Bashkirs had <u>pitched</u> their tents. It was all just as the peddler had said. The people lived by a river on the steppes in felt–covered tents.

> *put up, built*

Stop & Think

How much land did the peddler buy?

KEY WORDS

- **unpleasantness** ugliness; a bad situation
- **pitch** to put up a tent
- **felt–covered tent** a tent that has felt on it
- **uneducated** having no schooling
- **make up one's mind** to decide
- **steppe** a plain; a grassland
- **despite** in spite of

They were a simple people. They did not farm at all.
The men merely sat around, drank tea, ate lamb, and
<u>~~~~</u>⟶ only, just
played their pipes to make music. Still, despite being
in spite of ⟵
uneducated and knowing no Russian, they were good–
<u>~~~~</u>⟶ not educated
natured enough.
warm–hearted, kind–hearted ⟵

lamb

As soon as they saw Pahom, they came out of their
tents and gathered around their visitor. An interpreter
translator ⟵
was found, and Pahom told them he had come about
some land. They took Pahom and led him into one of
the best tents. Pahom took some presents out

cart

of his cart and distributed
gave, passed out ⟵
them among the Bashkirs.
The Bashkirs were
delighted.
⌐
very happy, pleased

CHECK UP Put the right words.

> tents   peddler   visit   interpreter

1 The _____ said that the Bashkirs sold their land for cheap prices.
2 Pahom decided to _____ the land of the Bashkirs.
3 The Bashkirs pitched their _____ beside a river.
4 Pahom told the _____ that he had come about some land.

GRAMMAR POINT

which (relative pronoun)

• So Pahom began looking out for *land* **which** he could buy.
↑_____⌐

• He was just returning from *the land of the Bashkirs*, **which** was far away.

present

crowded

exhausted

point out

The Bashkirs talked for a while and then told the interpreter to translate. "They wish to tell you," said the interpreter, "that they like you, and that it is our custom to do all we can to please a guest and to repay him for his gifts. You have given us presents. Now tell us which of the things we possess please you best so that we may present them to you."

interpret ←--- --→ *want to*

pay back ←---

have, own →

give, award →

"What pleases me best here," answered Pahom, "is your land. Our land is crowded, and the soil is exhausted; but you have plenty of land, and it is good land." The interpreter translated.

full of people →

used up, old →

The Bashkirs talked among themselves for a while. Then, they were silent and looked at Pahom while the interpreter said, "They wish me to tell you that in return for your presents, they will gladly give you as much land as you want. You have only to point it out with your hand, and it is yours."

quiet →

as payment for →

Stop & Think

What did Pahom say about the Bashkirs' land?

KEY WORDS

- **translate** to interpret
- **possess** to have; to own
- **crowded** full of people (≠ empty)
- **in return for** as payment for something
- **have a dispute** to argue
- **rise to one's feet** to stand up

- **repay** to pay a person back for something
- **present** to give; to award
- **exhausted** used up; spent; old
- **point out** to show
- **in one's absence** while one is not around
- **address** to speak to

The Bashkirs talked again for a while and began to have a dispute. Pahom asked what they were arguing about. The interpreter told him that some of them thought they ought to ask their chief about the land and ought not to act in his absence.

> argue
> should
> while he is not around

dispute

While the Bashkirs were arguing, a man in a large fox–fur cap appeared on the scene. They all became silent and rose to their feet. The interpreter said, "This is our chief himself."

> on the spot
> stood up *rise–rose–risen

dressing gown

Pahom immediately took out the best dressing gown and five pounds of tea, and he offered these to the chief. The chief accepted them and seated himself in the place of honor. The Bashkirs at once began telling him something. The chief listened for a while and addressed himself to Pahom. Speaking in Russian, he said, "Well, let it be so. Choose whatever piece of land you like. We have plenty of it."

> gave
> at the top seat
> spoke to

Stop & Think

What did Pahom give to the chief?

CHECK UP Choose the right words.

1 The Bashkirs wanted to _____ Pahom for his gifts. (repay | replay)
2 The Bashkirs told Pahom to _____ the land he wanted. (point out | purchase)
3 The _____ arrived while the Bashkirs were arguing. (interpreter | chief)
4 Did the chief speak to Pahom in Russian? (Yes | No)

GRAMMAR POINT

ought to / ought not to

• They **ought to** ask their chief about the land and **ought not to** act in his absence.

deed

"How can I take as much as I like?" thought Pahom. "I must get a deed to make it secure, or else they may say, 'It

certain, safe ⟵┄┄ ┄┄⟶ *if not, otherwise*

is yours,' and afterward they may take it away again."

┄┄⟶ *later*   ┄┄⟶ *take back, steal*

To the chief, he said, "I must get a deed as a guarantee,

promise ⟵┄┄

or else you may take the land away from me in the future."

The chief said, "We will go to the town with you and make a deed for the land."

"And what will be the price?" asked Pahom.

The chief answered, "Our price is always the same: one thousand rubles a day."

calculation
↑

Pahom did not understand. "A day? What measure is that? How many acres would that be?"

┄┄⟶ *calculate*

The chief said, "We don't know how to figure out the acres, so we sell land by the day. As much as you can go round on your feet in a day is yours, and the price is one thousand rubles a day."

Stop & Think

How much was the land Pahom wanted to buy?

KEY WORDS

- **deed** a paper that gives a person ownership of property
- **take away** to take back; to steal
- **measure** a calculation
- **tract** an area of land
- **spot** a place
- **enormous** huge; very large
- **guarantee** a promise
- **figure out** to calculate
- **condition** a requirement
- **set** to go down
- **imagine** to think about; to picture

Pahom said, "But you can walk around a large tract of land in a single day." one day area

circle

The chief laughed and then answered, "It will all be yours. But there is one condition: If you don't return to the spot where you started on the same day, your money is lost. You must make a circle. **You may make as large a circle as you wish,** but you must return to your starting point before the sun sets. Then, all of the land that you walked around will be yours."

requirement place goes down

imagine

Pahom agreed to the chief's conditions, and they decided to start the next morning.

That night, Pahom lay in bed thinking about the land. He thought, "I can cover an enormous amount of land. I can easily walk thirty–five miles in one day. Imagine how much land that will be."

huge Think, Suppose

Stop & Think

What was the condition the chief gave Pahom?

CHECK UP Answer the questions.

1 What did Pahom want the chief to give him with the land?
   a. a deed   **b.** some money   **c.** some servants

2 How far did Pahom think he could walk in one day?
   a. 20 miles   **b.** 35 miles   **c.** 50 miles

GRAMMAR POINT

as . . . as . . .

- How can I take **as much as** I like?
- **As much as** you can go round on your feet in a day is yours.
- You may make **as large** a circle **as** you wish.

lie awake

doze off

hoof

horn

> → *did not sleep *lie–lay–lain*   → *fell asleep for a short time*

Pahom lay awake all night and dozed off only just before dawn. Hardly were his eyes closed when he had a dream.
> →*Scarcely*

In his dream, the chief of the Bashkirs was sitting in front of a tent and laughing. "What are you laughing at?" he asked the chief. But the chief was no longer there. Instead, it was the peddler who had stopped at his house and told him about the Bashkirs. Then, the peddler disappeared, and the peasant who
> ----→ *vanished*

had told him about the land beyond the Volga River suddenly appeared. Then, he saw that it was not the
> ----→ *came into sight*

peasant either, but the Devil himself with hoofs and horns, sitting there and chuckling. There was a man
> ----→ *laughing*

lying dead in front of the Devil, and it was Pahom himself. He awoke horror–struck.
> ----→ *very shocked and afraid*

Looking round, he saw through the open door that the dawn was breaking. "It's time to wake them up," he thought. "We ought to be starting."

Pahom, the chief, and the other Bashkirs met on the land early in the morning. The chief stretched his arms
> ----→ *extended*

out and said, "All of this land—as far as you can see—belongs to us. You may have any part of it you like."

Stop & Think

What happened to Pahom in his dream?

KEY WORDS

- **lie awake** to lie in bed but not to sleep
- **appear** ≠ disappear
- **stretch out** to extend
- **dawn** the time when the sun rises
- **horror–struck** extremely shocked and afraid
- **spade** a shovel

The chief took off his fox–fur cap, placed it on the
ground, and said, "This will be the mark. Start from
here and return here again. All the land you go around
shall be yours." Pahom took out his money and put it
on the cap.

took off → ≠ put on
placed it → put

mark

Pahom stood ready to start with a spade in his hand.
He considered for some moments which way he had
better go. Then, he concluded, "I will go toward the
rising sun."

spade

Stop & Think

What did the chief put down to mark the starting spot?

CHECK UP Finish the sentences.

1 Pahom had a dream
2 The Devil was
3 Pahom put his money

a. on the fox–fur cap.
b. the night before the contest.
c. laughing in Pahom's dream.

GRAMMAR POINT

hardly . . . when . . .

- **Hardly** were his eyes closed **when** he had a dream.
  (= His eyes were **hardly** closed **when** he had a dream.)

girdle

ant

noon

lie down

Pahom started walking neither slowly nor quickly. After having gone a thousand yards, he stopped, dug a hole, and placed pieces of turf one on another to make it more visible. Then, he went on. Now that he had

> *can be seen ≠ invisible*

walked off his stiffness, he quickened his pace. After a

> *walked enough to soften*
> *moved faster*

while, he dug another hole.

The weather was getting warmer. He looked at the sun. It was time to think of breakfast. "It is too soon yet to turn. I will just take off my boots," he said to himself. He sat down, took off his boots, stuck them

> *put, pushed *stick-stuck-stuck*

into his girdle, and went on. It was easy to walk now.

> *belt*
> *kept walking*

"I will go on for another three miles," he thought, "and then turn to the left. This land here is so nice that it would be a pity to lose it."

> *shame*

He went straight on for a while, and then he looked

> *went right ahead ≠ went backward*

back. The people on the hill where he had started were as small as ants. "Ah, I have gone far enough in this direction," he thought. "It's time to turn and go another direction. Besides, I'm getting tired and need something to drink."

- **turf** grass; sod
- **quicken one's pace** to move faster (≠ slow down)
- **go straight** to go right ahead of oneself
- **lie down** to get down on the ground
- **damp** wet

- **stiffness** a feeling of inflexibility
- **a pity** a shame; a sad situation
- **look back** to look behind (≠ look ahead)
- **perceive** to notice
- **hollow** a valley

He looked at the sun and saw that it was noon. He sat down, ate some bread, and drank some water. But he did not lie down as he thought that if he did, he might fall asleep. After sitting for a little while, he went on again. It had become terribly hot, and he felt sleepy. Still, he went on, thinking, "An hour to suffer, a lifetime to live."

saw → knew, noticed
thought → because
terribly → extremely
suffer → endure pain

hollow

horizon

He went a long way in this direction also and was about to turn to the left again when he perceived a damp hollow. "It would be a pity to leave that out," he thought. So he went on past the hollow and dug a hole on the other side of it.

perceived → noticed
damp → wet
hollow → valley
leave that out → not include, omit

square

"Ah!" thought Pahom, "I have made the sides too long; I must make this one shorter." And he went along the third side as he moved faster. He looked at the sun. It was nearly halfway to the horizon, and he had not yet done two miles of the third side of the square. He was still ten miles from his goal.

nearly → almost

Stop & Think

Why did Pahom not lie down at lunch?

CHECK UP   True or false?

1 Pahom walked for 100 yards on the first side of the square. _____
2 Pahom did not stop to have lunch. _____
3 Pahom made the first side and the second side of the square too long. _____

GRAMMAR POINT

it would be a pity to . . .

- This land here is so nice that **it would be a pity to** lose it.
- **It would be a pity to** leave that out.

straight line

bare feet

bruised

flask

rush to get back

"I've got to hurry back in a straight line now. I shouldn't go too far," he thought. "Besides, I already have a huge amount of land." So Pahom turned and hurried toward the hill that he had started from.

was defeated by

But he now walked with difficulty. He was done in by the heat, his bare feet were cut and bruised, and his legs began to fail. He longed to rest, but it was impossible if he meant to get back before sunset. The sun waits for no man, and it was sinking lower and lower.

give out, not to work any longer

injured, black and blue

wanted to

going down ≠ rising

"Oh dear," he thought, "if only I had not blundered by trying for too much. What if I am too late?"

made a mistake

He looked toward the hill and at the sun. He was still far from his goal, and the sun was already near the rim.

edge

Pahom walked on and on. It was very hard to walk, but he went quicker and quicker. He began running. He threw away his coat, his boots, his flask, and his cap and kept only the spade which he used as a support.

discarded, got rid of *throw–threw–thrown

Stop & Think
What did Pahom throw away while he was returning to the hill?

KEY WORDS

- **hurry back** to rush to get back
- **bruised** injured; black and blue
- **blunder** to make an error
- **soaking** very wet
- **give way** to fail

- **be done in by** to lose to; to be defeated by
- **long to** to desire; to want to
- **breathless** unable to breathe
- **parched** very dry

grabbed, seized ←

"What shall I do?" he thought again. "I have grasped too much and ruined the whole affair. I can't get there before the sun sets." This fear made him still more breathless.

destroyed ← — — — → *event*

— — — → *unable to breathe*

Pahom went on running. His soaking shirt and trousers stuck to him, and his mouth was parched. His chest was working like a blacksmith's bellows, his heart

→ *very wet*

→ *attached *stick–stuck–stuck*

→ *very dry*

trousers

blacksmith

was beating like a hammer, and his legs were giving way as if they did not belong to him. Though afraid of death, he could not stop. He gathered the rest of his strength and ran on.

→ *hitting*

→ *failing*

hammer

Stop & Think

What was Pahom afraid of as he returned to the hill?

CHECK UP Put the right words.

support   land   heart

1 Pahom thought he had tried for too much _____.
2 Pahom kept his spade and used it as a _____.
3 Pahom's _____ was beating like a hammer.

GRAMMAR POINT

–er and –er (double comparatives)

• The sun waits for no man, and it was sinking **lower and lower**.
• It was very hard to walk, but he went **quicker and quicker**.

hold one's sides

The sun was close to the rim. Now, yes now, it was about to set. The sun was quite low, but he was also near his aim. Pahom could already see the people on the hill waving their arms to hurry him up. He could see the fox–fur cap on the ground and the money on it, and the chief sitting on the ground holding his sides. And Pahom remembered his dream.

→ was near to

→ goal

"There is plenty of land," he thought, "but will God let me live on it? I have lost my life. I shall never reach that spot."

→ died

Pahom looked at the sun, which had reached the earth. With all his remaining strength, he rushed on.

KEY WORDS

- **hold one's sides** to laugh badly
- **labor** work
- **take a long breath** to breathe deeply
- **flow** to come from
- **bury** to put a dead person into the ground
- **lose one's life** to die
- **in vain** for no use; without gain
- **fellow** a person; a guy
- **click one's tongue** to make a clicking noise
- **six feet** about two meters; the depth at which a person is buried

*became dark *grow–grew–grown

Just as he reached the hill, it suddenly grew dark. He looked up — the sun had already set. He gave a cry. "All my labor has been in vain," he thought.

→ work → for no use

He was about to stop, but he heard the Bashkirs still shouting. He realized that the sun seemed to have set, but the Bashkirs on the hill could still see it. He took a long breath and ran up the hill. It was still light there.

→ was going to
→ appeared to
→ took a deep breath

He reached the top and saw the cap. He fell forward and reached the cap with his hands.

blood

grave

"Ah, that's a fine fellow!" exclaimed the chief. "He has gained much land."

→ nice guy

Pahom's servant came running up and tried to raise him, but he saw that blood was flowing from his mouth. Pahom was dead.

→ coming from

The Bashkirs clicked their tongues to show their pity.

His servant picked up the spade and dug a grave long enough for Pahom to lie in and buried him in it. Six feet from his head to his heels was all he needed.

→ lifted
→ dig–dug–dug
→ rest in
→ 1.8 meters

Stop & Think

How much land did Pahom need?

CHECK UP Choose the right words.

1 The sun set at the bottom of the hill _____ than at the top. (slower | faster)

2 The _____ said that Pahom had gained much land. (chief | interpreter)

3 Pahom's servant saw that he was _____. (alive | dead)

4 Did the Devil win his contest with Pahom? (Yes | No)

GRAMMAR POINT

enough . . . to . . .

• His servant dug a grave long **enough** for Pahom **to** lie in.

Step

5

A Christmas Carol
— Charles Dickens

A Christmas Carol

♪ 07

foggy

greedy

beggar

One Christmas Eve, Scrooge sat busy in his office. It was cold and foggy weather. The city clocks had just rung three times, but it was already quite dark.

---> ring-rang-rung

Scrooge was an old man. He was known by everyone

---> not nice ≠ kind   *a person who sins <---*

to be mean, miserly, and cold. He was a greedy sinner.

---> stingy

No warmth could warm him, and no cold could chill

make cold <---

him. Nobody ever stopped Scrooge on the street to say, "My dear Scrooge, how are you?" No beggars implored

begged <---

him to give them some money. Even the dogs seemed to know him, and they avoided him, too. But Scrooge

---> kept away from

did not care at all. He liked it that way. People avoided him, and he avoided people.

He had worked in the same dark office for many years. Once it had been the office of *Scrooge and Marley*. Scrooge and Marley had been partners for many years. And even now, seven years after Marley had died, those names were still on the door.

It was a very small room with a very small fire. The only other person in the office was Bob Cratchit,

Stop & Think

How did people feel about Scrooge?

KEY WORDS

- **miserly** acting like a miser; refusing to spend money
- **greedy** wanting more money
- **implore** to beg; to plead
- **sinner** a person who sins; a bad person
- **bah, humbug** an expression of unhappiness or disgust

Scrooge's clerk. Bob was very cold. Scrooge did not give Bob much wood for his fire because he did not like to spend money. So the clerk put on his coat and tried to warm himself by the light of a candle.

merry

Scrooge did not like anything. He especially hated Christmas.

"Merry Christmas, Uncle," cried a cheerful voice. It was the voice of Scrooge's nephew Fred.

→ happy, pleasant

→ ≠ niece

"Bah, humbug," said Scrooge.

"Oh, come on, Uncle," said Fred. "I'm sure you don't mean it."

you don't intend to do it ←

"I do," said Scrooge. "Why are you merry? You're a poor man."

→ happy

"Well, why aren't you merry? You're a very rich man. And it's Christmas!"

"Bah, humbug," said Scrooge again. "You keep Christmas in your own way, and let me keep it in mine."

as you like ←

CHECK UP True or false?

1 Scrooge was a greedy man. _____
2 Scrooge and Marley still worked together. _____
3 Bob Cratchit was Scrooge's boss. _____

GRAMMAR POINT

no + noun (emphasis)

- **No warmth** could warm him, and **no cold** could chill him.
- **No beggars** implored him to give them some money.

A Christmas Carol **45**

portly

books

bow

"Don't be so angry, Uncle. Come and have dinner with us tomorrow."

Scrooge merely answered, "Goodbye."
> only, simply

"I don't want to be angry with you, Uncle," said Fred. "So a Merry Christmas, Uncle."

"Goodbye," Scrooge only said.

After Scrooge's nephew left, the clerk let two other people in. They were portly gentlemen. They had books and papers in their hands and bowed to Scrooge.
> rather fat

"Excuse us. May I ask, are you Mr. Scrooge or Mr. Marley?" said one of the gentlemen.

"Mr. Marley has been dead these seven years. He died seven years ago this very night," answered Scrooge.

"Mr. Scrooge then," said the man. "At this festive season of the year, it is nice for everyone to give something to people who have nothing–no homes, no food."

Christmas season <----

"Are there no prisons? Any orphanages?" said Scrooge.

jails <----   ----> places where orphans live

"There are. But they always need a little more. So a few of us are raising funds to buy the poor some meat,
> raising money

drink, and means of warmth. What shall I put you down for?"
> tools, equipments

> write down, record

Stop & Think

What did Scrooge's nephew ask him to do?

KEY WORDS

- **portly** overweight; rather fat
- **raise funds** to raise money
- **anonymous** of unknown name (≠ signed)
- **excuse** a reason
- **orphanage** a place where orphans live
- **put down** to write down; to note
- **all day off** not having to work for an entire day
- **pick a man's pocket** to steal money from a man

"Nothing!" answered Scrooge. → a gift without a name

"You wish to give an anonymous gift?"

"No. I wish to be left alone. I don't make merry at Christmas, and I can't afford to make lazy fools merry. I have my work to worry about." → don't have money to

lazy

After the men left, Scrooge turned to his clerk. "You'll want all day off tomorrow, I suppose?" he asked.
→ do not go to work → guess, think

"If that's convenient, sir," the clerk responded.
→ suitable, okay

empty

"It's not convenient, and it's not fair. Yet you'll still expect me to pay you a day's wages for no work, won't you?"
→ unfair
→ money that is paid for work

"It's only once a year, sir."

"That's a poor excuse for picking a man's pocket every
bad reason ← twenty–fifth of December. But I suppose you must have the whole day. Be here early the next morning."
→ stealing money from a man

The clerk promised that he would arrive early. Scrooge walked out of the office and went back to his empty home.
→ ≠ full

Stop & Think

What did Scrooge give Bob Cratchit for Christmas?

CHECK UP Put the right words.

money   wages   died   early

1 Scrooge said that Marley _____ seven years ago.
2 The men asked Scrooge to give them some _____.
3 Scrooge paid Bob Cratchit his day's _____ for Christmas.
4 Bob Cratchit promised to arrive _____ the day after Christmas.

GRAMMAR POINT

dead (adjective) / die (verb)

• Mr. Marley has **been dead** these seven years.
• He **died** seven years ago this very night.

knocker

dressing gown

nightcap

drag

cask

When Scrooge got to his building, he put the key into the lock of the door. But when he looked at the knocker, he did not see a knocker but Marley's face. Scrooge stared for a moment, and then it was a knocker again. He said, "Pooh, pooh!" and closed the door with a bang.

> looked at

> with a very loud sound

Scrooge went up to his room, and carefully locked the door. He checked twice to see if the door was locked and then made a little fire in the fireplace. He put on his dressing gown, slippers, and nightcap, and sat down before the very low fire. As he threw his head back in his chair, he heard something in the house. It was far away, but it was coming closer. It sounded as if some person were dragging a heavy chain over the casks in the wine merchant's cellar. Then, he heard the noise much louder on the floors below. Then, it came up the stairs, and then it came straight toward his door. It came right through the heavy door, and a ghost passed into the room before his eyes. The face! He recognized it right away as Marley's. It was Marley's ghost.

> whether

> started a fire

> leaned his head back

> distant ≠ near

> like

> spirit

> knew

> immediately

Stop & Think

What went into Scrooge's room?

KEY WORDS

- **knocker** an old–fashioned doorbell
- **drag** to pull something on the ground
- **caustic** sarcastic
- **dreadful** frightening; scary
- **linger** to remain in one place

- **low fire** a fire that is not hot
- **straight toward** directly at something
- **as ever** as usual
- **apparition** a ghost
- **stay away from** to keep away from; to avoid

"How now," said Scrooge, caustic and cold as ever. "What do you want with me?"

> sarcastic
> as usual

"Much." Marley's voice, no doubt about it.

"Who are you?"

"Ask me who I was."

"Who were you then?" said Scrooge, raising his voice.

"In life, I was your partner, Jacob Marley."

"Mercy! Dreadful apparition, why do you trouble me? What do you want?" Scrooge's voice trembled as he spoke.

> ghost
> shook

"I have been traveling since I died. Though I am dead, I must walk through the world of the living. I cannot rest. I cannot stay. I cannot linger anywhere."

> stay, remain

"Why?" asked Scrooge.

"Because I'm unhappy. I was very bad to people when I was alive. If a man stays away from other people while he is alive, that man becomes like me," said Marley's ghost.

> keeps away from, avoids

dreadful

CHECK UP   Answer the questions.

1 What kind of noise did Scrooge hear?
   a. a screaming man   **b.** a dragging chain   **c.** a laughing woman

2 What could Marley not do?
   a. rest   **b.** speak   **c.** move

GRAMMAR POINT

as if . . . (subjunctive)

• It sounded **as if** some person **were dragging** a heavy chain over the casks.

escape

chain

bell

wide open

"I am here tonight to warn you that you have yet a chance and hope of escaping my fate," said Marley's ghost.

↳ destiny

"This is the chain I made during my lifetime. Every time I refused to help those in need, the chain became

↳ rejected   ↳ poor, needy

longer and heavier. When I died, our chains were about the same, Scrooge, but now, after seven years, yours is much longer than mine. I want to help you not to be unhappy like me when you die."

"How?" asked Scrooge.

"You will be visited by three more ghosts," answered Marley's ghost. "Expect the first tonight when the bell

↳ Anticipate

tolls one. Expect the second tomorrow night at the

↳ rings

same hour. The third will come the next night, when the last stroke of twelve has rung."

↳ beat   ↳ ring-rang-rung

The ghost began floating out the window.

↳ flying out

"But wait. Will I see you again? Can't you tell me more?"

↳ will not

"No, Scrooge, you won't see me again. Remember what I told you, for your own sake, or you will soon see your own heavy chain."   ↳ for your own good

The ghost disappeared out the window, which was wide open.   ↳ vanished

Stop & Think

How many ghosts will visit Scrooge?

KEY WORDS

• **escape** to avoid; to get away from
• **in need** poor; needy
• **float out** to fly out by being carried by the wind
• **be drawn aside** to be opened

• **fate** destiny
• **stroke** a knock; a beat
• **troubled sleep** a restless sleep
• **figure** a form or shape; the human form

As Scrooge went to the window to see where Marley had gone, he suddenly heard some crying down below. Again, Scrooge's heart froze. The voices came not from people, but from ghosts. He quickly closed the window. He tried to say, "Humbug," but he stopped at the first syllable.

> freeze–froze–frozen

> a part of a word

flash up

"This couldn't have happened. I will go to sleep, and tomorrow everything will be fine," he thought. Then, he went to bed and fell into a troubled sleep.

> can't be true, can't be possible

> restless sleep

figure

When Scrooge awoke, it was still so dark. "Was it all a dream?" he wondered. Just then, the clock tolled a deep, dull, hollow one.

> woke up *awake–awoke–awoken

> rang

> instantly, at once

≠ sharp ← → empty

green holly

Light flashed up in the room in an instant, and the curtains of his bed were drawn aside by a strange figure. The ghost was an old man with long white hair. He held a branch of fresh green holly in his hand. From the top of his head, a bright clear jet of light sprang.

> opened

> appeared

> *spring–sprang–sprung

"I am the Ghost of Christmas Past," he said.

"Whose past?"

> a ray of light

"Your past," answered the ghost.

"What do you want?"

Stop & Think

What was the first ghost to visit Scrooge?

"Rise and walk with me."

> Stand up

CHECK UP Choose the right words.

1 Marley said that Scrooge's _____ was longer than his own. (life | chain)
2 The first ghost was going to come at _____ in the morning. (one | three)
3 The first ghost looked like _____. (an old man | a young man)

GRAMMAR POINT

be + p.p. (passive)

- You will **be visited by** three more ghosts.
- The curtains of his bed **were drawn** aside **by** a strange figure.

⟶ hold–held–held

hold one's hand

decoration

tears

Scrooge got up from his bed. He held the ghost's hand, and they passed through the wall together. Suddenly,

⟶ went through

they were standing in the country where he had lived as a boy. It was clear enough by the decorations in the shops that there, too, it was Christmastime.

They saw many boys and girls going home across the fields, happily shouting "Merry Christmas" to each other. Scrooge remembered the happiness and joy when he was a child. He could feel tears on his cheek.

"Are you sad?" asked the ghost.

"No, no, I am . . . happy," said Scrooge.

"They are not real. They are only spirits from Christmas past. They cannot see us."

⟶ ghosts

But Scrooge knew the spirits, just as he knew the streets, the houses, and the townspeople. Then, they

⟶ alone, by himself

saw Scrooge as a boy, reading on his own in an empty classroom. Seeing himself as he had once been, Scrooge sat down at a desk next to him and began to cry.

"It's me. Once when I was a boy, I was left alone here on Christmas. My father and mother weren't at home. Now,

Stop & Think

What time of year did the ghost take Scrooge to?

KEY WORDS

- **get up** to rise; to stand up
- **on one's own** alone (≠ together)
- **grow quiet** to become quiet
- **prepare** to get ready; to make something ready
- **decoration** an ornament
- **be left alone** to be by oneself
- **get angry** to become upset
- **apprentice** a person who is learning a skill

suddenly, I wish I would . . ." Scrooge's voice grew quiet.
→ *became quiet*

"What do you wish?" the ghost asked.

apprentice

"Last night, a young boy came to my office window and sang me a Christmas carol. I just got angry and told
→ *became upset*
him to leave. I wish I'd given some money to that poor boy," said Scrooge with heavy sadness.

The ghost smiled. "Let's see another Christmas," he said.

This time, Scrooge saw the office where he had first worked. He saw Mr. Fezziwig, the man whom he had worked for. Young Scrooge was helping them prepare the office for a Christmas party. Soon, there
→ *get ready*
were many young people there. They were his fellow
companion ←
apprentices. They were enjoying
→ *learners*
themselves and dancing. Even he, Scrooge himself, was dancing and enjoying himself.

CHECK UP Finish the sentences.

1 Scrooge and the ghost
2 The images Scrooge saw
3 Scrooge once worked

a. were not real.
b. in an office for Mr. Fezziwig.
c. passed through the wall together.

GRAMMAR POINT

where (relative adverb)

- Suddenly, they were standing in *the country* **where** he had lived as a boy.

- This time, Scrooge saw *the office* **where** he had first worked.

A Christmas Carol **53**

in pain

shadow

At the end of the party, Mr. and Mrs. Fezziwig said "Merry Christmas" to everybody.

"It's old Mr. Fezziwig's office. He was such a happy, kind boss." → supervisor, head

The ghost looked at Scrooge and asked, "What's the matter?"

"I was thinking of my clerk, Bob Cratchit. I wish I'd said something to him yesterday," said Scrooge.

The ghost smiled again. "Come, my time grows short," said the ghost. "Another Christmas," he said. → becomes

The scene changed. Scrooge again saw himself. He was older now—a man in the prime of life. He was sitting with a young woman. She had once been his girlfriend. She was crying. → view → the best years of life

"No, it's too late. You have another love now," she said.

"What? What other love?" Scrooge asked.

"Money. You love only money now, not me. Goodbye."

"No more! Ghost! Please remove me from this place," Scrooge cried in pain. → take me away from

"No, Scrooge. I told you that these were shadows of the things that have been," said the ghost. "There is one more scene."

Stop & Think

Who did Scrooge see with himself?

KEY WORDS

- **the prime of life** the best years of one's life
- **bear** to stand
- **struggle with** to fight with
- **be interested in** to like; to care about
- **haunt** to follow around
- **drowsiness** sleepiness

Years had passed since the last scene. Scrooge saw a beautiful woman smiling with her children in a warm house. The door opened, and the father came in. His arms were full of Christmas presents. He gave one to
→ were filled with
each of his children. The children laughed and shouted as they opened the presents.

haunt

Scrooge looked at the mother. She was the woman from Scrooge's past. She had left him because he had been more interested in money than in her. Looking at
→ liked, cared about
the happy family, Scrooge realized what he had lost.

exhausted

"No more! Leave me, ghost," shouted Scrooge.

"This was your life. These things happened and cannot be changed. Only the future can be changed," the ghost said.

drowsiness

stand
→
"Please, ghost, I cannot bear it. Haunt me no longer!"
→ Follow around
Scrooge shouted sadly.
→ fought with

As Scrooge struggled with the spirit, he suddenly became exhausted. He was overcome by drowsiness and
→ got tired   → defeated by   → sleepiness
sank into a heavy sleep.
→ fell into *sink–sank–sunk

Stop & Think
What did Scrooge tell the ghost?

CHECK UP True or false?

1 Scrooge never had a girlfriend in his entire life. _____
2 Scrooge loved money more than people. _____
3 The beautiful woman Scrooge saw was his mother. _____
4 Scrooge asked the ghost to show him some more scenes. _____

GRAMMAR POINT

I wish . . . (subjunctive)

• **I wish I'd said** something to him yesterday.

bowl of punch

couch

torch

robe

Scrooge awoke in his bedroom. It was one in the morning again—time for the second ghost. He looked around his bedroom. There was nobody there. He went to the door of his living room.

"Come in, Ebenezer Scrooge," said a voice.

He opened the door and saw something very surprising. The room looked so different. The walls were covered with Christmas trees. Heaped upon the floor *Piled* *filled with* were turkeys, geese, pigs, sausages, plum puddings, chestnuts, apples, and great bowls of punch. Upon the couch in the center of the room sat a happy giant, holding a glowing torch which lit the room. *light–lit–lit*

burning

"Come in. Come in. I am the Ghost of Christmas Present," said the giant.

"Ghost, I learned a lot from the ghost last night. Tonight, if you have something to teach me, take me anywhere you want," said Scrooge.

"Touch my robe," said the giant.

Stop & Think

Who was the second ghost?

KEY WORDS

- **heaped upon** piled on
- **light** to make light
- **crutch** a stick one uses to help one walk
- **gather** to get together

- **couch** a long sofa
- **bless** to say something good about
- **complain** to grumble; to criticize
- **propose** to offer

crutch

gather

> find–found–found

Scrooge did as he was told. Scrooge found they were walking in a London street on Christmas morning. The ghost took him to the Cratchits' house. At the door, the ghost smiled and stopped to bless Bob Cratchit's dwelling.

> the Cratchit family's

> ≠ curse

Mrs. Cratchit, Bob's wife, was preparing their Christmas dinner. Just then Bob Cratchit was coming back from church with the youngest son, Tiny Tim. Tiny Tim was ill and used a crutch to walk.

The family sat down to eat their meal. They had only one goose, some potatoes, and a small Christmas pudding. It seemed very small for such a large family, but nobody complained. Though it was a very simple Christmas meal, they were still as happy as if they had eaten a king's meal. After dinner, all the Cratchit family gathered around the fire. Bob proposed, "A Merry Christmas to us all, my dears. God bless us!"

> grumbled

> got together

> offered

> *Stop & Think*
>
> **What did Bob Cratchit's family have to eat?**

CHECK UP Put the right words.

| giant | Tiny Tim | touch | enjoyed |

1 There was a _____ sitting in the middle of Scrooge's living room.
2 The ghost told Scrooge to _____ his robe.
3 _____ needed to use a crutch to walk.
4 The Cratchits had a simple meal, but they _____ it.

GRAMMAR POINT

such a/an + adjective + noun (high degree)

• It seemed very small for **such a large family**.

A Christmas Carol **57**

"God bless us everyone!" said Tiny Tim. Tiny Tim sat very close to his father's side upon his little stool. He was very sick. Bob held his withered little hand in his

→ thin and dry, shrunken

as if he loved the child and wished to keep him by his side, but he dreaded that Tiny

→ feared, was afraid

Tim might be taken from him.

→ be taken away from

"Will he be here next Christmas?" Scrooge asked.

"With help," replied the ghost.

Scrooge raised his head when he heard his name spoken.

"Let's drink to Mr. Scrooge," said Bob.

→ turned red

"To Scrooge?" Mrs. Cratchit's face reddened, and she said, "Why should we drink to that old, stingy, unfeeling man?"

miserly ←   → unkind

"My dear," was Bob's mild answer, "it's Christmas Day."

"Well, you are right. I'll drink to him. But nothing we do could make that mean old man feel happy or merry," said Mrs. Cratchit.

stool

Stop & Think

Who did Bob Cratchit propose a toast to?

(KEY WORDS)

• **withered** shrunken
• **stingy** greedy; miserly
• **cast a shadow** to darken; to make dark
• **dig up** to unearth

• **dread** to fear; to be afraid of
• **unfeeling** having no emotions; unkind
• **take away** to remove
• **vanish** to disappear

The mention of his name cast a dark shadow on the party, which lasted for a full five minutes. After some time, the Cratchits became cheerful again. They were not a handsome family. They were not well dressed. But they were happy, grateful, and pleased with one another.

→ made dark

→ happy, pleasant

wearing nice clothes ←

→ thankful   → happy with

cheerful

The ghost took Scrooge away from the Cratchits' house. The two of them walked through the streets of London. People were going to parties with their friends and families. Suddenly, they were in a cold, dark, empty place. They looked through the window of a small house. Inside, there was a big family in a very small room. Yet they were happy and were singing Christmas carols together.

→ looked into

look through

miner

Scrooge asked, "Who are they?"

"They are poor miners," answered the ghost. "They have hard lives working inside the Earth to dig up coal."

dig up

Slowly, the scene vanished, and Scrooge suddenly heard a hearty laugh. It was his nephew Fred's house. Fred was telling everyone about his visit to his uncle.

→ disappeared

→ cheerful laugh

hearty laugh

CHECK UP Answer the questions.

1 How did Mrs. Cratchit feel about drinking to Scrooge?
   a. pleased   **b.** nervous   **c.** unhappy

GRAMMAR POINT

which (relative pronoun) : referring to a previous clause

- The mention of his name cast a dark shadow on the party, **which** lasted for a full five minutes.

phantom

mist

**bend down
upon one's knee**

"So when I said 'Merry Christmas' to him, he replied 'Bah, humbug!'" said Fred. Everyone laughed.

"He's a strange old man," said Fred. "He is rich, but he doesn't do anything good with his money. He even lives like he's poor. I invite him to have Christmas dinner with us every year, but he never comes. Someday, perhaps he will change his mind. And someday perhaps he will pay poor Bob Cratchit more money as well."

> *as if*
> *maybe, possibly*
> *think differently*

For the rest of the evening, Scrooge and the ghost watched his nephew and friends enjoy their Christmas party. Then, the clock struck twelve. Scrooge looked around for the ghost, but he saw the ghost no more. Then, he remembered Marley's prediction, and he lifted his eyes.

> *rang *strike–struck–struck*
> *a guess about the future*

Scrooge saw a solemn phantom coming like a mist along the ground toward him. Unlike the others, he could not see this one's face or body. It was covered from head to toe in a long black garment. The only visible part of the phantom was one outstretched hand.

> *quiet and serious*
> *fog*
> *not like*
> *a piece of clothing*
> *extended*

The phantom moved slowly and silently. As it came near him, Scrooge bent down upon his knee, for the ghost seemed to scatter gloom and mystery as it moved. The ghost did not speak at all.

> *kneeled*
> *spread*
> *unhappiness*

KEY WORDS

- **prediction** a guess about the future
- **phantom** a ghost
- **garment** a piece of clothing
- **scatter** to spread
- **yet to come** the future
- **solemn** quiet and serious
- **mist** fog
- **outstretched** extended
- **gloom** unhappiness; sadness
- **funeral** a ceremony held for a dead person

→ in front of, nearby

"I am in the presence of the Ghost of Christmas Yet to Come," said Scrooge. "You are about to show me the things which have not happened yet, but will happen in the time before us," Scrooge said, looking at the strange ghost. "Is that so, Spirit?"

→ future

point with one's hand

The ghost silently moved its head a little and pointed with its hand. Scrooge suddenly found himself in the middle of the city. The ghost stopped beside a group of businessmen. Scrooge could hear some of them talking.

funeral

"I don't know much about it. I only know he's dead," said one great fat man.

"When did he die?" inquired another.

"Last night, I believe."

→ asked

"What has he done with his money?" asked a red-faced gentleman.

"I haven't heard," responded the first man. "He didn't leave it to me though. That's all I know."

"At least his funeral will be very cheap," said one man.

Stop & Think

Who was the third ghost?

CHECK UP Choose the right words.

1 Fred wanted Scrooge to give Bob Cratchit more _____. (money | food)
2 The third ghost wore _____ clothes. (black | white)
3 The third ghost said _____. (many things | nothing)
4 Were the people the ghost showed Scrooge talking about a marriage? (Yes | No)

GRAMMAR POINT

for + S + V (reason) : given as an afterthought

• Scrooge bent down upon his knee, **for** the ghost seemed to scatter gloom and mystery.

old rag

shopkeeper

"That's true. He had no friends. No one liked him, so nobody will go to his funeral."

Scrooge did not understand why the ghost wanted him to listen to this conversation, but he knew the ghost would not answer him, so he did not ask.

⤍ little known

They left the busy scene and went to an obscure part of the town. The streets were dark and small. They visited a dirty shop full of horrible old things you can

⤍ awful, terrible

imagine—iron, old rags, bottles, clothes, and bones. It was a place where people came to sell their things when they needed money.

Scrooge watched as three people brought things to sell to the shopkeeper. They were from the same dead man's house.

"What have you got to sell?" asked the shopkeeper.

One woman took out some towels, silver teaspoons, and other small things, and said, "He doesn't need these now."

"No indeed, ma'am," answered the shopkeeper.

⤍ certainly, surely

Stop & Think

Where did the three people get the items they were selling?

KEY WORDS

- **obscure** little known
- **in horror** in fear; in disgust
- **pale light** a dim light
- **uncared for** not taken care of
- **tenderness** kindness; mercy
- **be not likely to** be unlikely to
- **bare** having nothing; empty
- **unwept** not mourned
- **as silent as ever** quiet like usual
- **connected with** related to; concerning

"Take a look at these," said the other woman. "Bed curtains and blankets. He isn't likely to catch a cold without them now."
→ doesn't seem to, is unlikely to

blanket

Scrooge listened to this dialogue in horror. "Ghost, I see. The case of this unhappy man might be my own."
→ in fear
→ situation, condition

The scene had suddenly changed, and Scrooge found himself in another terrible room. There was a bare bed with no blankets or curtains around it. A pale light from outside fell straight upon the bed. On it, unwatched, unwept, and uncared for, was the dead body of the unknown man. He was covered by a thin sheet.
→ having nothing, empty
→ dim light
→ not watched
→ not mourned
→ not taken care of

catch a cold

The ghost, as silent as ever, merely pointed at the body. Scrooge realized that the ghost wanted him to look at the face of the dead man, but he could not do it.
→ quiet like usual

sheet

"I cannot look at his face," cried Scrooge. "Let me see some tenderness connected with this death, or this dark chamber will be forever in my memory."
→ kindness, mercy
→ related to
→ large room

The scene changed to another home. A woman stood up as her husband entered the room. "Have you gotten any news?" she asked.
→ got up
→ Have you heard

chamber

CHECK UP   Finish the sentences.

1 The shopkeeper asked the women   a. what they had to sell.
2 One woman was selling   b. bed curtains and blankets.
3 The ghost pointed at   c. a dead body covered by a sheet.

GRAMMAR POINT

be likely to . . . / it is likely that . . .

• He **isn't likely to** catch a cold without them now.
  = It **isn't likely that** he will catch a cold without them now.

flow down

churchyard

grave

→ discover, learn

"When I visited him to find out if we could pay the money one week later," he answered, "an old woman told me he was dead."

"That's great news," she said. "I'm sorry for saying that. I mean that now we have time to get the money that we have to pay."

→ feel bad about

"No, ghost! Show me someone who's sorry about a death, not someone who's happy because of a death," shouted Scrooge.

The ghost took him to poor Bob Cratchit's house. Scrooge saw the family sitting quietly around the fire. They were talking about Tiny Tim.

"I met Fred, Mr. Scrooge's nephew," said Bob. "And he said that he was very sorry to hear about Tiny Tim."

Bob turned to his family and said, "We must never forget what a good boy Tiny Tim was."

"No, never father," shouted all the children.

Then, Bob Cratchit broke down all at once. He couldn't help it as the tears flowed down his face.

started to cry ← ・ → suddenly

was unable to stop doing it ←

"Ghost," said Scrooge, "something informs me that

→ tells

Stop & Think

Why was the Cratchit family sad?

our parting moment is at hand. Tell me. Who was the
dead man we saw?"

> the time to leave
> near, close

The Ghost of Christmas Yet to Come took Scrooge to
a churchyard. The ghost stood among the graves and
pointed down to one. Scrooge crept toward it, trembling
as he went, and followed the finger to read the name
on the neglected grave: EBENEZER SCROOGE.

> move slowly *creep–crept–crept
> ignored, uncared for

"Am I that man who lay upon the bed? No, ghost!
Oh no, no. I am not the man I was. I will not be the
man I must have been but for this evening. Why show
me this if I am past all hope?
Assure me that I may yet
change these shadows."

> lie–lay–lain
> if not, without
> if I cannot be saved
> Promise, Tell   still

CHECK UP True or false?

1 The Ghost of Christmas Yet to Come took Scrooge to a churchyard.   _____
2 Scrooge wanted to know who the dead man was.   _____
3 The name on the grave was Scrooge's.   _____

GRAMMAR POINT

relative pronoun

● Now we have time to get *the money* **that** we have to pay.

● Show me *someone* **who**'s sorry about a death, not *someone* **who**'s happy because of a death.

● Who was *the dead man* **(whom)** we saw?

● Am I *that man* **who** lay upon the bed?

butcher's shop

butcher

Scrooge continued, "I will honor Christmas in my heart and try to keep it all the year. I will live in the past, present, and future. I will never forget the lessons that I have been taught."

> keep, remember

> teach–taught–taught

Then, the phantom began to disappear, and Scrooge realized that he was back in his own bedroom. Best and happiest of all, time was before him. He had time to make amends.

> make up for the mistakes

Scrooge heard the church bells ringing loudly. Running to the window, he opened it and put out his head. It was a clear, bright, stirring, golden day.

> exciting, thrilling

"What day is it today?" cried Scrooge to a boy down on the street.

"Today? It's Christmas Day, sir," answered the boy.

"Christmas!" Scrooge was surprised. All of the visits from the ghosts had taken place in one night.

> occurred, happened

"Do you know the butcher's shop down the street?" Scrooge asked. "Please go and tell the butcher I'll buy a big goose. Come back with the man, and I'll give you a nice tip." The boy ran off quickly.

"I'll send it to Bob Cratchit's. He won't know who

Stop & Think

What did Scrooge tell the boy to do?

KEY WORDS

- **honor** to keep; to remember
- **stirring** exciting, thrilling
- **dress oneself** to put on one's clothes
- **a dozen times** 12 times
- **make amends** to make up for a past mistake
- **butcher's shop** a store that sells meat
- **one's Sunday best** one's finest clothes
- **courage** bravery

is sending it. It's twice the size of Tiny Tim," Scrooge thought to himself.

delighted

→ put on his finest clothes

Scrooge then dressed himself in his Sunday best and went out onto the streets. Many people were on the streets, and Scrooge gave each of them a delighted smile. He said, "Good morning, sir," or "A Merry Christmas to you," to everyone he passed.

pleased ⟵

knock

Later in the afternoon, he walked toward his nephew's house. He passed the door a dozen times before he had the courage to go up and knock. But he finally did.

→ 12 times; many times

→ bravery

Fred was very surprised to see his uncle. "Uncle, why are you here?" he asked.

→ ↔ aunt

"I have come to dinner. Will you let me in, Fred?" Scrooge asked.

"Of course you may!" cried out Fred.

Fred was very happy, and so were his wife and all their friends. They had a wonderful party together.

CHECK UP Put the right words.

| the goose | one night | have dinner |

1 Scrooge realized that all three ghosts had visited him in _____.
2 Scrooge sent _____ to Bob Cratchit's house.
3 Scrooge went to his nephew's house to _____.

GRAMMAR POINT

So am I.

- You are happy. **So am I.** (= I **am also happy**.)
- Fred was very happy, and **so were** his wife and all their friends.
  = Fred was very happy, and **his wife and all their friends were also very happy**.

salary

assist

The next day, Scrooge went to the office early in the morning. He wanted to be there before Bob got there. Bob was eighteen minutes late. As Bob walked in, Scrooge said, "Hello. What do you mean by coming here at this time of day?"

arrived

"I'm very sorry, sir. I'm late," replied Bob.

"Yes, I think you are," said Scrooge.

"Now, I'll tell you what, my friend," said Scrooge. "I'm not going to stand this sort of thing any longer. And therefore . . . therefore, I am going to pay you more money!"

this kind of thing

Scrooge continued, "I'll raise your salary and assist your struggling family. We will discuss your affairs this very afternoon," Scrooge said with a nice smile.

increase · *help, aid*

having a hard time · *personal or business interests*

That afternoon, Scrooge took Bob out for a drink and explained how he was going to help him.

Stop & Think

What did Scrooge tell Bob Cratchit he was going to do?

KEY WORDS

- **raise salary** to give more money for working
- **struggling** having a hard time
- **this very afternoon** today; now
- **do not mind** to not care
- **ever afterward** forever
- **assist** to aid; to help
- **affairs** personal or business interests
- **laugh at** to make fun of; to tease
- **dealing with** a relationship with

Scrooge was better than his word. He did everything he said he was going to do and more. He became a friend of the Cratchit family, and to Tiny Tim, who did not die, he was like a second father. He became as good a friend, as good a master, and as good a man as the city ever knew.

> a person who acts like a father

laugh at

Some people laughed at him because he had changed. Scrooge did not mind. Scrooge's own heart laughed, and that was quite enough for him. He had no further dealings with ghosts, but he lived happily ever afterward.

> did not care

> spirit

> relationship with

> forever

Stop & Think

How did Scrooge act toward Tiny Tim?

CHECK UP   Answer the questions.

1 What did Scrooge promise Bob Cratchit?
   a. a bigger house   **b.** a healthy family   **c.** a higher salary

2 What kind of man did Scrooge become?
   a. a greedy man   **b.** a good man   **c.** a silly man

GRAMMAR POINT

as . . . as . . . ever . . .

• He became **as good** a friend, **as good** a master, and **as good** a man **as** the city **ever** knew.

A Christmas Carol   **69**

Step

6

The Last Leaf

— O. Henry

The Last Leaf

♩ 10

In a little district west of Washington Square, the
streets have run crazy and broken themselves into small
strips called "places." These "places" make strange
angles and curves. One street crosses itself a time or
two. An artist once discovered a valuable possibility on
this street. Suppose a collector with a bill for paints,
paper, and canvas should, in taking this route, suddenly
meet himself coming back, without a cent having been
paid on account.

So, to quaint old Greenwich Village, the art people
soon came prowling, hunting for north windows and
eighteenth-century gables and Dutch attics and low
rents. Then, they imported pewter mugs and a dish or
two from Sixth Avenue and became a "colony."

region → run crazy
split into
Imagine
following this way
old-fashioned
gathered around
brought in
village

angle

gable

attic

Stop & Think

What kind of people went to old Greenwich Village?

KEY WORDS

- **run crazy** to move in a strange way
- **quaint** old-fashioned
- **colony** an area where a group of similar-minded people live
- **pneumonia** an inflammation of the lungs
- **boldly** bravely
- **victim** someone who has been hurt or killed

- **possibility** a chance; an opportunity
- **prowl** to move around looking for something
- **stride** to walk with quick, long steps
- **scores of** large numbers of (1 score = 20)
- **tread** to walk slowly

At the top of an ugly, three–story brick house, Sue and Johnsy had their studio. "Johnsy" was a nickname for Joanna. One was from Maine; the other from California. They had met at the restaurant Delmonico's on Eighth Street and had found that their tastes in art, food, and clothes were so similar that the joint studio resulted.

> having three floors

> workroom

three–story

That was in May. In November, a cold, unseen stranger, whom the doctors called Pneumonia, visited the colony, touching one here and there with his icy fingers. Over on the east side, this ravager strode boldly, claiming scores of victims, but his feet trod slowly through the maze of the narrow and moss–grown "places."

> very cold fingers

stride–strode–stridden

> many

tread–trod–trodden

labyrinth

fingers

maze

Mr. Pneumonia was not what you would call a gentleman. A small woman with blood thinned by the warm California zephyrs was no match for the tough and deadly illness.

> a pale complexion

breeze, gentle wind

> not able to compete against

moss–grown

Stop & Think

What happened in the colony in November?

CHECK UP Choose the right words.

1 There were "_____" in Washington Square. (places | attics)
2 People went to old Greenwich Village looking for low _____. (rents | houses)
3 Sue and _____ lived together. (Delmonico | Johnsy)
4 Did many people get pneumonia in May? (Yes | No)

GRAMMAR POINT

one / the other

• **One** was from Maine; **the other** from California.

But he attacked Johnsy, and she lay, scarcely moving, on her painted iron bedstead, looking through the small Dutch windowpanes at the blank side of the next brick house.

→ empty

One morning, the busy doctor invited Sue into the hallway.

→ a ten−percent chance; 10%

"She has one chance in—let us say, ten," he said, as he shook down the mercury in his clinical thermometer.

→ shake−shook−shaken

"And that chance is for her to want to live. Sometimes when people give up trying to live, it doesn't matter what medicines I give. Your friend has made up her mind that she's not going to get well. Has she anything on her mind?"

→ quit, stop
→ decided, determined
→ get better
→ Is there anything she cares about?

"She . . . she wanted to paint the Bay of Naples some day," said Sue.

→ nonsense

"Paint? Bosh! Does she have anything on her mind worth thinking about twice, like a man, for instance?"

→ important, valuable

"A man?" said Sue, with a hard sound in her voice.

windowpane

Stop & Think

What did the doctor say Johnsy needed to do?

KEY WORDS

- **deadly** causing death; lethal
- **one chance in ten** a ten−percent chance, 1/10
- **have on one's mind** to think about something
- **weakness** a weak point; problem (≠ strength)
- **subtract** to take away; to remove
- **swagger** to walk; to stride

- **windowpane** the glass part of a window
- **make up one's mind** to decide
- **bosh** nonsense; pshaw
- **accomplish** to do; to complete
- **one−in−five chance** a twenty−percent chance, 1/5
- **popular tune** a well−known song

"Is a man worth–but, no, Doctor. There is nothing of the kind."

"Well, it is the weakness then," said the doctor. "I will do all that science, so far as it may be employed by me, can accomplish. But whenever my patient begins to count the carriages in her funeral procession, I subtract fifty percent from the power of medicine to cure. If you can get her to ask one question about the new winter styles in cloak sleeves, I will promise you a one–in–five chance for her instead of one in ten."

weak point, problem
as much as what I can do
do
take away
heal
a twenty–percent chance; 20%
rather than

clinical thermometer

carriage

After the doctor left, Sue went into the workroom and cried a napkin to a pulp. Then, she swaggered into Johnsy's room with her drawing board, whistling a popular tune.

cried very hard
strode
popular song
without moving

drawing board

Johnsy lay, scarcely making a move under the bedclothes, with her face toward the window. Sue stopped whistling, thinking she was asleep.

Stop & Think

What did the doctor want Sue to do?

CHECK UP Put the right words.

medicine	cried	live

1 The doctor said Johnsy had one chance in ten to _____.
2 _____ is less effective when patients think about death.
3 Sue _____ very hard after the doctor left.

GRAMMAR POINT

participle clause

- she lay, scarcely **moving**, . . . **looking** through the small Dutch windowpanes . . .
- Johnsy lay, scarcely **making** a move under the bedclothes, . . .
- Sue stopped whistling, **thinking** she was asleep.

count backwards

10 9 8 7 6 5 4 3 ...

ivy vine

skeleton branch

She arranged her board and began a pen–and–ink *→ set up* drawing to illustrate a magazine story. Young artists must pave their way to art by drawing pictures for the *→ draw a picture* magazine stories that young authors must write to pave *→ make a path* their way to literature.

As Sue was sketching a pair of elegant horseshow riding trousers and a monocle on the figure of the hero, an Idaho cowboy, she heard a low sound, several times repeated. She quickly went to the bedside. *→ said again*

Johnsy's eyes were open wide. She was looking out the window and counting backwards. "Twelve," she said, *→ were wide awake* and a little later, "eleven"; and then "ten," and "nine"; *→ ≠ forwards* and then "eight" and "seven" almost together.

Sue looked out the window. What was there to count? There was only a bare, dreary yard to be seen, *having nothing ←* *→ dull, dark, gloomy* and the blank side of the brick house twenty feet away. An old, old ivy vine, twisted and decayed at the roots, *→ rotten* climbed halfway up the brick wall. The cold breath of autumn had taken most of its leaves from the vine until *the cold autumn wind ←* its skeleton branches clung, almost bare, to the bricks.

"What is it, dear?" asked Sue. *→ cling–clung–clung*

KEY WORDS

- **pave one's way** to make a path
- **bare** having nothing
- **blank** bare; empty
- **cling to** to hold on to
- **ten to one** a ninety–percent chance
- **eyes be open wide** to be wide awake
- **dreary** dark; gloomy
- **skeleton branches** branches that have no leaves
- **have to do with** to be concerned with
- **as good a chance as** very good odds

"Six," said Johnsy, in almost a whisper. "They're falling faster now. Three days ago, there were almost a hundred. It made my head ache to count them. But now it's easy. There goes another one. There are only five left now."

gave me a headache

"Five what, dear. Tell your Sudie."

"Leaves. On the ivy vine. When the last one falls, I must go, too. I've known that for three days. Didn't the doctor tell you?"

silliness

"Oh, I have never heard of such nonsense," complained Sue, with magnificent scorn. "What have old ivy leaves to do with your getting well? And you used to love that vine so, you naughty girl. Don't be

be concerned with

streetcar

like that. Why, the doctor told me this morning that your chances for getting well real soon were–let's see

Well, You know

exactly what he said–he said the chances were ten to one. Why, that's almost as good a chance as we have in New York when we ride on the streetcars or walk past a new building."

ninety percent; 90%

Stop & Think

What was Johnsy counting?

CHECK UP True or false?

1 Johnsy was counting backward.   _____
2 Johnsy said she would die when the last leaf fell.   _____
3 Sue said Johnsy's chances of living were ten to one.   _____

GRAMMAR POINT

the subject of gerund

• What have old ivy leaves to do with **your/you** getting well?

The Last Leaf   **77**

broth

pork chop

"Try to have some broth now, and let Sudie go back to her drawing, so she can sell it to the editor. Then, I'll buy port wine for her sick child and pork chops for her greedy self."

"You don't need to get any more wine," said Johnsy, keeping her eyes *fixed* out the window.

> attached to, set on

"There goes another. No, I don't want any broth. That leaves just four. I want to see the last one fall before it gets *dark*. Then, I'll go, too."

becomes dark ←

> leaning over

"Johnsy, dear," said Sue, *bending over* her, "will you promise to keep your eyes closed and not to look out the window until I am done working? I must *hand* my drawings *in* by tomorrow. I need the light, or I would pull the *shade* down."

> turn in, submit

> curtain

"Couldn't you draw in the other room?" Johnsy asked coldly.

> I would prefer to

"I'd *rather* be here beside you," said Sue. "Besides, I don't want you to keep looking at those *silly* ivy leaves."

foolish, ridiculous

Stop & Think

What did Sue ask Johnsy to do?

KEY WORDS

- **port wine** a type of wine
- **bend over** to lean over
- **be tired of** to be sick of
- **beard** facial hair on a man's chin and cheeks
- **except for** not including

- **fixed** attached to; set on
- **hand in** to turn in; to submit
- **hermit** a man who lives by himself
- **noteworthy** important; remarkable
- **minor** ≠ major

"Tell me as soon as you have finished," said Johnsy, closing her eyes, and lying white and still as a fallen statue, "because I want to see the last one fall. I'm tired of waiting. I'm tired of thinking. I want to turn loose my hold on everything and go sailing down, down, just like one of those poor, tired leaves."

> not moving
> sick of
> let go

"Try to sleep," said Sue. "I must call Behrman up to be my model for the old hermit–miner. I'll just be gone for a minute. Don't try to move until I come back."

> contact
> a person who lives alone

Old Behrman was a painter who lived on the ground floor beneath them. He was past sixty and had a long beard like Michelangelo's Moses curling down from his wide head. Behrman was a failure in art. He had been painting for forty years, but he had never produced anything noteworthy. He had always been about to paint a masterpiece, but he had never yet begun it. For several years, he had painted nothing except for minor advertisements here and there.

> loser
> remarkable, significant
> a great work
> small ≠ major

statue

miner

beard

Moses

Stop & Think

Who was Behrman?

CHECK UP Answer the questions.

1 What did Johnsy ask Sue to do?
   a. draw in another room   **b.** give her some broth   **c.** pull the shade down

2 What kind of an artist was Behrman?
   a. a successful one   **b.** an average one   **c.** a failed one

GRAMMAR POINT

not to + V

- Will you promise to keep your eyes closed and **not to look** out the window?

juniper berry

canvas

easel

He earned a little by serving as a model for those young artists in the colony who could not pay for a professional. He drank gin to excess and still talked about his coming masterpiece. *[too much]* For the rest, he was a *[Also]* fierce little old man, who made fun of anyone who was *[very aggressive]* *[laughed at]* soft and who regarded himself as a bulldog ready to protect the two young artists living in the studio above him. *[thought of himself as]*

Sue found Behrman smelling strongly of juniper *[not bright]* *[a small quiet room]* berries in his dimly lit den below. In one corner was a blank canvas on an easel that had been waiting there for twenty-five years to receive the first line of the masterpiece. She told him about Johnsy's fancy and *[imagination]* how she feared she would, indeed, light and fragile as a *[was afraid]* *[easily breakable]* leaf herself, float away when her slight hold upon the world grew weaker. *[small, weak]*

Old Behrman, with his red eyes plainly streaming, *[clearly]* shouted about how silly Johnsy's idea was. *[flowing]*

"What!" he cried. "Are there people in this world so foolish to believe that they will die when a leaf falls off *[drops]*

> **Stop & Think**
>
> What did Behrman drink too much of?

KEY WORDS

- **to excess** too much (≠ in moderation)
- **regard oneself as** to think of oneself as
- **den** a small quiet room
- **float away** to be carried away by the wind
- **stream** to flow
- **horrid** awful; horrible

- **fierce** ≠ meek
- **dimly lit** not bright; dark
- **fragile** easily breakable
- **plainly** clearly; obviously
- **pose as a model** to sit for someone to use as a model
- **lie sick** to be sick in bed

a vine? I have never heard of such a thing. No, I will not pose as a model for you. Why did you allow such a silly thought to enter her head? Oh, that poor little Miss Johnsy."

"She is very ill and weak," said Sue, "and the fever has
> has allowed
left her mind filled with thoughts of death and other horrible things. Very well, Mr. Behrman, if you do not care to pose for me, you don't have to. But I think you are a horrid old man."
> you don't need to
> awful, very bad

"You are just like a woman!" yelled Behrman. "Who said I will not pose? Go on. I will go with you. For half an hour, I have been trying to say that I am ready to pose. God, this is not a place in which someone as pretty as Miss Johnsy should lie sick. Someday, I will
> be sick in bed
paint a masterpiece, and we shall all go away. God, yes."
> leave

pose as a model

CHECK UP   Finish the sentences.

1 Behrman worked as
2 There was a blank canvas
3 Behrman thought Johnsy's idea
4 Behrman decided to

a. in one corner of Berhman's den.
b. pose as a model for Sue.
c. a model for artists in the colony.
d. was silly.

GRAMMAR POINT

relative pronoun : separating a noun from its relative pronoun

- . . . for *those young artists* in the colony **who** could not pay for a professional

- . . . *a blank canvas* on an easel **that** had been waiting there for twenty–five years . . .

♪ 12

windowsill

peer out

serrated

decay

Johnsy was sleeping when they went upstairs. Sue pulled the shade down to the windowsill and motioned
drew down · *gave a signal*
Behrman to go into the other room. In there, they fearfully peered out the window at the ivy vine. Then,
looked out
they looked at each other for a moment without speaking. A persistent, cold rain was falling along with
constant
some snow. Behrman, in his old blue shirt, took his seat
sat down
as the hermit–miner on an upturned kettle for a rock.
upside–down

When Sue awoke from an hour's sleep the next morning, she found Johnsy with dull, wide–open eyes staring at the drawn green shade.
draw–drew–drawn

"Pull it up. I want to see," she ordered in a whisper.
Open it. / Raise it.
Wearily, Sue obeyed.
followed
≠ *Energetically*
But, incredibly, despite the beating rain and fierce
amazingly · *in spite of*
gusts of wind that had lasted throughout the entire
strong winds
night, there still remained one ivy leaf against the wall.
It was the last one on the vine. Still dark green near its stem, but, with its serrated edges tinted yellow as it was
colored

Stop & Think

What did Johnsy tell Sue to do when she woke up?

KEY WORDS

- **motion** to give a signal; to make a motion
- **peer out** to look out at something
- **upturned** upside–down; turned over
- **gusts of wind** strong winds
- **hang** to hold on to; to cling

- **fearfully** in a scared manner; with fear
- **persistent** constant; continual
- **incredibly** amazingly
- **decay** to rot
- **lean . . . down** to bend down; to bend over

rot

beginning to decay, it hung bravely from a branch some
twenty feet above the ground.   clung *hang–hung–hung

worn face

"It is the last one," said Johnsy. "I thought it would
surely fall during the night. I heard the wind. It will fall
today, and I shall die at the same time."

weary

"Dear, dear!" said Sue, leaning her worn face down to
the pillow. "Think of me, if you won't think of yourself.
What would I do?"

bending

Stop & Think

What did Johnsy and Sue see outside?

CHECK UP   Choose the right words.

1   Sue and Behrman looked out the _____ at the ivy vine. (window | door)
2   There was still _____ left on the vine. (one leaf | two leaves)
3   Johnsy thought the last leaf would fall during the _____. (day | night)
4   Was Johnsy ready to die? (Yes | No)

GRAMMAR POINT

despite (= in spite of)

• **Despite** the beating rain and fierce gusts of wind . . . , there still remained one ivy leaf against the wall.

tie

twilight

eave

stir

But Johnsy did not answer. The most lonesome thing `----> lonely` in the entire world is a soul when it is making ready to go on its mysterious, far journey. The fancy seemed to possess her more strongly as, one by one, the ties that `----> distant ≠ near` `----> connections` bound her to friendship and to Earth were loosed. `----> take up` `----> tied *bind-bound-bound` `----> were freed`

The day passed, and even in the twilight, they could see the lone ivy leaf clinging to its stem against the `----> hanging` wall. And then, with the coming of the night, the north wind again began to blow while the rain still beat against the windows and ran down the eaves. `hit`

When it was light enough, Johnsy, the merciless, commanded that the shade be raised. `----> ordered` `without mercy, cruel`

The ivy leaf was still there. `----> pulled up`

Johnsy lay for a long time looking at it. And then she called to Sue, who was stirring her chicken broth over the gas stove. `----> mixing, blending`

"I've been a bad girl, Sudie," said Johnsy. "Something has made that last leaf stay there to show me how

Stop & Think

What did Sue and Johnsy see the next morning?

KEY WORDS

- **mysterious** strange; unknown
- **twilight** the period of time when the sun goes down
- **command** to order
- **wicked** evil; very bad
- **sit up** to sit while one is in bed
- **be loosed** to be let go; to be freed
- **merciless** without mercy; cruel
- **stir** to mix; to blend
- **sin** a bad deed; a wrong act
- **even chances** a fifty-percent chance

wicked I was. It is a sin to want to die. You may bring
> evil, bad   > bad deed, wrong act
me a little broth now and some milk with a little port in
                                    port wine <
it, and . . . No, bring me a hand–mirror first, and then
pack some pillows about me, and I will sit up and watch
> set
you cook."

hand–mirror

An hour later, she said, "Sudie, someday I hope to
paint the Bay of Naples."

The doctor came in the afternoon, and Sue had an
excuse to go into the hallway as he left.   made an excuse

pillow

"Even chances," said the doctor, taking Sue's thin,
> a fifty–percent chance; 50%
shaking hand in his. "With good nursing, you'll win.
> trembling   > care
And now I must see another case I have downstairs.
Behrman, his name is–some kind of an artist, I believe.
Pneumonia, too. He is an old, weak man, and the attack
is acute. There is no hope for him, but he goes to the
> ≠ chronic
hospital today to be made more comfortable."

CHECK UP Put the right words.

> the last leaf   nutrition   pneumonia   wicked

1 Johnsy looked at _____ for a long time.
2 Johnsy said it was _____ for her to want to die.
3 The doctor told Sue that Behrman had _____.
4 The doctor said that Johnsy needed _____ and care.

GRAMMAR POINT

command that + S (+ should) + V

• Johnsy, the merciless, **commanded** that the shade **(should) be raised**.

knit

janitor

The next day, the doctor said to Sue, "She's out of danger. You've won. Nutrition and care now–that's all she needs."

→ safe

→ healthy food   → nursing

That afternoon, Sue went to the bed where Johnsy lay, contentedly knitting a very blue and very useless woolen shoulder scarf, and she put one arm around her, pillows and all.

→ happily

"I have something to tell you, my dear," she said. "Mr. Behrman died of pneumonia in the hospital today. He was ill for only two days. The janitor found him on the morning of the first day in his room downstairs helpless

→ caretaker

Stop & Think

What happened to Behrman?

KEY WORDS

- **out of danger** safe
- **janitor** a person who looks after a building; a cleaning man
- **helpless** unable to help oneself
- **dreadful** awful; horrible
- **flutter** to move, often because of the wind
- **contentedly** happily
- **be soaked** to be very wet
- **scattered** spread out

with pain. His shoes and clothing were soaked and icy

→ *were very wet*

cold. They couldn't imagine where he had been on such

a dreadful night. And then they found a lantern, still

→ *awful, horrible*

lit, a ladder that had been dragged from its place, some

→ *drawn*

scattered brushes, and a palette with green and yellow

→ *spread out*

colors mixed on it, and–look out the window, dear, at

the last ivy leaf on the wall. Didn't you wonder why

it never fluttered or moved when the wind blew? Ah,

→ *moved by wind*

darling, it's Behrman's masterpiece. He painted it there

the night that the last leaf fell."

lantern

ladder

palette

CHECK UP   True or false?

1 The janitor saw Behrman painting outside. _____
2 Behrman was found with his shoes and clothes soaking wet. _____
3 Behrman painted the last leaf. _____
4 The last leaf was Behrman's masterpiece. _____

GRAMMAR POINT

die of / die from

- Mr. Behrman **died of** pneumonia in the hospital today.
- She **died from** injuries after the car accident.

The Last Leaf   **87**

Super
Reading
Story
Training
Book

TRAINing
BOOK

Table of
Contents

《經典文學故事》

《 童話寓言故事 》

Super
Reading
Story
Training
Book

Step

4

What Men Live By

— Leo Tolstoy

•

How Much Land Does
a Man Need?

— Leo Tolstoy

What Men Live By

There was once / a poor shoemaker / named Simon. He had no house or land. He lived in a hut / with his wife and children. One morning, / he went to the village / to buy some sheepskins / for a winter coat. He had only three rubles, / but he planned / to visit some of his customers / on the way. They owed him five rubles / for work / he had already done.

Simon visited several customers' houses, / but he could not collect any money. He went to the store / and asked if he could buy the sheepskins / on credit. But the shopkeeper refused / to give them to Simon.

Simon felt downhearted / and started walking homeward. "Though I have no sheepskin coat, / I don't care. I can live / without a coat. Yet my wife will surely fret," he thought.

While he was walking home, / he passed by a church / at the bend in the road. Simon saw something white / behind the church. He did not know / what it was. He came closer, / and, to his surprise, / it was a naked man. He was sitting against the church / without any clothes on.

Suddenly, / Simon felt afraid. "Robbers must have killed him / and stolen his clothes. If I interfere, / I will have a big problem," Simon thought.

Simon continued walking, / but when he looked back, / he saw / the man was moving. Simon felt more frightened.

"If I go there, / he might kill me / for my clothes. Even if he doesn't attack me, / what can I do for him?" thought Simon.

He ran down the road. But he suddenly stopped.

·hut 木屋　·sheepskin 羊皮　·ruble 盧布（俄國的錢幣單位）·customer 客人
·on the way 在路上　·owe 欠　·collect 收帳　·on credit 賒帳　·refuse 拒絕
·feel downhearted 覺得沮喪　·pass by 經過　·naked 光著身子　·robber 強盜
·interfere 介入　·have a big problem 惹上大麻煩　·look back 回頭看
·frightened 受驚的　·attack 攻擊

CLOSE UP

1　**owed him five rubles** 欠他五盧布
〈owe＋人＋錢〉是「向某人借多少錢」、「欠某人多少錢」的意思。

2　**to his surprise** 出乎他所料
to one's surprise是「出乎某人意料之外」、「令人訝異的是」的意思。
例 To my surprise, he was alive.（出乎我所料，他竟還活著。）

3　**must have killed him and (must have) stolen his clothes** 一定殺了他、搶了他的衣服
〈must have p.p.〉是「一定已經……了」的意思，用於對過去的事作很有把握的推測時。

人靠什麼存活

　　從前 once 有一個貧窮的鞋匠 a poor shoemaker 叫西門 named Simon，他沒有房子，也沒有土地 have no house or land，他和妻子、孩子 with his wife and children 住在一棟小木屋裡 live in a hut。有天早晨 one morning，他到村莊裡 go to the village 買些羊皮 buy some sheepskins 想做一件冬天的大衣。他只有三個盧布 only three rubles，他計劃 plan 在路上 on the way 拜訪 visit 他的幾個顧客 some of his customers，他幫他們做鞋 for work he does，他們還欠他五個盧布 owe him five rubles。

　　西門拜訪了幾個客戶的家，但收不到半毛錢 cannot collect any money。他到商店裡 go to the store 問能不能賒帳 on credit 買羊皮，但店主 the shopkeeper 拒絕把羊皮賣給西門 refuse to give them to Simon。

　　西門覺得很沮喪 feel downhearted，於是往回家路上走 walk homeward。「儘管我沒有羊皮大衣 have no sheepskin coat，我不在乎 don't care，我沒有大衣 without a coat 也活得下去 can live，但我太太 my wife 一定會很憂愁 will surely fret。」他想。

　　當他走回家的時候，在路上的轉彎處 at the bend 經過一間教堂 pass by a church，西門看到有個白白的東西 something white 在教堂後面 behind the church，他不知道那是什麼，他走近 come closer 一看，很訝異 to his surprise。那是一個光著身子的男子 a naked man，一絲不掛地 without any clothes on 背靠著教堂坐著 sit against the church。

　　突然間 suddenly，西門很害怕 feel afraid。「強盜 robbers 一定殺了他 kill him，搶了他的衣服 steal his clothes。如果我插手 interfere，我會惹上大麻煩 have a big problem。」西門想。

　　西門繼續走 continue walking，但他回頭 look back 一看，他看到那個人動了，西門更害怕 feel more frightened 了。

　　「如果我去那裡 go there，他可能會為了我的衣服 for my clothes 把我殺掉 kill me。即使他沒有攻擊我 attack me，我又能為他做什麼呢？」他想。

　　他往前跑 run down the road，但他突然停下來 suddenly stop。

"What am I doing? The man could be dying!" He felt guilty, / so he turned around / and went back to the church.

When Simon went behind the church, / he saw / that the stranger was a young man. He was freezing and frightened. Simon immediately took off his coat / and put it around the man. Then, / he put boots on the man. Simon had / an extra pair of boots.

"Can you walk?" asked Simon. "It's too cold / to stay here. I will take you / to my home. Here is a stick for you / to lean on / while you walk."

The man stood up / and looked kindly at Simon. But he did not speak. As they walked to Simon's home, / Simon asked him / where he was from / and how he got to the church. The man replied / with a calm voice, "I'm not from around here. God has punished me."

Simon was surprised by the response. But he said, "Well, God rules all men. Come home with me / and at least / make yourself warm." As Simon walked with the stranger, / he felt glad / to help another person.

Simon's wife was preparing dinner / when Simon and the man / came into the house. Matryna noticed / that the man had no hat / and was wearing felt boots. And he was wearing her husband's coat. Simon had no sheepskins. Her heart was ready to break / with disappointment. "He has been out drinking, / and now he has brought another drunk home / with him," she thought.

Simon took off his hat / and sat down on the bench / as if things were all right. Then, he said, "Have a seat, my friend, / and let us have some dinner."

Matryna became very angry / and said, "I cooked dinner, / but not for you. You went out / to buy some sheepskins / but bring a strange man home / instead. He doesn't even have / any clothes of his own. You must have spent / all our money / on vodka. I have no supper / for drunkards like you."

·feel guilty 覺得愧疚　·turn around 轉身　·go back 回去　·stranger 陌生人
·freezing 凍死人的　·take off 脫下　·extra 多的　·stick 枴杖　·lean on 靠著
·stand up 站起來　·calm 平靜的　·punish 懲罰　·be surprised by 對……感到驚訝
·response 回應　·at least 至少　·notice 注意　·felt boots 毛氈靴子
·disappointment 失望　·bring 帶　·drunk 喝醉的　·supper 晚餐
·drunkard 醉漢

CLOSE UP

1 **her heart was ready to break** 她的心要碎了
〈be ready to . . .〉是「快要……」的意思。

2 **as if things were all right** 好像一切都很好的樣子
〈as if . . .〉是「有如……」的意思。

3 **any clothes of his own** 任何屬於他自己的衣服
of one's own是「屬於某人的」的意思。例 a shop of my own（屬於我的店）

「我在做什麼？那個人快死 be dying 了！」他感到愧疚 feel guilty，於是轉身 turn around 走回教堂 go back to the church。

當西門走到教堂後面 go behind the church，他看到那個陌生人 the stranger 是個年輕男子 a young man，他凍僵了 freezing，而且很害怕 frightened。西門立刻脫下他的大衣 take off his coat，把它披在男子的身上 put it around the man，然後，西門多帶了一雙靴子 have an extra pair of boots，他幫男人穿上了靴子 put boots on the man。

「你能走嗎？」西門問：「留在這裡太冷了，我帶你回我家 take you to my home，這裡有一根枴杖 a stick 你可以撐著走 lean on。」

那人站了起來 stand up 和藹地看著西門 look kindly at Simon，一語不發 do not speak。他們往西門的家走去 walk to Simon's home。西門問他從哪裡來 where he was from，又是怎麼到教堂的 how he got to the church。那人用平靜的聲音 with a calm voice 回答：「我不是附近這一帶 from around here 的人，神 God 懲罰了我 punish me。」

他的回答 by the response 讓西門很驚訝 be surprised，但他說：「好吧，神掌管所有人 rule all men，跟我回家吧 come home with me，至少 at least 能讓你溫暖 make yourself warm。」西門和陌生人一起走 walk with the stranger，幫助別人 help another person 讓他覺得很開心 feel glad。

西門和那人走進屋裡 come into the house 的時候，西門的妻子 Simon's wife 正在準備晚餐 prepare dinner。瑪琪娜 Matryna 注意到那人沒戴帽子 have no hat，腳上穿著毛氈靴子 wear felt boots，身上穿著他丈夫的大衣 wear her husband's coat。西門沒有羊皮 have no sheepskins。她的心 her heart 因失望 with disappointment 快要碎了 be ready to break。「他一定是去喝酒 be out drinking 了，現在他帶了一個醉漢 another drunk 回來。」她想。

西門脫下帽子 take off his hat，坐在板凳上 sit down on the bench，好像一切都很好的樣子，然後他說：「請坐 have a seat，我的朋友，我們一起吃晚餐 have some dinner 吧！」

瑪琪娜生氣 become angry 了，她說：「我煮了晚餐 cook dinner，但不是給你吃的 not for you，你去買羊皮，卻帶了一個陌生人回來 bring a strange man home。他甚至連一件自己的衣服 any clothes of his own 都沒有。你一定把我們所有的錢拿去買伏特加 spend all our money on vodka 了。我不把晚餐 have no supper 給像你們這樣的酒鬼 drunkards like you 吃。」

假設疑問句 ⇨ 〈疑問詞＋主詞＋動詞〉

• Simon asked him **where he was** from and **how he got** to the church.
西門問他從哪裡來，又是怎麼到教堂的。

• He saw something white. He did not know **what it was**.
他看到白白的東西，不知道那是什麼。

Simon tried to explain / to his wife / how he had met the man, / but she did not listen. She angrily walked out the door, / but then she stopped undecidedly; she wanted to work off her anger, / but she also wanted to learn / what sort of a man / the stranger was. She was curious about the man.

"If he were a good man, / he would not be naked. Where is he from?" she asked.

"That's just / what I'm trying to tell you," answered Simon. "When I passed the church, / I saw him sitting there / naked and frozen. God made me / go to help him, / or he would have died. What should I have done? So I helped him get up, / gave him my coat, / and brought him here. Don't be so angry with me. Anger is a sin."

As Matryna listened to her husband, / she looked closely at the man. He sat on the bench / without moving. His hands were folded / on his knees, / and he looked down at the floor. His eyes were closed / as if he were in pain.

"Matryna, / don't you love God?" asked Simon.

Suddenly, / her heart softened / toward the stranger. She went back into the kitchen. She set the table / and served dinner. While they were eating, / Matryna felt pity for the stranger. She did not feel angry / anymore. She even began to like him. At that moment, / the man looked at Matryna / and smiled at her. A light seemed to / come from his face.

When they had finished supper, / she asked the man / where he was from. But the man said / he did not know. All he said / was, "God punished me. I was naked and freezing cold. Then, Simon saw me, / took pity on me, / and brought me here. You have fed me / and pitied me, too. God will reward you."

· undecidedly 猶豫地　·work off 消除　·anger 憤怒　·frozen 冰凍的　·sin 罪
· be folded 交疊　·be in pain 很痛苦　·soften 軟化　·serve 送上
· feel pity for 為⋯⋯感到同情　·seem to 似乎　·take pity on 憐憫⋯⋯　·feed 餵
· reward 回報

CLOSE UP

1　**She was curious about the man.** 她對那人感到好奇。
　〈be curious about . . .〉是「對⋯⋯感到好奇」的意思。

2　**felt pity for the stranger** 同情陌生人 / **took pity on me** 憐憫我 / **pitied me** 憐憫我
　〈feel pity for . . .〉、〈take pity on . . .〉、〈pity . . .〉全都是「對⋯⋯感到同情/憐憫」的意思。

西門想把他怎麼遇到那個人的經過解釋 **try to explain** 給她太太聽，但她不想聽 **do not listen**，她很生氣地 **angrily** 走出門 **walk out of the door**，但她猶豫不決地 **undecidedly** 停了下來 **stop**，她想要平息她的憤怒 **work off her anger**，但又想了解那個陌生人到底是什麼樣的人 **what sort of a man**。她對那人感到好奇 **be curious about the man**。

「如果他是一個好人，他不該光著身子，他從哪兒來？」她問。

「這正是我想跟妳說的事 **what I'm trying to tell you**，」西門回答，「我經過教堂的時候，我看到他坐在那裡光著身子 **naked**，凍僵了 **frozen**。神讓我去幫助他 **go to help him**，不然他可能會死，我應該怎麼做？所以我扶他站起來 **help him get up**，把我的大衣給他穿 **give him my coat**，把他帶回來 **bring him here**。不要這麼生我的氣 **don't be so angry with me**。怒氣 **anger** 是一種罪 **a sin**。」

瑪琪娜趁丈夫 **listen to her husband** 說話的時候，仔細地看著那人 **look closely at the man**。他坐在板凳上 **sit on the bench** 一動也不動 **without moving**，他的雙手 **his hands** 疊 **be folded** 在膝蓋上 **on his knees**，然後低頭看著地板 **look down at the floor**。他的雙眼 **his eyes** 閉著 **be closed**，好像很痛苦 **be in pain** 的樣子。

「瑪琪娜，難道妳不愛神嗎？」西門問。

突然間，她心軟了 **soften**，回到廚房 **go back into the kitchen**，擺好桌子 **set the table**，端上晚餐 **serve dinner**。他們正在吃飯的時候，瑪琪娜對陌生人起了憐憫之情 **feel pity for the stranger**，她不再生氣，她甚至開始喜歡他 **like him**。那一刻 **at that moment**，那人看著瑪琪娜 **look at Matryna** 對著她笑 **smile at her**，他的臉上 **from his face** 似乎散發著一抹光芒 **a light**。

他們用完晚餐以後，她問那人他從哪裡來，但那人說他不知道，他只是一直說：「神處罰我，我光著身子，快凍僵 **freezing cold** 了，然後，西門看到我、同情我 **take pity on me**，把我帶來這裡 **bring me here**。妳給我食物 **feed me**，憐憫我 **pity me**，神會回報你的 **reward you**。」

if . . .（假設語氣）⇨ 有「過去式」和「過去完成式」。

- **If** he **were** a good man, he **would** not **be** naked. 如果他是好人，他不可能赤身露體。
  （過去式：和現在事實相反的假設，if子句的be動詞要用were，不用was。）

- God made me go to help him, or he **would have died**.
  (= **If** God **had** not **made** me go to help him, he **would have died**.)
  如果神沒有讓我去幫助他，他就會死去。
  （過去完成式：和過去事實相反的假設）

Matryna gave the man some clothes, / and he went to get some sleep. Then, / she and Simon went to bed, too, / but Matryna could not sleep. She could not get the stranger / out of her mind. Then, / she suddenly remembered / that they had eaten / their last piece of bread, / so there was nothing left / for tomorrow. She felt grieved.

"Simon, / what will we do tomorrow?"

"As long as we are alive, / we will find something to eat," Simon answered.

The next morning, / Simon and Matryna woke up / and saw / that the stranger was already awake. He looked much better / than the day before.

Simon said, "Well, friend, / we have to work / for a living. What work do you know?"

"I do not know anything," answered the man.

Surprised, / Simon said, "A man / who wants to learn / can learn anything."

"Then I will learn / how to work."

"What is your name?" asked Simon.

"Michael."

"Well, Michael, / if you work with me, / I will give you food and shelter," offered Simon.

"May God reward you," answered Michael. "Show me / what to do."

Simon showed Michael / how to make boots. Michael learned quickly / and was very skilled. He ate little food / and almost never went anywhere.

He made boots so well / that many people came to Simon's shop. Soon, / Simon began to make a lot of money.

A year passed. Michael lived and worked / with Simon. One day, / Simon and Michael / were working hard / when a carriage / drawn by three horses / drove up to the hut. A servant opened the door, / and a gentleman / wearing a fur coat / got out. He strode into the hut / and asked, "Which of you / is the master bootmaker?"

· **get . . . out of one's mind** 將……趕出腦海中   · **feel grieved** 感到哀傷
· **wake up** 醒來   · **awake** 醒著的   · **surprised** 驚訝的   · **shelter** 住處
· **skilled** 技術良好的   · **carriage** 馬車   · **drawn by** 被……拉著   · **drive up to** 驅車往
· **servant** 僕人   · **stride into** 大步走   · **master bootmaker** 製靴大師

CLOSE UP

1 **how to work** 怎麼工作 / **what to do** 做什麼 / **how to make boots** 如何製靴
〈how to . . .〉是「如何去……（的方法）」的意思。〈what to . . .〉是「要去……」的意思。

2 **May God reward you.** 願神獎賞你。
〈May＋主詞＋動詞原形〉是「願某人怎麼樣」的意思。 例 May God be with you.（願神與你同在。）

3 **He made boots so well that many people came to Simon's shop.**
他做靴子做得非常好以致大家都來西門的店裡光顧。
〈so . . . that . . .〉是「如此……以致於……」的意思。

瑪琪娜拿了一些衣服給那人 give the man some clothes，他睡覺 get some sleep 去了，然後她和西門也上床睡覺 go to bed，但瑪琪娜睡不著 cannot sleep，陌生人在她腦中揮之不去 cannot get the stranger out of her mind，然後她突然想起，他們吃了最後一塊麵包 their last piece of bread，明天沒有半點食物 nothing left 可以吃，她覺得很哀傷 feel grieved。

　　「西門，我們明天該怎麼辦？」

　　「只要我們還活著 be alive，我們會找到東西吃的 find something to eat。」西門回答。

　　隔天一早 the next morning，西門和瑪琪娜醒來 wake up，看到陌生人已經醒了 be awake，他看起來比前一天好很多 look much better than the day before。

　　西門說：「好吧，朋友，我們得工作 have to work 賺錢過活 for a living，你會做什麼工作？」

　　「我什麼也不會 do not know anything。」那人回答。

　　西門很驚訝地 surprised 說：「願意學習 want to learn 的人就能學會任何事 can learn anything。」

　　「那麼我願意學習怎麼工作 how to work。」

　　「你叫什麼名字 your name？」西門問。

　　「麥可 Michael。」

　　「好吧，麥可，如果你跟我一起工作 work with me，我會給你食物和住宿的地方 food and shelter。」西門提議 offer。

　　「願神獎賞你 may God reward you，」麥可回答，「請教我 show me 怎麼做 what to do。」

　　西門教麥可怎麼做靴子 how to make boots，麥可學得很快 learn quickly，而且手藝很好 be very skilled，他吃得很少 eat little food，且哪也不去 never go anywhere。

　　他做的靴子很棒 make boots so well，許多人 many people 來光顧西門的店 come to Simon's shop。不久，西門開始賺很多錢 make a lot of money。

　　一年 a year 過去了 pass，麥可和西門一同生活、工作 live and work with Simon。有一天 one day，正當西門和麥可認真工作 work hard 的時候，一輛有三匹馬拉著 drawn by three horses 的馬車 a carriage 向小木屋駛來 drive up to the hut。一個僕人 a servant 打開車門 open the door，一個紳士 a gentleman 身穿毛皮大衣 wearing a fur coat 走了出來 get out，大步走進小木屋 stride into the hut，他問：「你們哪一個 which of you 是靴子師傅 the master bootmaker？」

GRAMMAR POINT

主動的現在分詞（V-ing）/ 被動的過去分詞（V-en）

⇨ 分詞可以修飾名詞。現在分詞（V-ing）含有主動的含意，過去分詞（V-en）含有被動的含意。

- A gentleman **wearing** a fur coat got out. 一個穿著毛皮大衣的紳士走了出來。

- A carriage **drawn** by three horses drove up to the hut.
　一輛由三匹馬拉著的馬車驅車前往　小木屋。

"I am, sir," Simon answered.

Then the gentleman said, "Do you see this leather here?"

"Yes, it is good leather, sir."

"You fool," laughed the gentleman. "It is the finest leather. It comes from Germany / and is extremely expensive. I want you to make me / a pair of boots / that will last for years. If they lose their shape / or fall apart, / I will throw you into prison. After one year, / if the boots are still good, / I will pay you ten rubles / for them," said the rich man.

Simon was terrified, / but Michael advised him / to make the boots. So Simon agreed, / and then he measured the gentleman's feet. While he was doing that, / Simon saw / Michael was gazing behind the rich man / as if someone were there. Suddenly, / Michael smiled, / and his face turned bright.

"What are you grinning at, / you fool?" shouted the man. "You had better make these boots / on time. I will come back / in two days."

"They will be ready," answered Michael.

After he left, / Simon looked at Michael / and said, "Michael, / we must be cautious / with this expensive leather. We cannot make a single mistake."

Michael started cutting the leather, / but he did not cut it / for boots. Instead, / he started to make soft slippers. Simon saw / what Michael was doing, / and he was shocked.

"What are you doing, / Michael? The gentleman ordered boots, / not slippers. You've ruined that leather. What's going to happen to me now?"

·fool 傻瓜　·extremely 非常地　·last 持續　·lose one's shape 變形
·fall apart 裂開　·throw . . . into prison 把⋯⋯丟進大牢　·terrified 嚇人的
·advise 建議　·measure 測量　·gaze 盯　·grin at 對⋯⋯微笑　·on time 準時
·cautious 謹慎的　·make a mistake 犯錯　·ruin 毀掉

CLOSE UP

1　**a pair of boots that will last for years** 一雙可以穿好幾年的靴子
這裡的 last 是動詞「夠用」、「（功能）持續」的意思，that will last for years 是修飾 a pair of boots 的關係子句。

2　**advised him to make the boots** 建議他做靴子
〈advise . . . to . . .〉是「建議⋯⋯去⋯⋯」的意思。

3　**You had better make these boots on time.** 你最好準時做完這雙靴子。
〈had better＋動詞原形〉是「最好⋯⋯」的意思，表警告，意指如果不這樣做的話，可能會有不好的事發生。
〈on time〉是「準時地」、「沒有耽誤時間地」的意思。

「我是，先生。」西門回答。

紳士說：「你看到這些皮 **see this leather** 了嗎？」

「是的，這是很好的皮 **good leather**。」

「你這個傻子 **you fool**，」紳士笑，「這是最好的皮 **the finest leather**，從德國來的 **come from Germany**，非常地昂貴 **be extremely expensive**。我要你幫我做一雙可以穿上好幾年 **last for years** 的靴子 **make a pair of boots**。如果它們變形 **lose their shape** 或裂開 **fall apart**，我就把你關進大牢 **throw you into prison**。一年後 **after one year**，如果這靴子還完好如初 **be still good**，我會付你10個盧布 **pay you ten rubles**。」富人說。

西門嚇壞了 **be terrified**，但麥可建議他做這雙靴子，於是西門同意了 **agree**，然後他量了那個人的雙腳 **measure the gentleman's feet**。西門做這些事的時候，他看到麥可盯著富人的身後 **gaze behind the rich man** 看，好像有人 **someone** 在那裡 **be there** 似的。忽然間，麥可笑了，他的臉 **his face** 變亮了 **turn bright**。

「你在對誰笑 **grin at**？你這個傻子，」富人大叫，「你最好準時 **on time** 完成，我過兩天 **in two days** 再來 **come back**。」

「我們會把靴子準備好 **be ready**。」麥可回答。

他走了以後，西門看看麥可，說：「麥可，我們用這麼貴的皮 **with this expensive leather**，一定要謹慎處理 **be cautious**，不能出半點差錯 **cannot make a single mistake**。」

麥可開始裁切皮革 **cut the leather**，但不是拿來做靴子，相反地，他開始做一雙柔軟的拖鞋 **make soft slippers**。西門看到麥可正在做的事 **what Michael is doing**，非常震驚 **be shocked**。

「你在做什麼，麥可？那個紳士訂製的是靴子 **order boots**，不是拖鞋 **not slippers**。你已經毀了那塊皮 **ruin that leather**。我會出什麼事呢？」

GRAMMAR POINT

as if ...（假設語氣）：就像……一樣 ⇨ 好像是那樣，但事實上並不是。

- Michael was gazing behind the rich man **as if** someone **were** there.
  麥可盯著那有錢人的後面，好像有人在那裡一樣。（過去式：表與現在事實相反的假設）

- Michael was staring at the girls **as if** he **had known** them before.
  麥可盯著女孩們，好像他曾經認識她們一樣。（過去完成式：表與過去事實相反的假設）

At that very moment, / the gentleman's servant / rushed into the hut.

"My master does not need boots anymore," he announced. "He is dead. He did not even make it home alive / as he died in the carriage. My master's wife / sent me here / to cancel the order for boots. Instead, / she wants you to quickly make / a pair of soft slippers / for his corpse."

Simon was amazed. Michael took / the pair of soft slippers / he made / and handed them to the servant.

More time passed, / and Michael had now lived with Simon / for six years. He never went anywhere, / and he was always quiet. He had only smiled / two times in six years: / once / when Matryna gave him food / and a second time / when the rich man was in their hut. Simon adored Michael / and was afraid / that Michael would leave him.

One day, / one of Simon's sons / came running to Michael. "Uncle Michael," he cried, "Look! A lady / with two little girls / is coming, / and one of the girls / is lame."

Michael immediately stopped work / and looked out the window. Simon was surprised / since Michael never looked outside. Simon also looked out / and saw / that a well-dressed woman / with two little girls / was coming to his hut. One of the girls / was crippled / in her left leg.

The woman came in / and said, "I want leather shoes / for these two girls / for spring."

Simon answered, "I have never made / such small shoes, / but my assistant Michael / is a master at making shoes, / so he can do it."

Michael was staring at the girls / as if he had known them before. Simon was confused, / but he began to measure the girls' feet. The woman mentioned / that the girls were twins.

Simon asked, "How did it happen to her? Was she born this way?"

"No," the woman answered. "Her mother crushed her leg. Their father died / one week before they were born. And their mother died / right after she gave birth to them."

·rush 趕去 ·cancel 取消 ·corpse 屍體 ·amazed 驚訝的 ·hand . . . to 把……交給
·adore 很喜歡 ·be afraid 很害怕 ·lame 跛腳的 ·crippled 跛腳的
·assistant 助理 ·master 大師 ·stare at 盯著 ·confused 困惑的 ·mention 提到
·twins 雙胞胎 ·crush 壓壞

CLOSE UP

1 **did not even make it home alive** 甚至沒有活著回到家
〈make it to . . .〉是「到……地方」、「（勉強地）在時間內到……」的意思，這裡的home是副詞，所以不加to。

2 **is a master at making shoes** 是做鞋子的大師
master是對某事相當通達的「達人、大師」的意思。
〈be a master at＋V-ing〉是「擅長做……」、「做……的達人」的意思。

3 **Was she born this way?** 她生來如此嗎？ / **she gave birth to them** 她生下她們
〈be born〉是「被生出來」的意思。〈give birth to . . .〉是「生孩子」的意思。

那一刻 at that very moment，紳士的僕人 the gentleman's servant 飛奔進小木屋 rush into the hut。

「我的主人 my master 不再需要靴子 do not need boots 了。」他宣布，「他死了 be dead，他甚至沒有活著回家，就死在馬車上了 die in the carriage。我主人的妻子 my master's wife 派我來這裡 send me here，取消訂單 cancel the order。她希望你為他的遺體 for his corpse 趕緊 quickly make 改做一雙軟拖鞋 a pair of soft slippers。」

西門很驚訝 be amazed，麥可把他做的那雙軟拖鞋拿給僕人 hand them to the servant。

日子 more time 又過去了 pass，麥可和西門 with Simon 一起住了六年 for six years，麥可哪裡都不去 never go anywhere，總是很安靜 be quiet。六年之中 in six years 只微笑 smile 了兩次 two times：一次 once 是瑪琪娜給他食物 give him food，第二次是 a second time 富人 the rich man 到他們的木屋 be in their hut 時。西門很喜歡麥可 adore Michael，很怕麥可有天會離開他。

有一天，西門其中一個兒子跑來找麥可，「麥可叔叔 Uncle Michael，」他喊：「你看 look！一位女士 a lady 帶著兩個小女孩 with two little girls 走過來，其中一個女孩 one of the girls 的腿瘸了 be lame。」

麥可立刻停下工作 stop work 往窗外一看 look out the window。西門很驚訝，因為麥可從不看窗外。西門也往外看，看到一個穿得很體面的女人 a well-dressed woman，帶著兩個小女孩，往他的木屋走來 come to his hut，其中一個女孩左腿 in her left leg 瘸了 be crippled。

女人進來以後說：「我想要做皮鞋 want leather shoes 給這兩個女孩春天穿的 for these two girls for spring。」

西門回答：「我從來沒做過這麼小的鞋子，但我的助理 my assistant 麥可是製鞋巧匠 a master at making shoes，他能幫妳做鞋子。」

麥可盯著兩個小女孩 stare at the girls，猶如他之前認識她們 know them before。西門很困惑 be confused，但他開始量女孩們的腳 measure the girls' feet。女人說兩個小女孩是雙胞胎 twins。

西門問：「她發生了什麼事？她生來如此 be born this way 嗎？」

「不，」女人回答，「她母親 her mother 壓壞她的腳 crush her leg，她們的父親在她們出世前一週過世，而母親生下她們 give birth to them 之後也過世了。」

She continued, "My husband and I / were their neighbors. When I visited their hut, / I found / that the mother, / when dying, / had rolled on this child / and crushed her leg. The babies were left alone. What could I do? I was the only woman / in the village / with a baby, / so I took both girls / and nursed them / as well."

"I thought / the crippled one / would die, / so I did not feed her / at first. But I had so much milk / that I could feed my son and both girls. Then, / my own son died / when he was two." She sighed.

"I thank God / for giving me these two girls. I would be very lonely / without them. They are precious to me."

She wiped some tears / from her face / as she told the story.

Then, Matryna said, "The old proverb is true. 'One may live / without father or mother, / but one cannot live / without God.'"

As they talked, / suddenly a bright light / filled the room. They looked at Michael, / who was the source of this light. He was smiling / and looking up at the heavens.

After the woman left / with the girls, / Michael bowed low / to Simon and Matryna. "Farewell," he said. "God has forgiven me. I ask your forgiveness, too, / for anything / I have done wrong."

They saw / a light was shining from Michael. Simon bowed to Michael / and said, "I see / that you are not an ordinary man. But please tell me. When I first met you / and brought you home, / you were quite gloomy. But you smiled at my wife / after she gave you some food. Then, / when the rich man came / and ordered boots, / you smiled again. Finally, / when the woman brought the girls, / you smiled a third time. And now / you have become / as bright as day. Why is your face shining like that, / and why did you smile / those three times?"

- neighbor 鄰居　- roll on 翻身　- nurse 養育　- sigh 嘆氣　- lonely 孤單的
- precious 珍貴的　- wipe tears 拭淚　- proverb 箴言　- source 來源
- look up 向上看　- the heavens 天堂；天上　- bow 鞠躬　- farewell 道別；再見
- forgive 原諒　- shine 發光　- ordinary 平凡的　- gloomy 憂鬱的
- three times 三次

1 **thank God for giving me these two girls** 感謝神給我這兩個女孩
〈thank . . . for . . . 〉是「對……因……表示感謝」的意思。

2 **bowed low to Simon and Matryna** 向西門和瑪琪娜深深鞠躬 /
bowed to Michael 向麥可鞠躬
〈bow to . . . 〉是「向……(彎腰)鞠躬」、「向……點頭示意」的意思。
bow low：「深深地彎腰一鞠躬」。

3 **have become as bright as day** 變得像白天一樣明亮
〈as bright as day〉是「像白天一樣明亮」的意思。

她繼續説：「我丈夫和我 my husband and I 是他們的鄰居 their neighbors，當我去探視他們的木屋 visit their hut 時，我發現她們的母親快要死了，臨死前她轉身壓在這個孩子的身上，壓壞了她的腳。這一家只留下 be left alone 小嬰兒 the babies。我能怎麼辦？我是村裡 in the village 唯一 the only 有嬰兒 with a baby 的女人 woman，於是我把兩個女孩帶走 take both girls，養育她們 nurse them。」

「我以為瘸腿的女孩 the crippled one 會死，所以我一開始 at first 沒餵她 do not feed her，但我有很多奶水 have so much milk，所以我能餵飽我兒子和兩個女孩 feed my son and both girls。結果，我自己的兒子 my own son 兩歲 be two 時過世了 die。」女人嘆息 sigh。

「我感謝神 thank God 給我這兩個女孩，如果沒有她們 without them 我會很孤單 be very lonely，對我來說她們很寶貝 be precious。」

她一邊敘述 tell the story 一邊擦拭臉上的淚水 wipe some tears from her face。

瑪琪娜説：「一句古老的諺語 the old proverb 説的是真的 be true－『人可以活著 may live 沒有父母 without father or mother，但是不能活著 cannot live 沒有神 without God。』」

他們在聊天時，突然一道白光 a bright light 充滿了整個房間 fill the room，他們看著麥可 look at Michael，因為他是光芒的來源 the source of this light，他正微笑看著天上 look up at the heavens。

女人帶著兩個女孩離開以後，麥可向西門和瑪琪娜深深鞠躬 bow low。「再見 farewell，」他説：「神已經原諒我了 forgive me。如果我曾做錯什麼 do wrong，我也請求你們的原諒 ask your forgiveness。」

他們看到一道光 a light 從麥可身上 from Michael 散發出來 shine。西門向麥可鞠躬 bow to Michael 説：「我知道你不是凡人 an ordinary man，但請告訴我 tell me，我第一次遇見你 first meet you、帶你回家 bring you home 時，你看起來很憂鬱 be quite gloomy，但當我妻子給你食物 give you some food 後，你卻對她微笑 smile at my wife，接著富人 the rich man 來訂靴子 order boots 的時候，你再次微笑 smile again，最後，那婦人 the woman 帶兩個女孩 bring the girls 來的時候，你第三次微笑 smile a third time。現在你如白晝般明亮 as bright as day，為什麼你的臉會這樣發光 shine like that 呢？你為什麼微笑那三次 smile those three times 呢？」

Michael answered, "Light is shining from me / because I was punished, / but now God has forgiven me. I smiled three times / because God sent me here / to learn three truths, / and I have learned them. I learned the first / when your wife pitied me, / so I smiled then. I learned the second / when the rich man ordered the boots, / so I smiled again. And I learned the third / when I saw the little girls, / so I smiled for the third time."

Simon asked, "Michael, / why did God punish you? And what are the three truths? I would like to learn them / for myself."

Michael answered, "God punished me / because I disobeyed Him. I was an angel in Heaven, / but I disobeyed God. God sent me / to take the soul of a woman. I came down to Earth / and saw a sick woman / lying alone. She had just given birth to twin girls. The woman saw me / and said, 'Angel of God, / my husband has just died, / and there is no one / to look after my girls. Do not take my soul. Let me live / to care for my babies. Children cannot live / without father or mother.'"

Michael continued, "I put one child at her breast / and put the other in her arms. Then, / I returned to Heaven. I told God, 'I could not take the mother's soul. Her husband died, / and the woman has twins / and prays to stay alive.'"

"But God said, 'Go back / and take the woman's soul, / and learn three truths: Learn / what dwells in man. Learn / what is not given to man. And learn / what men live by. When you learn all three things, / you may return to Heaven.'"

- **be punished** 受罰　• **truth** 真理　• **the third time** 第三次　• **disobey** 違背
- **Heaven** 天堂　• **take a soul** 取走靈魂　• **lie alone** 獨自躺著　• **care for** 照顧
- **breast** 胸部　• **pray** 祈求　• **stay alive** 活下去　• **dwell** 住　• **live by** 靠……活著

CLOSE UP

1. **sent me here to learn three truths** 派我來這學習三件事 /
   sent me to take the soul of a woman 派我帶走女人的靈魂
   〈send . . . to . . .〉是「派……去……」的意思。

2. **I would like to learn them** 我想學它們
   〈I would like to . . .〉是「我想要……」的意思。

3. **look after my girls** 照顧我的女兒 / **care for my babies** 照顧我的寶寶
   〈look after . . .〉和〈care for . . .〉是「照顧/照料……」的意思。

麥可回答：「我之前受神懲罰 be punished，但如今神已經原諒我 forgive me 了，所以光從我身上散發出來，我微笑是因為我已經學會神差我來這裡 send me here 要我學的三項真理 learn three truths。你妻子憐憫我 pity me 的時候，我學會了第一件事 the first，所以我笑了；當富人來訂靴子 order the boots 的時候，我學會了第二件事 the second，所以我又笑了；當我看到兩個小女孩 see the little girls 的時候，我學會了第三件事 the third，所以我笑了第三次。」

　　西門問：「麥可，為什麼神要懲罰你？那三項真理又是什麼呢？我也想學那三件事。」

　　麥可回答：「因為我違背祂 disobey Him，所以受到神的懲罰，我曾是天堂裡的天使 an angel in Heaven，但我沒有順服神。神派我把一個女人的靈魂帶走 take the soul of a woman，於是我來到人間 come down to Earth。我看到一個生病的女人 a sick woman 獨自躺著 lie alone，剛剛生下一對雙生女嬰 just give birth to twin girls。女人看見我 see me，就說：「神的天使 Angel of God，我丈夫 my husband 剛死 just die，沒有人 no one 可以照顧我女兒 look after my girls，請不要帶走我的靈魂，讓我活下來 let me live 照顧我的寶寶 care for my babies。孩子們沒有父母會活不了。」

　　麥可繼續說：「我把一個孩子 one child 放在她的胸部上 at her breast，另一個 the other 放在她的手臂中 in her arms，然後，我便回到天堂 return to Heaven。我告訴神：『我不能帶走那位母親的靈魂，她的丈夫死了，留下一對雙胞胎 have twins，她祈求能繼續活下去 pray to stay alive。』」

　　「但神說：『回去 go back，帶回那個女人的靈魂，學習三項真理 learn three truths：認識什麼住在人裡面 what dwells in man；認識神沒有賜給人什麼 what is not given to man；認識人靠什麼活著 what men live by。當你學會這三件事，你才能回到天堂。』」

be + p.p.（被動語態）

⇨ 主詞「承受」動詞的行為時使用，行為者放在 by 之後，從句意就能知道行為者是誰的話，這時一般都會將行為者省略。

- I **was punished** (by God), but now God has forgiven me.
  我被神懲罰，但如今神已經原諒我了。

- Learn what **is** not **given** to man. 認識神沒有賜給人什麼。

"So I flew back to Earth / and took the mother's soul. The babies fell from her breast. Her body rolled over on the bed / and crushed one of the baby's legs. I tried to fly up to Heaven / with the mother's soul, / but my wings suddenly dropped off. Then, / I fell to Earth. That is / how you found me, Simon."

Simon and Matryna now understood / who had been living with them, / so they began to cry for joy.

The angel Michael said, "I was alone in the field / and naked. I had never known / cold or hunger / until I became a man. I crawled to a church. Then, / I saw a man / coming down the road.

"He frowned / as he passed me, / but he came back / a few minutes later. He gave me some clothes / and brought me to his house. When I entered the house, / his wife seemed very angry. She wanted to send me back into the cold, / but her husband mentioned God to her. The woman changed / at once. When she brought me some food, / I looked at her. I noticed / she had changed. She had become alive, / and God was in her.

"Then, / I remembered the first lesson / God had sent me. God told me, 'Learn / what dwells in man.' I understood. It was love. Love lives in men. God had shown me the first truth, / so I smiled."

"After a year, / a rich gentleman came / to order some boots. I looked at him / and saw the Angel of Death / standing behind him. Only I could see the Angel of Death, / so I knew / that he would die soon. The man was about to die, / yet he wanted boots / that would last for years.

"Then, / I remembered God's second order: 'Learn / what is not given to man.' I learned / that men are not given the knowledge / to know / what they need. So I smiled / for a second time."

·**fly back** 飛回去   ·**drop off** 脫落   ·**joy** 歡樂 ≠ sadness   ·**crawl** 爬   ·**frown** 皺眉
·**alive** 活著   ·**stand** 站

CLOSE UP

1   **that is how you found me** 那就是你找到我的經過
    〈that is how . . .〉是「那就是⋯⋯的整個經過情形」的意思，表示事件的整個來龍去脈。

2   **the man was about to die** 那人將要死
    〈be about to . . .〉是「即將⋯⋯」、「很快就會⋯⋯」的意思。

3   **the knowledge to know what they need** 明白他們需要什麼的能力
    knowledge（知識、分析能力）是 know（知道）的名詞。

「於是我飛回人間 fly back to Earth，帶走那位母親的靈魂 take the mother's soul。小寶寶從她的胸前掉下來 fall from her breast，她的身體在床上翻了過去 roll over on the bed，壓壞了其中一個寶寶的腳 crush one of the baby's legs。我試著帶母親的靈魂 with the mother's soul 飛回天堂 fly up to Heaven，但我的雙翼 my wings 突然掉落 drop off，我掉到人間 fall to Earth，這就是你發現我 find me 的經過，西門。」

西門和瑪琪娜現在明白誰和他們住在一塊，於是他們高興地大叫 cry for joy。

天使麥可 the angel Michael 說：「我在田裡 in the field 孤單一人 alone 赤身露體 naked。變成人 become a man 之前，我從不知道什麼是寒冷或飢餓 cold or hunger，我爬到教堂 crawl to a church，看到一個人沿途走來。

「他經過我 pass me 的時候，皺著眉頭 frown，但幾分鐘後 a few minutes later 他走回來 come back，給了我一些衣服 give me some clothes，帶我回到他家 bring me to his house。我進到他家 enter the house 的時候，他的妻子看起來很生氣 seem very angry，她想把我送回寒冷的屋外 send me back into the cold，但她丈夫向她提到神 mention God。那女人的態度立刻 at once 轉變了 change，她給我一些食物 bring me some food 時，我看著她 look at her，我注意到她改變了。她變得生氣勃勃 become alive，是神在她裡面 be in her。

「然後，我記起神要我學的第一課 remember the first lesson，神告訴我『認識住在人裡面的是什麼。』我明白了，是愛 love，愛住在人裡面。神將第一項真理啟示給我看，於是我笑了。」

一年過後 after a year，一個有錢的紳士 a rich gentleman 來訂製靴子 order some boots，我看著他，看到他身後站了 stand behind him 死亡天使 the Angel of Death，只有我能看見死亡天使，於是我知道他不久就死了。那人都快要死了 be about to die，他卻想要一雙可以穿很多年的靴子。

「於是，我想起神的第二個命令 God's second order：『認識神沒有賜給人什麼。』我認識人不知道自己所需的是什麼 not given the knowledge to know what they need，於是我又笑了。」

not/never . . . until . . . ：直到……才……

- I had **never** known cold or hunger **until** I became a man.
  在變成人之前，我從不知道什麼是寒冷或飢餓。

- I did **not** realize how much I loved him **until** he died.
  直到他死了以後，我才明白我有多麼愛他。

"I still did not know the third truth, / so I have waited / for God to reveal it.

"In my sixth year here, / the woman and the two girls / came. I recognized the girls / and listened to / how the woman had kept them alive. After she told the story, / I realized / that the woman had loved two children / who were not her own. I saw the living God in her, / and then I learned the last lesson: I learned / what men live by. I knew / God had revealed it to me / and had forgiven me, / so I smiled / for a third time."

Just then, / Michael's body / was surrounded by a bright light. He said, "I have learned / that all men live / not by care for themselves / but by love. I did not die / because a man and his wife / took pity on me / and loved me. The orphans stayed alive / because of the love of a woman / who was not their mother. And all men live / because love is in them. A person / who has love / is in God, / and God is in that person / because God is love."

Then, / the roof opened, / and a ray of light / fell down from Heaven. Michael spread his wings / and flew up in the light. Simon stood there, / gazing after him. After a while, / the roof was closed. No one / but Simon and his family / remained.

·reveal 啟示；揭示　·recognize 認得　·be surrounded by 被圍繞　·orphan 孤兒
·ray of light 光芒　·spread 展開　·fly up 飛上去　·remain 剩下

CLOSE UP

1　**I have waited for God to reveal it** 我等候神向我啟示它
〈wait . . . to . . .〉是「等候……去……」的意思。

2　**how the woman had kept them alive** 那女人如何讓她們存活下來
〈keep＋受詞＋補語〉是「讓……維持／保持著……的狀態」的意思。

3　**not by care for themselves but by love** 不是靠他們對自己的照顧，而是靠著愛
〈not . . . but . . .〉是「不是……而……」的意思；這裡的 care for themselves 是「自己照顧自己」也就是「愛護自己」的意思。這裡的 love 是照顧、愛護他人的心，也就是「愛心」。

「我還不知道第三項真理是什麼，於是我繼續等候神的啟示 reveal it。」

「我在這裡的第六年 in my sixth year here，婦人和兩個女孩來了。我認得那兩個女孩 recognize the girls，聽婦人說明她如何養活她們 keep them alive，她說完事情經過 tell the story 以後，我明白那婦人愛這兩個不是她親生的孩子 love two children who were not her own，在她裡面 in her 我見到永活的神 the living God，學會了第三個功課 learn the last lesson：我知道人靠什麼而活。我知道神已向我啟示、原諒我，所以我微笑了第三次。」

此時，麥可的身體 Michael's body 被亮光圍繞 be surrounded by a bright light，他說：「我認識到所有人 all men 不是憑著他們的照料 care for themselves 而活，而是靠著愛而活 live by love 我沒有死是因為一個男人和他的妻子 a man and his wife 憐憫我 take pity on me，並且愛我 love me；那兩個孤兒 the orphans 活下來 stay alive 是因為一個女人的愛 the love of a woman，而她並不是他們的親生母親。人活著是因為愛在他們裡面，有愛 have love 的人在神裡面 be in God，神也在那個人裡面 be in that person，因為神就是愛 God is love。」

於是，屋頂 the roof 開了 open，一道光 a ray of light 從天而降 fall down from Heaven，麥可展開他的雙翼 spread his wings 飛到光中 fly up in the light，西門站在那裡 stand there，盯著他的身影 gaze after him。過了一會兒 after a while，屋頂關上 be closed 了，只有西門和他的家人 but Simon and his family 還留 remain 在那裡。

GRAMMAR POINT

because ＋主詞＋動詞：因為……　**because of** ＋名詞：因為……

⇨ because 後接子句；because of 後接名詞。

- I did not die **because** a man and his wife took pity on me and loved me.
  因為有個人和他的妻子憐憫我、愛我，所以我沒有死。

- The orphans stayed alive **because of** the love of a woman.
  因為一個女人的愛，孤兒活下來了。

- All men live **because** love is in them. 因為人裡面有愛，所以人能存活。

How Much Land Does a Man Need?

An elder sister / went to visit her younger sister / in the country. The elder sister was married / to a tradesman in town / and the younger sister / to a peasant in the village. As the sisters sat over their tea talking, / the elder began to boast about / the advantages of town life. She talked about / how comfortably they lived there, / how well they dressed, / what good things they ate and drank, / and how she went to the theater and other types of entertainment.

The younger sister was annoyed / and in turn / mocked the life of a tradesman. She stood up for / the life of a peasant.

"I would not change my way of life / for yours," she said. "We may live roughly, / but at least / we are free from anxiety. You live in a better style / than we do, / but though you often earn more / than you need, / you are very likely to lose / all you have."

She continued, "We know the proverb / 'Loss and gain are brothers twain.' It often happens / that people / who are wealthy one day / are begging for their bread the next. Our way is safer. Though a peasant's life is not a fat one, / it is long."

Pahom, / the master of the house, / was lying on the top of the stove, / and he listened to the women's chatter.

"It is perfectly true," he said. "Busy as we are from childhood / farming Mother Earth, / we peasants have no time / to let any nonsense settle in our heads. Our only trouble is / that we haven't got enough land. If I had plenty of land, / I wouldn't fear the Devil himself!"

The women finished their tea, / chatted a while about dresses, / and then cleared away the tea things / and lay down to sleep. But the Devil had been sitting behind the stove / and had heard all / that was said.

· be married to 嫁給　·tradesman 商人　·peasant 農夫　·boast 誇口
·advantage 好處；優點　·entertainment 娛樂　·annoyed 煩人的　·in turn 接著
·mock 嘲諷　·stand up for 捍衛……　·one's way of life 人的生活方式
·anxiety 憂慮　·proverb 諺語　·twain 雙生子　·beg for 乞求
·the master of the house 屋主　·lie 躺　·chatter 聊天　·Mother Earth 大地
·settle 停留　·the Devil 撒旦　·clear away 清理

CLOSE UP

1 **we are free from anxiety** 我們免於憂慮
〈be free from . . .〉是「不再……」的意思，這裡的free指「沒有不愉快或痛苦」、「自由自在」。

2 **you are very likely to lose all you have** 你很可能會失去你所有的一切
〈be likely to . . .〉是「很可能會……」、「……的可能性很高」的意思，likely前面加very的話，表可能性非常高。〈all you have〉是「你擁有的全部」，也就是「你全部的財產」的意思。

3 **busy as we are from childhood** 如同孩童時期起就很忙碌
〈形容詞＋as＋主詞＋動詞〉是「如……那麼的……」的意思。

人需要多少土地？

　　有一個姊姊 an elder sister 去拜訪她住在鄉下的妹妹 visit her younger sister。姊姊嫁給鎮上的商人 be married to a tradesman，妹妹嫁給村裡的一個農夫 to a peasant。當姊妹倆坐在一塊喝茶談天 sit over their tea talking，姊姊開始誇耀 boast 鎮上生活的好處 the advantages of town life，說他們在那裡住得 live 有多舒服 how comfortably，穿得 dress 有多好 how well，吃的、喝的 eat and drink 有多好 what good things，還有戲院 the theater 和其他各種娛樂 other types of entertainment。

　　妹妹聽了覺得很煩 be annoyed，接下來 in turn 她嘲諷 mock 商人的生活 the life of a tradesman，捍衛 stand up for 農夫的生活 the life of a peasant。

　　「我才不會改變自己的生活方式 change my way of life，換成你們那樣的 for yours，」她說：「我們可能過得很差 live roughly，但至少 at least 我們無須擔憂 be free from anxiety。你們過得比我們好 live in a better style，賺的錢比所需的還多 earn more than you need，但你們有可能失去 be very likely to lose 所有的一切 all you have。」

　　她繼續說：「我們都知道諺語 know the proverb 說：『失去和獲得 loss and gain 是孿生兄弟 brothers twain』，它通常發生在今天 one day 很有錢 be wealthy，明天 the next 卻要乞討維生 beg for their bread 的人身上。我們的生活方式比較安全，雖然農夫的生活並不優渥 be not fat one，卻比較長久 be long。」

　　房子的主人 the master of the house，帕霍姆 Pahom，躺在爐子上面 lie on the top of the stove，聽見女人們的談話。

　　「這真是完全正確，」他說：「從小 from childhood 忙著耕地 farm Mother Earth，我們農夫沒有時間讓 have no time to let 任何無意義的事 any nonsense 停留在我們腦中 settle in our heads，我們唯一的煩惱 our only trouble 是土地不夠多 haven't got enough land。如果我們有足夠的土地 have plenty of land，我才不怕 wouldn't fear 撒旦本人 the Devil himself！」

　　女人喝完茶 finish their tea，聊了一會衣服 chat about dresses，收拾完 clear away 茶具 the tea things 以後，就躺下睡覺 lie down to sleep。撒旦 the Devil 一直坐在爐子後面 sit behind the stove，聽見 hear 所有的談話 all that is said。

當作主詞、補語、受詞來用的 that 子句

- **It** often happens **that** people who are wealthy one day are begging for their bread the next.
  它通常發生在今天很有錢，明天卻要向人乞討維生的人身上。
  （that子句當主詞：一般都會用虛主詞it放在句首，真主詞that子句則出現主要動詞後。）

- Our only trouble is **that** we haven't got enough land.
  我們唯一的煩惱是土地不夠多（that子句當補語：放在be動詞後。）

- Pahom heard (that) a neighbor was going to buy fifty acres of land.
  帕霍姆聽說他的鄰居要買50畝地（that子句當受詞：這時的that可以省略。）

He was pleased to hear / that the man had boasted / that if he had plenty of land, / he would not fear the Devil himself.

"All right," thought the Devil. "We will have a contest. I'll give you enough land, / and by means of that land, / I will get you into my power."

One day, / Pahom heard / that a neighbor was going to buy fifty acres of land, / so he felt envious. Pahom and his wife / sold some of their property / and borrowed some money. Then, / they bought a farm of forty acres.

So now / Pahom had land of his own. He borrowed seed / and sowed it on the land / he had bought. The harvest was a good one, / and within a year, / he had managed to pay off his debts. So he became a landowner. When he went out to plow his fields / or to look at his growing corn, / his heart would fill with joy.

However, / over time, / some of the peasants in the neighborhood / began to trespass across Pahom's land / with their cows and horses. For a long time, / Pahom forgave the owners. But at last / he lost patience / and complained to the district court. He thought, "I cannot go on overlooking it, / or they will destroy / all I have. They must be taught a lesson."

Pahom began to fine his neighbors / for trespassing on his land. This made them very upset with him, / so they started to trespass on his land / on purpose. Sometimes, / they even sneaked onto his land at night / and chopped down his trees. Pahom was furious.

He tried to figure out / who was doing it, / and he decided / that it was probably Simon. He took Simon to court, / but Pahom had no evidence / against Simon. The judges let Simon go, / so Pahom got angry at them / and quarreled with the judges / and with his neighbors. Threats to burn his building / began to be uttered.

- **have a contest** 比賽　**by means of** 藉由　**feel envious** 覺得嫉妒　**property** 財產
- **sow** 種　**manage to** 設法　**pay off one's debts** 還清債務　**landowner** 地主
- **neighborhood** 鄰近地區　**trespass** 穿過　**lose patience** 失去耐性
- **district court** 地區法院　**overlook** 忽視　**be taught a lesson** 記取教訓　**fine** 罰錢
- **upset with** 對……很不高興　**on purpose** 故意　**sneak** 偷溜　**chop down** 砍下
- **furious** 盛怒的　**figure out** 找出　**take . . . to court** 帶到法庭　**evidence** 證據
- **judge** 法官　**threat** 威脅　**utter** 說出

1　**by means of that land** 靠著那塊土地
〈by means of . . .〉意「利用……」、「藉由……的幫助」，這裡的 means 指「手段」、「方法」。

2　**he had managed to pay off his debts** 他成功地還清他的債務
〈manage to . . .〉是「設法去……」、「順利地完成……」、「用任何方法去……」。
〈pay off〉是「還清」、「償還」債務等的意思。

3　**I cannot go on overlooking it** 我不能繼續坐視不理。
〈go on＋V-ing〉是「繼續／持續去……」的意思。

他很高興 be pleased 聽到那男人誇口自己若有許多土地 plenty of land，便不怕撒旦。「好吧 all right，」撒旦想，「我們來個比賽 have a contest，我會給你足夠的土地 give you enough land，藉著土地，我會讓你擁有我的力量 get you into my power。」

有天 one day，帕霍姆聽説他的鄰居 neighbor 要買50畝地 fifty acres of land，他很嫉妒 feel envious。帕霍姆和妻子把他們一部分的財產賣掉 sell some of their property，借了一些錢 borrow some money，買了一塊40畝的農地 a farm of forty acres。

所以現在帕霍姆有自己的土地了 land of his own，他借了一些種子 borrow seed，把它們種 sow 在他買的田地裡。由於田裡的收成 harvest 很好，他在一年內 within a year 便還清了債務，於是他變成地主 become a landowner。當他出去耕田 plow his fields，或是去看他種的玉米 his growing corn，他的心充滿歡喜 fill with joy。

不過，時間一點一滴的過去 over time，附近有些農夫 some of the peasants 開始帶著他們的牛和馬 with their cows and horses 穿越帕霍姆的土地 trespass across Pahom's land。好長一段時間，帕霍姆都原諒了那些牛馬的主人 forgive the owners，但最後 at last，他失去了耐心 lose patience，向地方法庭申訴 complain to the district court。他想「我不能再坐視不理 overlook it，不然他們會毀掉我所有的一切 destroy all I have，他們必須學到教訓 be taught a lesson。」

只要鄰居穿越他的土地 trespass on his land，他就罰他們錢 fine his neighbors。這讓他們很生氣，所以他們故意 on purpose 穿過他的土地。有時候，甚至晚上偷溜到他的土地上 sneak onto his land，砍下他的樹 chop down his trees，帕霍姆氣得火冒三丈 be furious。

他試圖查明 figure out 是誰做的，他判定大概是西門 probably Simon，他帶西門到法院 take Simon to court，控告西門，但是帕霍姆沒有證據 have no evidence。法官 the judges 放了西門 let Simon go，所以帕霍姆很氣他們 get angry at them。他和法官及鄰居起了爭執 quarrel，有人開始恐嚇 threat 要燒毀他的家。

About this time, / there was a rumor / that many people were moving to a new place. "There's no need / for me / to leave my land," thought Pahom. "But some of the others / might leave our village, / and then there would be more room for us. I would take over their land myself / and make my estate a bit bigger."

One day, / Pahom was sitting at home / when a peasant / passing through the village / happened to call on him. The peasant was allowed to stay the night, / and supper was given to him. Pahom had a talk with this peasant / and asked him / where he had come from. The stranger answered / that he had come from beyond the Volga River, / where he had been working. He said / that many people were moving there. Anyone / who moved to the village / was given twenty-five acres of land / for free.

"The land there / is very good," said the peasant. "One peasant moved to the village / with nothing at all, / but now he is very wealthy."

Pahom's heart / was filled with desire. He thought, "Why should I suffer / in this narrow hole / if one can live so well elsewhere? I will sell my land here, / and with the money I get, / I will start all over again / with more land. But I must first go / and find out all about it myself."

So Pahom went down / to the land beyond the Volga. It was / just as the stranger had said. The peasants owned plenty of land. The village gave each person / twenty-five acres of land, / and people could also buy / as much land as they could afford. Pahom moved with his family / to the new settlement.

Pahom had much more land / than before. In fact, / he was ten times better off / than he had been. This made Pahom very happy. But after he got used to it, / he began to think / that even here he did not have enough land. He grew tired of / having to rent other people's land / every year. Wherever there was good land to be had, / the peasants would rush for it / and argue about the land.

- **rumor** 傳言　　**room** 空間　　**take over** 接手　　**estate** 產業　　**pass through** 經過
- **call on** 拜訪　　**beyond** 在……的那一邊　　**for free** 免費　　**suffer** 受苦
- **start all over again** 重頭來過　　**find out** 找出　　**afford** 付得起　　**settlement** 居住地
- **better off** 更有餘裕的　　**get used to** 習慣於　　**grow tired of** 對……厭煩　　**rush** 搶購

CLOSE UP

1　**There's no need for me to leave my land.** 我不需要離開我的土地。
〈there's no need to . . . 〉是「沒必要去……」的意思，
to 不定詞的行為者要用〈for＋受格〉的形式，放在 to 不定詞前。

2　**could also buy as much land as they could afford** 也可以買很多自己負擔得起的地
〈as much/many . . . as. . . 〉是「像……一樣多的……」的意思。

3　**he was ten times better off than he had been** 他比以前富裕 10 倍
time 可以用來表倍數，例如 three times（三倍）、four times（四倍）；表兩倍的話，twice 比 two times 更常用。

這時候 about this time，有傳言 rumor 説許多人 many people 要遷居到一個新的地方 move to a new place。「我不需要 there's no need 離開我的土地 leave my land，」帕霍姆想，「但有些人 some of the others 可能會離開我們的村莊 leave our village，那麼就會有更多地方讓我們耕種，我將親自接手他們的土地 take over their land，讓我的產業更大 make my estate a bit bigger。」

有一天，帕霍姆坐在家裡 sit at home，有一個農夫經過村莊 pass through the village 突然來拜訪他 call on him，帕霍姆讓這個農夫留宿一晚 stay the night，招待他吃晚餐。帕霍姆和這位農夫聊天 have a talk，問他從哪裡來，這個陌生人 the stranger 回答他從伏加河的另一頭來到這裡 come from beyond the Volga River，他曾在那裡工作。許多人都要搬去那裡 move there，任何搬進那座村莊的人 move to the village，就可以免費 for free 獲得 25 畝地 twenty–five acres of land。

「那裡的土地 the land there 很肥沃 be very good，」那個農夫説：「有一個農夫一開始一貧如洗 with nothing，搬到那個村莊以後，現在很有錢 be very wealthy。」

帕霍姆心裡 Pahom's heart 充滿了慾望 be filled with desire，他想，「如果人可以在其他地方過得這麼好，為什麼我要擠在這個窄洞裡 in this narrow hole 受苦 suffer？我要把我的土地賣掉 sell my land，用我所得到的錢 with the money I get，從頭來過 start all over again，得到更多土地 with more land，但是我得先去，親自打探消息 find out all about it。」

於是帕霍姆來到 go down 伏加河另一邊的土地，如陌生人所説的，那裡的農夫擁有許多田地 own plenty of land，村莊給每個人 25 畝地，大家也可以買自己能負擔得起的土地 as much land as they can afford。帕霍姆帶著全家 with his family 搬到新的居住地 to the new settlement。

帕霍姆比以前擁有更多地 have much more land，事實上，他比以前富裕 10 倍 be ten times better off，這讓帕霍姆相當開心，但是等他習慣 get used to it 以後，他又開始覺得他在這裡沒有足夠的田地 do not have enough land。他很厭煩 grow tired of 每年都要跟別人租地 rent other people's land。哪裡有好田地可以買 good land to be had，農夫就會急忙去搶購 rush for it，為土地爭吵 argue about the land。

where（關係副詞）：……的地方 　 **wherever**（關係副詞）：任何……的地方

⇨ 關係副詞 where 接在表場所的名詞之後，形成關係子句修飾該名詞，此時子句的功能是要説明一個不可以省略的必要資訊，稱為限定用法；當 where 引導的關係子句只是附帶説明與該場所有關的事時，稱為非限定用法，這時 where 前面要加逗號來區隔用法。

- He went to *a place* **where** they had pitched their tents. 他到他們紮營的地方去。
  （限定用法）

- He had come from *beyond the Volga River*, **where** he had been working.
  他從伏加河的另一頭來到這裡，他曾在那裡工作。（非限定用法：where 前要加逗點）

- **Wherever** there was good land to be had, the peasants would rush for it.
  哪裡有好田地可以買，農夫就會急忙去搶購。

"If it were my own land," thought Pahom, "I would be independent, / and there would not be all this unpleasantness."

So Pahom began looking out for land / which he could buy. One day, / a peddler went by his house. He said / that he was just returning / from the land of the Bashkirs, / which was far away. There, / he had bought / thirteen thousand acres of land / for one thousand rubles.

"That area has so much land / that you could walk for a year / and still be in the land of the Bashkirs. They sell their land / for very cheap prices. All one has to do / is / make friends with the chief. The land lies near a river, / and the whole prairie is virgin soil."

Pahom was curious, / so he made up his mind / to visit the land of the Bashkirs. Before he went there, / he bought some gifts. The peddler had told him / that it was their custom / to give gifts.

On the seventh day of his travels, / he came to a place / where the Bashkirs had pitched their tents. It was all / just as the peddler had said. The people lived by a river / on the steppes / in felt-covered tents.

They were a simple people. They did not farm at all. The men merely sat around, / drank tea, / ate lamb, / and played their pipes to make music. Still, / despite being uneducated and knowing no Russian, / they were good-natured enough.

As soon as they saw Pahom, / they came out of their tents / and gathered around their visitor. An interpreter was found, / and Pahom told them / he had come about some land. They took Pahom / and led him into one of the best tents. Pahom took some presents out of his cart / and distributed them among the Bashkirs. The Bashkirs were delighted.

- independent 獨立的　　- unpleasantness 不愉快　　- look out for 向外尋找
- peddler 小販　- virgin soil 處女地　- make up one's mind 下定決心　- custom 習俗
- pitch 紮營　- steppe 大草原　- felt-covered tent 毛氈的帳棚　- farm 耕地
- merely 只是　- despite 除了　- uneducated 沒受過教育的
- good-natured 善良溫厚的　- interpreter 通譯員　- take . . . out of . . . 從……拿出
- distribute 分送　- delighted 高興的

CLOSE UP

1　**All one has to do is (to) make friends with the chief.** 你只須要跟首領交朋友。
〈all . . . have to do is (to) . . . 〉是「……要做的事就只是……」、「……只要做……就可以了」的意思。

2　**he made up his mind to visit the land of the Bashkirs**
他下定決心要探訪巴什基爾人的地
〈make up one's mind to . . . 〉是「決定／下定決心要去……」的意思，也可以換成〈decide to……〉

3　**as soon as they saw Pahom** 他們一看到帕霍姆
〈as soon as . . . 〉是「一當……」的意思。

「如果那是我自己的地 my own land，」帕霍姆想，「我就獨立 be independent 了，這一切的不愉快 all this unpleasantness 就會消失了。」

於是帕霍姆開始到處去找尋他買得起的土地 look out for land。有一天 one day 有一個小販 a peddler 經過他的家 go by his house，他說他剛 just 從巴什基爾人的地 the land of the Bashkirs 回來 return，那在很遠的地方 be far away，他在那裡用 1000 盧布 for one thousand rubles 買下 13000 畝地 thirteen thousand acres of land。

「那個地區 that area 有很多土地 have so much land，你可以走上一年 walk for a year，卻還在巴什基爾人的地上 be in the land of the Bashkirs。他們用很便宜的價錢 for very cheap prices 販賣土地 sell their land。你只需要 all one has to do 跟首領交朋友 make friends with the chief。那片地在河附近 lie near a river，整個草原 the whole prairie 都是處女地 virgin soil。」

帕霍姆很好奇 be curious，於是他下定決心 make up his mind 要去探訪那片土地 visit the land，他出發前買了一些禮物 buy some gifs，小販告訴他送禮 give gifts 是他們的習俗 their custom。

旅途的第七天 on the seventh day，他來到巴什基爾人紮營的地方 pitch their tents，正如小販所說，他們住在河邊 by a river 的大草原上 on the steppes，住在毛氈的帳棚裡 in felt-covered tents。

他們是一群單純的人 simple people，不需要耕地 do not farm，只是坐在一起 sit around，喝茶 drink tea，吃羊肉 eat lamb，吹笛 play their pipes 作樂 make music。除了沒受過教育 be uneducated，不會說俄文 know no Russian，他們相當善良溫厚 good-natured enough。

他們一看到帕霍姆 see Pahom 就走出帳棚 come out of their tents 圍在這位訪客旁邊 gather around their visitor。他們找了一名通譯員 an interpreter，帕霍姆告訴他們，他是為了土地而來 come about some land。他們帶帕霍姆 take Pahom 進到其中一個最好的帳棚 into one of the best tents。帕霍姆從他的推車上 out of his cart 拿出了一些禮物 take some presents，分送給他們 distribute them。巴什基爾人很高興 be delighted。

GRAMMAR POINT

which（關係代名詞）

⇨ 代替前面出現的事物（先行詞）。which 引導的關係子句說明一個不可以省略的必要資訊，稱為限定用法；附帶說明和該事物有關的事項，稱為非限定用法。

- So Pahom began looking out for *land* **which** he could buy.

  於是帕霍姆開始到處去找尋他買得起的土地。（限定用法）

- He was just returning from *the land of the Bashkirs*, **which** was far away.

  他剛從巴什基爾人的地回來，那在很遙遠的地方。（非限定用法：which前要加逗點）

The Bashkirs talked for a while / and then told the interpreter to translate. "They wish to tell you," said the interpreter, "that they like you, / and that it is our custom / to do all we can / to please a guest / and to repay him for his gifts. You have given us presents. Now tell us / which of the things we possess / please you best / so that we may present them to you."

"What pleases me best here," answered Pahom, "is your land. Our land is crowded, / and the soil is exhausted; / but you have plenty of land, / and it is good land." The interpreter translated.

The Bashkirs talked among themselves / for a while. Then, / they were silent / and looked at Pahom / while the interpreter said, "They wish me to tell you / that in return for your presents, / they will gladly give you / as much land as you want. You have only to point it out / with your hand, / and it is yours."

The Bashkirs talked again for a while / and began to have a dispute. Pahom asked / what they were arguing about. The interpreter told him / that some of them thought / they ought to ask their chief about the land / and ought not to act in his absence.

While the Bashkirs were arguing, / a man in a large fox-fur cap / appeared on the scene. They all became silent / and rose to their feet. The interpreter said, "This is our chief himself."

Pahom immediately took out / the best dressing gown and five pounds of tea, / and he offered these to the chief. The chief accepted them / and seated himself in the place of honor. The Bashkirs at once / began telling him something. The chief listened for a while / and addressed himself to Pahom. Speaking in Russian, / he said, "Well, let it be so. Choose / whatever piece of land / you like. We have plenty of it."

·translate 翻譯　·wish to 希望　·repay 回報　·possess 擁有　·present 禮物
·crowded 擁擠的　·exhausted 疲乏的　·in return for 作為回報　·point out 指出
·have a dispute 爭吵　·ought to 應該　·chief 首領　·in one's absence 某人不在時
·fox-fur cap 狐皮帽　·on the scene 出現　·rise to one's feet 起身
·in the place of honor 上席；主位　·at once 立刻　·address 說話

CLOSE UP

1　**so that we may present them to you** 這樣我們就能把它送給你
〈so that . . .〉是「這樣就能……」、「以便……」的意思。

2　**in return for your presents** 作為你送我們禮物的回報
〈in return for . . .〉是「作為……的回報」、「作為……代價」的意思。

3　**you have only to point it out** 你只需要用手指出來
〈have only to . . .〉是「只要做……就可以了」的意思。

4　**addressed himself to Pahom** 開口跟帕霍姆說話
〈address oneself to . . .〉是「對……說話」的意思。

巴什基爾人談了一會兒 talk for a while，請通譯員翻譯 translate：「他們想告訴你 wish to tell you，」翻譯說：「他們喜歡你 like you。我們的習俗 our custom 是盡我們所能的 all we can 讓賓客高興 please a guest，報答他的禮物 repay him for his gifts。你為我們帶了禮物 give us presents，現在告訴我們，我們哪一樣東西 the things we possess 讓你最滿意 please you best，我們會把它送給你 present them to you。」通譯員如此說。

「這裡最讓我滿意 what pleases me best 的是你們的土地 your land。」帕霍姆回答：「我們的土地 our land 很擁擠 be crowded，土壤 the soil 貧乏了 be exhausted，但你們有許多土地 have plenty of land，而且是肥沃的地 good land。」通譯員翻譯道。

巴什基爾人之間 talk among themselves 討論了一會兒，然後他們靜默 be silent，看著帕霍姆 look at Pahom。通譯員說：「他們要我告訴你，作為你送禮的回報 in return for your presents，他們樂意給你土地，想要多少都可以 as much land as you want，你只需要用手 with your hand 指出你想要的地 point it out，那就是你的了。」

巴什基爾人談了一會兒，開始爭論 have a dispute。帕霍姆問他們在吵什麼，通譯員告訴他，他們其中有些人認為應該要問首領 ought to ask their chief，不應 ought not to 在他不在的時候 in his absence 自作主張 act。

當巴什基爾人爭吵的時候，一個男人頭戴狐皮製成的大帽子 in a large fox-fur cap，出現在他們眼前 appear on the scene。他們全都安靜下來 become silent，站起來 rise to their feet。通譯員說：「那是我們的首領 our chief。」

帕霍姆立刻拿出 take out 最上等的袍子 the best dressing gown 和五磅茶葉 five pounds of tea，把它們送給首領 offer these to the chief。首領接受這些禮物 accept them，坐在主位 seat himself in the place of honor。巴什基爾人立刻 at once 開始告訴他發生了什麼事 tell him something，首領聽了一會兒 listen for a while 開口跟帕霍姆說話 address himself to Pahom，用俄語說 speak in Russian：「好，就這麼做吧 let it be so，選 choose 一塊你喜歡的地 whatever piece of land you like，我們多的是。」

GRAMMAR POINT

ought to：應該要……　**ought not to**：不該……

⇨ 和助動詞 should 的意思非常像，表建議應該要去做什麼，或有義務要去做什麼。

- They **ought to** ask their chief about the land and **ought not to** act in his absence.
  他們應該要向首領稟報土地的事，不該在他不在時擅自作主。（not 要放在 to 前面）

- You don't look well. You **ought to** see a doctor. 你臉色很差，應該去看醫生。
- We **ought not to** break the rules. 你不應該違反規定。

"How can I take / as much as I like?" thought Pahom. "I must get a deed / to make it secure, / or else they may say, 'It is yours,' / and afterward / they may take it away again."

To the chief, / he said, "I must get a deed / as a guarantee, / or else / you may take the land away from me / in the future."

The chief said, "We will go to the town with you / and make a deed for the land."

"And what will be the price?" asked Pahom.

The chief answered, "Our price is always the same: one thousand rubles a day."

Pahom did not understand. "A day? What measure is that? How many acres would that be?"

The chief said, "We don't know / how to figure out the acres, / so we sell land / by the day. As much as you can go round / on your feet / in a day / is yours, / and the price is / one thousand rubles a day."

Pahom said, "But you can walk around / a large tract of land / in a single day."

The chief laughed / and then answered, "It will all be yours. But there is one condition: If you don't return to the spot / where you started / on the same day, / your money is lost. You must make a circle. You may make as large a circle / as you wish, / but you must return to your starting point / before the sun sets. Then, / all of the land / that you walked around / will be yours."

Pahom agreed to the chief's conditions, / and they decided to start / the next morning.

That night, / Pahom lay in bed / thinking about the land. He thought, "I can cover / an enormous amount of land. I can easily walk / thirty-five miles / in one day. Imagine / how much land / that will be."

·deed 契約　·secure 安全的　·or else 不然　·afterward 之後　·take away 拿走
·guarantee 保證　·measure 單位　·figure out 計算
·a large tract of land 一大片土地　·condition 條件　·spot 地方；點　·set 日落
·enormous 廣大的　·imagine 想像

CLOSE UP

1　**you may take the land away from me** 你可能從我這裡把土地拿走
〈take . . . away from . . .〉是「從……拿走……」的意思。

2　**how to figure out the acres** 畝怎麼算
這裡的 figure out 是「計算、算出」數量或費用等的意思。另外，figure out 也常拿來當作經過審慎思考後「理解／知道……」的意思。例 I can't figure out the answer.（我不知道答案。）

3　**we sell land by the day** 我們以日為單位來賣地
by 也能用來表單位。例 by the hour（以小時為單位）/ by the kilo（以公斤為單位）

「怎樣才能得到更多我想要的土地 as much as I like 呢？」帕霍姆想，「我一定要拿到契約 get a deed，這樣才安全 make it secure，不然 or else 他們可能會說：『那是你的』，然後之後 afterward 又把土地拿走 take it away。」

他對首領說：「我想要一份契約作保證 as a guarantee，不然你將來 in the future 可能從我這裡把土地拿走 take the land away from me。」

首領說：「我們會和你一起到鎮上 go to the town，立一份土地的契約 make a deed for the land。」

「那麼價錢 the price 怎麼算？」帕霍姆問。

首領回答：「我們的價錢一直以來都一樣 be always the same，一天1000盧布 one thousand rubles a day。」

帕霍姆不明白，「一天？這是什麼單位 what measure？這樣是多少畝 how many acres？」

首領說：「我們不知道畝怎麼算 figure out the acres，於是我們以日為單位 by the day 來賣地，只要一天之內 in a day 用腳 on your feet 能走多少 as much as you can go round 就都是你的，價錢都是一天1000盧布。」

帕霍姆說：「但光是一天內 in a single day 就可以走 walk around 一大片土地 a large tract of land。」

首領笑了，然後回答：「那麼土地就都是你的，但有一個條件 one condition，如果你同一天內 on the same day 回不到 don't return 你出發的地方 the spot where you start，你的錢 your money 就沒了 be lost。你一定要走一個圓 make a circle，你想要多大的圓都可以 as large a circle as you wish，但一定要在日落前 before the sun sets 回到起點 return to your starting point，那麼你所走完的土地就是你的了。」

帕霍姆同意首領的條件 agree to the chief's conditions，他們決定 decide 明天早上 the next morning 再開始 start。

那天晚上 that night，帕霍姆躺在床上 lie in bed 想著土地 think about the land，他想，「我可以走完 cover 一片廣大的土地 an enormous amount of land，我一天內 in one day 可以輕鬆走完35哩 walk thirty-five miles，想像 imagine 一下那會是多少地 how much land。」

GRAMMAR POINT

as . . . as . . . ：像……一樣……

- How can I take **as much as** I like? 怎樣才能得到更多我想要的土地？
- **As much as** you can go round on your feet in a day is yours.
  只要一天之內你用腳能走多少土地，就算你的。
- You may make **as large** a circle **as** you wish. 你想要走多大的圓都可以。
- The people on the hill were **as small as** ants. 山丘上的人看起來像螞蟻一樣小。

How Much Land Does a Man Need?　**33**

Pahom lay awake all night / and dozed off / only just before dawn. Hardly were his eyes closed / when he had a dream. In his dream, / the chief of the Bashkirs / was sitting in front of a tent / and laughing. "What are you laughing at?" he asked the chief. But the chief was no longer there. Instead, / it was the peddler / who had stopped at his house / and told him about the Bashkirs. Then, the peddler disappeared, / and the peasant / who had told him about the land beyond the Volga River / suddenly appeared. Then, / he saw / that it was not the peasant either, / but the Devil himself / with hoofs and horns, / sitting there and chuckling. There was a man / lying dead in front of the Devil, / and it was Pahom himself. He awoke horror-struck.

Looking round, / he saw through the open door / that the dawn was breaking. "It's time / to wake them up," he thought. "We ought to be starting."

Pahom, the chief, and the other Bashkirs / met on the land / early in the morning. The chief stretched his arms out / and said, "All of this land—as far as you can see– / belongs to us. You may have / any part of it / you like."

The chief took off his fox-fur cap, / placed it on the ground, / and said, "This will be the mark. Start from here / and return here again. All the land / you go around / shall be yours." Pahom took out his money / and put it on the cap.

Pahom stood / ready to start / with a spade in his hand. He considered / for some moments / which way he had better go. Then, he concluded, "I will go toward the rising sun."

·lie awake 清醒地躺著　·doze off 打瞌睡　·dawn 黎明　·hardly 幾乎　·appear 出現
·hoof 蹄　·chuckle 咯咯笑　·lying dead 橫屍　·horror-struck 驚恐萬分
·stretch out 伸出　·spade 鏟子

CLOSE UP

1 **the peddler disappeared** 那位小販消失 / **suddenly appeared** 突然出現
appear（出現）和disappear（消失不見）是相反的意思。

2 **It's time to wake them up.** 是時候把他們叫醒了
〈it's time to . . .〉是「該是……的時候了」的意思。

3 **all of this land–as far as you can see** 這裡所有的地，你能看多遠就有多遠
〈as far as . . .〉是距離、範圍、程度等的「直到……」的意思。

整晚 all night 帕霍姆清醒地躺著 lie awake，破曉前 just before dawn 才打了一會兒瞌睡 doze off，剛閉上雙眼，他就做了一個夢 have a dream。在夢裡 in his dream，巴什基爾人的首領 the chief of the Bashkirs 坐在帳棚前 sit in front of a tent，大笑 laugh。「你在笑什麼？」他問首領，但首領消失不見了 be no longer there，而是 instead，那個停留在他家 stop at his house、告訴他巴什基爾人 tell him about the Bashkirs 的那個小販 the peddler 出現了，然後小販又消失 disappear 了。那個跟他說伏加河另一邊土地 the land beyond the Volga River 的農夫 the peasant 突然出現了 suddenly appear。然後，他看了一下，又不是農夫，而是有蹄有角 with hoofs and horns 的撒旦本尊 the Devil himself，坐在那裡 sit there 咯咯笑 chuckle。有一個人橫屍 lie dead 在撒旦前面 in front of the Devil，是帕霍姆自己 Pahom himself。他又驚又怕地醒了 awake horror-struck。

他看看四周 look around，從半開的門 through the open door 看到黎明 the dawn 破曉 break。「是時候 it's time 把他們叫醒了 wake them up，」他想，「我們該開始了。」

帕霍姆、首領和其他巴什基爾人一大早在土地上碰面，首領伸出他的雙臂 stretch his arms out，說：「這裡所有的土地 all of this land，視線所達之處 as far as you can see，都屬於我們的 belong to us。你可以得到你想要的任何一部分 have any part of it。」

首領拿下他的狐皮帽 take off his fox-fur cap，放在地上 place it on the ground，說：「這個當作記號 the mark，從這裡開始 start from here，再回到這裡 return here，你走完的所有土地將會是你的。」帕霍姆拿出他的錢 take out his money，放在帽子上 put it on the cap。

帕霍姆站好準備開始 ready to start，他手拿一把鏟子 with a spade in his hand，他考慮 consider 了一會兒 for some moments 他應該走哪個方向 which way，然後，他決定 conclude，「我要朝日出的方向 toward the rising sun 走。」

GRAMMAR POINT

hardly . . . when . . . ：一⋯⋯就⋯⋯（倒裝句）

⇨ 有 hardly 的主要子句，時常都是用過去完成式的，也可以用 scarcely 來代替 hardly。

- **Hardly** were his eyes closed **when** he had a dream. 一閉上雙眼，他就做了一個夢。
  (= His eyes were **hardly** closed **when** he had a dream.
  = His eyes had **hardly** been closed **when** he had a dream.)

- **Hardly** had they seen me **when** they ran away. 他們一看到我，就跑走了。
  (= They had **hardly** seen me **when** they ran away.)

Pahom started walking / **neither slowly** / **nor quickly**. After having gone a thousand yards, / he stopped, / dug a hole, / and placed pieces of turf one on another / to make it more visible. Then he went on. **Now that he had walked off his stiffness,** / he quickened his pace. After a while, / he dug another hole.

The weather was getting warmer. He looked at the sun. It was time / to think of breakfast. "**It is too soon yet** / **to turn.** I will just take off my boots," he said to himself. He sat down, / took off his boots, / stuck them into his girdle, / and went on. It was easy / to walk now.

"I will go on / for another three miles," he thought, "and then turn to the left. This land here is so nice / that it would be a pity / to lose it."

He went straight on / for a while, / and then he looked back. The people on the hill / where he had started / were as small as ants. "Ah, I have gone far enough / in this direction," he thought. "It's time / to turn and go another direction. Besides, / I'm getting tired / and need something to drink."

He looked at the sun / and saw / that it was noon. He sat down, / ate some bread, / and drank some water. But he did not lie down / as he thought / that if he did, / he might fall asleep. After sitting for a little while, / he went on again. It had become terribly hot, / and he felt sleepy. Still, he went on, / thinking, "An hour to suffer, / a lifetime to live."

He went a long way / in this direction also / and **was about to turn to the left** again / when he perceived a damp hollow. "It would be a pity / to leave that out," he thought. So he went on past the hollow / and dug a hole / on the other side of it.

"Ah!" thought Pahom, "I have made the sides too long; I must make this one shorter." And he went along the third side / as he moved faster. He looked at the sun. It was nearly halfway to the horizon, / and he had not yet done / two miles of the third side of the square. He was still ten miles from his goal.

· **dig a hole** 挖個洞　· **turf** 草皮塊　· **walk off** 消除　· **stiffness** 僵硬　· **quicken** 加快
· **take off** 脫下　· **girdle** 皮帶　· **stick** 塞在　· **a pity** 可惜　· **go straight** 直走
· **look back** 往回看　· **lie down** 躺下　· **fall asleep** 睡著　· **suffer** 痛苦　· **lifetime** 一輩子
· **perceive** 看到　· **damp** 潮濕的　· **hollow** 山谷　· **horizon** 地平線　· **square** 正方形

1　**neither slowly nor quickly** 不慢也不快
〈neither . . . nor . . . 〉（不是……也不是……）。

2　**now that he had walked off his stiffness** 因為走路讓身體的僵硬消失了
〈now that . . . 〉（因為……）。

3　**It is too soon yet to turn.** 現在轉彎還太早了。
〈too . . . to . . . 〉（太……以致不能……）。

4　**was about to turn to the left** 是時候左轉了
〈be about to . . . 〉（正要去……的時候）。

帕霍姆不疾不徐地 neither slowly nor quickly 開始走 start walking，他走了 1000 碼（900公尺）go a thousand yards 以後，停下來 stop，挖個洞 dig a hole，放了幾塊草皮 pieces of turf，一塊疊一塊 one on another，讓它更明顯 make it more visible，然後他繼續走 go on，走到身體不再僵硬 walk off his stiffness，他就加快步伐 quicken his pace。過一會兒，他又挖了一個洞 dig another hole。

天氣變得暖和 get warmer，他看著太陽 look at the sun，是時候想想早餐了 think of breakfast。「現在轉彎還太早了，我要脫下我的靴子。」他跟自己說，他坐下 sit down，脫掉他的靴子 take off his boots 把它們塞在他的皮帶 stick them into his girdle 裡，然後繼續走 go on，現在好走多了。

「我要再繼續走三哩（五公里）another three miles，」他想，「然後再左轉 turn to the left。這裡的土地 this land here 太好了 be so nice，如果失去它 lose it 很可惜 a pity。」

過了一陣子 for a while 他又繼續往前走 go straight on，然後他往回看 look back，山丘上的人 the people on the hill 看起來像螞蟻一樣小 as small as ants。「啊，我往這個方向 in this direction 走得已經夠遠了 go far enough，」他想，「是時候轉彎，朝另一個方向走了 go another direction，而且 besides，我也累了 get tired，需要喝點水。」

他看看太陽，已經是中午 noon 了，他坐下來，吃了一點麵包 eat some bread，喝了一點水 drink some water，但他沒有躺下 do not lie down，因為他覺得如果他躺下，他可能會睡著 fall asleep。他坐了一會兒 sit for a little while，又繼續走 go on again。天氣變得非常地熱 become terribly hot，他覺得很睏 feel sleepy，但他仍然繼續走，心想「痛苦一小時 an hour to suffer，享受一輩子 a lifetime to live。」

他往這個方向走了很長一段路 go a long way，又該左轉了，然後他看到一個潮濕的山谷 perceive a damp hollow。「捨棄這個 leave that out 太可惜了 a pity。」他想，於是他繼續走過了山谷 past the hollow，在山谷的另一邊 on the other side of it 挖了一個洞 dig a hole。

「啊 ah！」帕霍姆想，「我把邊界弄得太長了 make the sides too long，我得把這邊弄短一點 make this one shorter。」他走第三邊 go along the third side 時加快了腳步 move faster，他看太陽，離地平線只剩一半的距離 nearly halfway to the horizon，而他還要走兩哩 have not yet done two miles（三公里），才走完正方形的第三邊 the third side of the square，他離目標還有 10 哩 ten miles from his goal。

"I've got to hurry back / in a straight line / now. I shouldn't go too far," he thought. "Besides, / I already have a huge amount of land." So Pahom turned / and hurried toward the hill / that he had started from.

But he now walked with difficulty. He was done in by the heat, / his bare feet were cut and bruised, / and his legs began to fail. He longed to rest, / but it was impossible / if he meant to get back / before sunset. The sun waits for no man, / and it was sinking lower and lower.

"Oh dear," he thought, "if only I had not blundered / by trying for too much. What if I am too late?"

He looked toward the hill / and at the sun. He was still far from his goal, / and the sun was already near the rim.

Pahom walked on and on. It was very hard to walk, / but he went quicker and quicker. He began running. He threw away / his coat, his boots, his flask, and his cap / and kept only the spade / which he used as a support.

"What shall I do?" he thought again. "I have grasped too much / and ruined the whole affair. I can't get there / before the sun sets." This fear / made him still more breathless.

Pahom went on running. His soaking shirt and trousers / stuck to him, / and his mouth was parched. His chest was working / like a blacksmith's bellows, / his heart was beating / like a hammer, / and his legs were giving way / as if they did not belong to him. Though afraid of death, / he could not stop. He gathered the rest of his strength / and ran on.

- **hurry back** 趕回去　　• **be done in by** 精疲力竭　　• **bare feet** 赤腳　　• **bruised** 瘀血的
- **fail** 走不動　　• **long to** 渴望　　• **sunset** 日落　　• **sink** 沉　　• **blunder** 犯錯
- **try for** 爭取　　• **rim** 邊緣　　• **throw away** 丟掉　　• **support** 支撐　　• **grasp** 抓
- **ruin** 毀　　• **affair** 事情　　• **fear** 恐懼感　　• **breathless** 快要不能呼吸　　• **soaking** 濕淋淋的
- **stick** 黏　　• **parched** 乾涸的　　• **blacksmith** 鐵匠　　• **bellows** 風箱　　• **give way** 支撐不住

1　**I've got to hurry back** 我必須趕回去
〈have got to . . .〉和〈have to . . .〉一樣，是「必須……」的意思，表必須和義務。

2　**he longed to rest** 他很想休息
long 當作動詞時，是「懇切地期望」的意思，要注意〈long to ＋原形動詞〉、〈long for ＋名詞〉。
例 He longed for peace.（他渴望和平的到來）

3　**if only I had not blundered** 要是我沒有犯錯
〈if only . . .〉是「要是……的話，就好了」的意思，表和事實相反的期望。

4　**What if I am too late?** 萬一我來不及怎麼辦？
〈What if . . . ?〉（要是……的話，該怎麼辦？）。

5　**as if they did not belong to him** 好像不屬於他自己的
〈as if . . .〉（就像……一樣）。

「我最好走直線 in a straight line 趕回去 hurry back，我不該走太遠 shouldn't go too far，」他想，「而且我已經有一大片土地 a huge amount of land 了。」於是帕霍姆轉彎，趕回他出發的山丘 hurry toward the hill。

但是現在他行走困難 walk with difficulty，高溫讓他精疲力竭 be done in by the heat。他赤腳 his bare feet 被割傷又瘀血 be cut and bruised，他的腿 his legs 開始走不動 fail，他很想休息 long to rest，但如果一定要 mean to 在日落前 before sunset 趕回去 get back，就不可能 be impossible 休息。太陽不等人 wait for no man，它愈來愈往下沉 sink lower and lower。

「哎啊 oh, dear」他想，「但願我沒有為了得到更多土地 try for too much 而犯錯 blunder。萬一我來不及 be too late 怎麼辦？」

他往山丘一看 look toward the hill，又看看太陽，離目標還有很遠 still far from his goal，但夕陽已經在邊緣 near the rim。

帕霍姆繼續走 walk on and on，走得很艱辛，但愈走愈快 go quicker and quicker，開始跑了起來 begin running。他把大衣、靴子、水壺、帽子 his coat, his boots, his flask, and his cap 都丟了 throw away，只留 keep only 用來支撐 as a support 他的鏟子 keep only the spade。

「我該怎麼做？」他又想，「我抓奪了太多 grasp too much，把一切都毀了 ruin the whole affair，日落前我到不了終點 can't get there。」這股恐懼感 this fear 讓他更無法呼吸 more breathless。

帕霍姆繼續跑 go on running，他濕淋淋的上衣和褲子 his soaking shirt and trousers 黏在他身上 stick to him。他的嘴巴 his mouth 渴得要命 be parched。他的胸 his chest 運轉 work 得像一個鐵匠的風箱 like a blacksmith's bellows。他的心臟 his heart 跳動 beat 得像鐵鎚 like a hammer 在敲打。他的雙腳 his legs 支撐不住了 give way，好像不屬於他自己的 do not belong to him。儘管很怕死 afraid of death，他也不能停 cannot stop，他凝聚 gather 所有剩餘的殘力 the rest of his strength，繼續跑 run on。

GRAMMAR POINT

比較級 and 比較級：愈來愈……地

- The sun waits for no man, and it was sinking **lower and lower**.
  太陽不等人，它愈沉愈低。

- It was very hard to walk, but he went **quicker and quicker**.
  他走得很艱辛，但愈走愈快。

The sun was close to the rim. Now, yes now, / it was about to set. The sun was quite low, / but he was also near his aim. Pahom could already see / the people on the hill / waving their arms / to hurry him up. He could see / the fox-fur cap on the ground / and the money on it, / and the chief / sitting on the ground / holding his sides. And Pahom remembered his dream.

"There is plenty of land," he thought, "but will God let me live on it? I have lost my life. I shall never reach that spot."

Pahom looked at the sun, / which had reached the earth. With all his remaining strength, / he rushed on. Just as he reached the hill, / it suddenly grew dark. He looked up / —the sun had already set. He gave a cry. "All my labor has been in vain," he thought.

He was about to stop, / but he heard the Bashkirs / still shouting. He realized / that the sun seemed to have set, / but the Bashkirs on the hill / could still see it. He took a long breath / and ran up the hill. It was still light there. He reached the top / and saw the cap. He fell forward / and reached the cap / with his hands.

"Ah, that's a fine fellow!" exclaimed the chief. "He has gained much land."

Pahom's servant / came running up / and tried to raise him, / but he saw / that blood was flowing / from his mouth. Pahom was dead.

The Bashkirs clicked their tongues / to show their pity.

His servant picked up the spade / and dug a grave long enough / for Pahom to lie in / and buried him in it. Six feet / from his head to his heels / was all he needed.

·aim 目標　·hold one's sides 捧腹大笑　·lose one's life 失去某人的性命　·labor 努力
·in vain 白費　·be about to 快要　·seem to 看起來　·take a long breath 深呼吸
·fellow 漢子　·servant 僕人　·raise 拉起　·flow 流出
·click one's tongue 舌頭發出嘖嘖聲　·grave 墳墓　·lie in 躺在裡面　·bury 埋
·six feet 六呎（180公分）

CLOSE UP

1　**had reached the earth** 落到地上 / **reached the hill** 到上丘上 /
reached the top 到山上 / **reached the cap** 摸到帽子
〈reach . . .〉是「到達／延伸到／擴展到……」的意思，也有「（伸出手去）抓住／拿……」的意思，
reach之後不能接to，要注意。

2　**All my labor has been in vain.** 我一切的努力都白費了。
〈be in vain〉是「變成白費」、「成為泡沫」的意思。

夕陽接近地平線 close to the rim，現在，就是現在，夕陽將要西沉 be about to set。夕陽很低 quite low，但他也接近目標了 near his aim，帕霍姆已經可以見到山丘上 on the hill 的人向他揮手 wave their arms，要他趕快 hurry him up。他看到地上的狐皮帽 the fox-fur cap 和上面的錢 the money on it。首領坐在地上 sit on the ground 捧腹大笑 hold his sides。帕霍姆想起了他的夢 remember his dream。

「那裡有許多地 plenty of land，」他想「但神會讓我住在其上 let me live on it 嗎？我失去了我的性命 lose my life，永遠也到不了終點 never reach that spot。」

帕霍姆看著太陽落到地平線上 reach the earth，用他剩餘的力氣 with all his remaining strength，他趕上了 rush on。他一到上丘上 reach the hill，天突然變黑 grow dark，他抬頭看 look up，太陽已經下山了 already set。他大叫 give a cry：「我一切的努力 all my labor 都白費了 be in vain。」

他快要停下來 about to stop 的時候，他聽到巴什基爾人還在大叫，他明白太陽看起來下山了 seem to have set，但是山丘上的巴什基爾人 the Bashkirs on the hill 還看得到太陽 can still see it。他深呼吸 take a long breath，跑上山丘 run up the hill，還有一點陽光，他到了山上 reach the top，看到帽子 see the cap，他往前倒 fall forward，用手 with his hands 碰到了帽子 reach the cap。

「啊 ah，真是條好漢 a fine fellow！」首領驚呼：「他得到很多土地 gain much land。」

帕霍姆的僕人 Pahom's servant 衝上前來 come running up，試著扶他起來 raise him，但他看到他口裡 from his mouth 流出 flow 鮮血 blood。帕霍姆死了 be dead。

巴什基爾人的舌頭發出嘖嘖聲 click their tongues，表達他們的遺憾 show their pity。

他的僕人撿起鏟子 pick up the spade，挖了一個墳墓 dig a grave，長得足以讓帕霍姆躺在裡面，然後把他埋進去 bury him in it。從頭到腳 from his head to his heels，他只需要 all he needs 六呎 six feet（180公分）。

GRAMMAR POINT

enough . . . to . . . ：有足夠的……可以去……

⇨ 要注意 enough 的位置，要在形容詞後或名詞前。

- His servant dug a grave long **enough** for Pahom **to** lie in.
  他的僕人挖了一個墳墓，長得足以讓帕霍姆躺在裡面。（形容詞後）

- That area has **enough** land for all of them **to** farm.
  這一帶有足夠的土地可以讓所有人耕種。（名詞前）

Step

5

A Christmas Carol

— Charles Dickens

A Christmas Carol

One Christmas Eve, / Scrooge sat busy / in his office. It was cold and foggy weather. The city clocks / had just rung three times, / but it was already quite dark.

Scrooge was an old man. He was known / by everyone / to be mean, miserly, and cold. He was a greedy sinner. No warmth could warm him, / and no cold could chill him. Nobody ever stopped Scrooge / on the street / to say, "My dear Scrooge, how are you?" No beggars implored him / to give them some money. Even the dogs seemed to know him, / and they avoided him, too. But Scrooge did not care / at all. He liked it / that way. People avoided him, / and he avoided people.

He had worked / in the same dark office / for many years. Once / it had been the office / of *Scrooge and Marley*. Scrooge and Marley / had been partners / for many years. And even now, / seven years after Marley had died, / those names were still on the door.

It was a very small room / with a very small fire. The only other person / in the office / was Bob Cratchit, / Scrooge's clerk. Bob was very cold. Scrooge did not give Bob / much wood for his fire / because he did not like to spend money. So the clerk put on his coat / and tried to warm himself / by the light of a candle.

Scrooge did not like anything. He especially hated Christmas.

"Merry Christmas, Uncle," cried a cheerful voice. It was the voice / of Scrooge's nephew Fred.

"Bah, humbug," said Scrooge.

"Oh, come on, Uncle," said Fred. "I'm sure / you don't mean it."

"I do," said Scrooge. "Why are you merry? You're a poor man."

"Well, why aren't you merry? You're a very rich man. And it's Christmas!"

"Bah, humbug," said Scrooge again. "You keep Christmas / in your own way, / and let me keep it / in mine."

·foggy 有霧的　·mean 小氣的；心地不好的　·miserly 吝嗇的　·greedy 貪心的
·sinner 罪人　·chill 變冷　·beggar 乞丐　·implore 乞求　·avoid 躲避
·do not care 不關心　·clerk 職員　·cheerful 歡樂的　·bah, humbug 呸！騙人的東西
·merry 快樂的

CLOSE UP

1　**He was known by everyone to be mean, miserly, and cold.**
大家都知道他很小氣、吝嗇、冷酷。
〈be known to . . .〉是「以……知名」的意思。by everyone 是為了強調所有人都這麼認為而插入的。

2　**You keep Christmas in your own way, and let me keep it in mine.**
你用你的方式過聖誕節，我用我的方式過。
〈in one's own way〉是「以……的方式」的意思。這裡的 in mine 是 in my own way 的縮寫。

聖誕頌歌

　　聖誕節前夕 **one Christmas Eve**，施顧己 **Scrooge** 在他的辦公室裡 **in his office** 坐著忙公事 **sit busy**。外面天氣又冷，霧又大 **cold and foggy**，市鐘 **the city clocks** 剛響了三次 **ring three times**，天色卻已經很暗了 **be quite dark**。

　　施顧己是一個老人 **an old man**，大家都知道他很小氣、吝嗇、冷酷 **mean, miserly, and cold**。他是一個貪心的罪人 **a greedy sinner**，沒有溫情 **no warmth** 可以溫暖他 **warm him**，沒有冷酷 **no cold** 可以讓他感到寒冷 **chill him**。沒有人 **nobody** 會在街上攔下他 **stop Scrooge** 說：「我親愛的施顧己，你好嗎 **how are you**？」沒有乞丐 **no beggars** 向他乞討 **implore**，求他給他們一點錢 **give them some money**。連狗 **even the dogs** 看起來好像認識他，也躲著他 **avoid him**，但施顧己一點也不在意 **do not care at all**。他喜歡這樣 **like it that way**，大家躲著他，他也躲著大家。

　　他在同一間陰暗的辦公室裡 **in the same dark office** 工作了好幾年 **for many years**，這間辦公室曾經是「施顧己和馬里 **Scrooge and Marley** 公司」。施顧己和馬里曾是好多年的合夥人 **partners**，就算現在馬里已經過世七年了，那些名字依然留在門上。

　　那是一間很小的房間 **a very small room**，裡面只有很小的火 **with a very small fire**。辦公室裡面唯一的另一個人 **the only other person** 是施顧己的職員 **Scrooge's clerk**。鮑伯‧克萊契 **Bob Cratchit** 很冷 **be cold**，施顧己沒有給他很多木頭生火 **much wood for his fire**，因為他不想花錢 **spend money**，於是職員穿上大衣 **put on his coat**，試著用蠟燭的火光 **by the light of a candle** 讓自己溫暖一點 **warm himself**。

　　施顧己討厭一切事物 **do not like anything**，特別是聖誕節 **hate Christmas**。

　　「聖誕快樂 **Merry Christmas**，舅舅。」一個興高采烈的聲音說，那是施顧己的外甥佛萊德 **Scrooge's nephew, Fred**。

　　「呸 **bah**！騙人的東西 **humbug**。」施顧己說。

　　「喔，拜託，舅舅，」佛萊德說：「我相信你不是認真的 **don't mean it**。」

　　「我是認真的，」施顧己說：「你有什麼好高興的 **be merry**？你是個窮人 **a poor man**。」

　　「好吧，你為什麼不快樂？你是個很有錢的人 **a rich man**，而且是聖誕節呀！」

　　「呸！騙人的玩意，」施顧己又說了一次，「你用你的方式 **in your own way** 過聖誕節 **keep Christmas**，我用我的方式過我的。」

GRAMMAR POINT

no + 名詞：任何⋯⋯也不能⋯⋯ ⇨ 想強調否定含意時使用。

- **No warmth** could warm him, and **no cold** could chill him.
  沒有溫情可以溫暖他，沒有冷酷可以讓他感到寒冷。
- **No beggars** implored him to give them some money.
  沒有乞丐向他乞討，求他給他們一點錢。

"Don't be so angry, Uncle. Come / and have dinner with us / tomorrow."
Scrooge merely answered, "Goodbye."

"I don't want / to be angry with you, / Uncle," said Fred. "So / a Merry Christmas, / Uncle."

"Goodbye," Scrooge only said.

After Scrooge's nephew left, / the clerk let two other people in. They were portly gentlemen. They had books and papers / in their hands / and bowed to Scrooge.

"Excuse us. May I ask, / are you Mr. Scrooge / or Mr. Marley?" said one of the gentlemen.

"Mr. Marley has been dead / these seven years. He died / seven years ago / this very night," answered Scrooge.

"Mr. Scrooge then," said the man. "At this festive season of the year, / it is nice / for everyone / to give something to people / who have nothing / –no homes, no food."

"Are there no prisons? Any orphanages?" said Scrooge.

"There are. But they always need / a little more. So / a few of us / are raising funds / to buy the poor / some meat, drink, and means of warmth. What shall I put you down for?"

"Nothing!" answered Scrooge.

"You wish / to give an anonymous gift?"

"No. I wish / to be left alone. I don't make merry / at Christmas, / and I can't afford / to make lazy fools merry. I have my work / to worry about."

After the men left, / Scrooge turned to his clerk. "You'll want / all day off / tomorrow, / I suppose?" he asked.

"If that's convenient, / sir," the clerk responded.

"It's not convenient, / and it's not fair. Yet you'll still expect me / to pay you a day's wages / for no work, / won't you?"

"It's only once a year, / sir."

"That's a poor excuse / for picking a man's pocket / every twenty-fifth of December. But I suppose / you must have the whole day. Be here early / the next morning."

The clerk promised / that he would arrive early. Scrooge walked out of the office / and went back to his empty home.

·merely 只是　·portly 肥胖的　·books 帳冊　·bow 鞠躬　·festive 歡樂的
·prison 監獄　·orphanage 孤兒院　·raise funds 募款　·means of ……的工具
·put down 寫下　·anonymous 匿名的　·can't afford to 付不起　·lazy 懶惰的
·all day off 整天休息　·convenient 方便的　·fair 公平的　·wages 工資　·poor 窮的
·excuse 藉口　·pick one's pocket 偷人的錢　·empty 空的

CLOSE UP

1   **let two other people in** 讓另外兩個人進來
    〈let . . . in〉是「讓……進來」的意思。

2   **You'll want all day off** 你要休假一整天
    off 是「不工作，休息」的意思。例 I have two days off this week.（我這星期有兩天休息。）

3   **expect me to pay you a day's wages** 期望我付你一天的工資
    〈expect . . . to . . .〉是「期望……去……」的意思。〈pay＋人＋錢〉是「付給……多少錢」的意思。

「不要這麼生氣，舅舅，來吧 come，明天和我們一塊吃晚餐 have dinner with us。」

施顧己只是回答：「再見 goodbye。」

「我不生你的氣，舅舅，」佛萊德說：「聖誕快樂，舅舅。」

「再見。」施顧己說。

施顧己的外甥離開了以後，職員讓另外兩個人進來 let two other people in，兩個胖胖的先生 portly gentlemen，手上 in their hands 拿著帳冊和紙 have books and papers，向施顧己鞠躬 bow to him。

「不好意思 excuse us，我可以請教一下 may I ask，你是施顧己先生，還是馬里先生呢？」其中一位先生開口說道。

「馬里先生 Mr. Marley 已經過世了 be dead 七年之久，七年前 seven years ago 的今晚 this very night 死去 die」施顧己回答。

「那麼施顧己先生，」那人說：「在一年最歡樂的季節當中 at this festive season of the year（festive season 指聖誕節及新年期間），能給 give 那些一無所有 have nothing 的人一些東西 something 是一件善舉 be nice——那些人沒有家 no homes、沒有食物 no food。」

「沒有監獄 no prisons 嗎？沒有孤兒院 any orphanages 嗎？」施顧己說。

「當然有，但他們需要更多一點 need a little more 幫助，所以我們幾個 a few of us 正為窮人 the poor 買肉 meat、飲料 drink 和保暖工具 means of warmth 而募款 raise funds，我該為你寫下 put you down 什麼？」

「什麼都不要 nothing！」施顧己回答。

「你想要以無名氏捐贈禮物 give an anonymous gift 嗎？」

「不，我希望你們讓我獨處 be left alone，我不會在聖誕節製造歡樂 make merry，我也沒有錢讓那些懶惰的笨蛋快樂 make lazy fools merry，我有我的工作要擔心。」

男人離開以後，施顧己轉向他的職員 turn to his clerk。「我猜你明天想要休息一整天 want all day off？」他問。

「如果那樣方便的話 if that's convenient，先生 sir。」職員回答。

「那一點也不方便，而且不公平 it's not fair，但你還是希望 expect 我在你不用上班 for no work 這天，付你一天的工資 pay you a day's wages，對吧？」

「一年只有一次 once a year，先生。」

「這對每年 12 月 25 日 every twenty–fifth of December 都從人的口袋裡把錢偷走 pick a man's pocket 來說，是一個很爛的藉口 a poor excuse，但我猜你想要放一整天的假 have the whole day。隔天早上 the next morning 要早一點來 be here early。」

職員答應 promise 他會早點到 arrive early，施顧己走出辦公室 walk out of the office，回到 go back 自己空蕩蕩的家 to his empty home。

GRAMMAR POINT

dead（形容詞）：死的　　**die（動詞）**：死

- Mr. Marley has **been dead** these seven years. 馬里先生已經過世七年了。
- He **died** seven years ago this very night. 他七年前的今晚過世了。

When Scrooge got to his building, / he put the key / into the lock of the door. But when he looked at the knocker, / he did not see a knocker / but Marley's face. Scrooge stared for a moment, / and then / it was a knocker again. He said, "Pooh, pooh!" / and closed the door / with a bang.

Scrooge went up to his room, / and carefully locked the door. He checked twice / **to see if the door was locked** / and then made a little fire / in the fireplace. He put on his dressing gown, slippers, and nightcap, / and sat down / before the very low fire. As he threw his head back in his chair, / he heard something in the house. It was far away, / but it was coming closer. It sounded / as if some person were dragging a heavy chain / over the casks / in the wine merchant's cellar. Then, / he heard the noise much louder / on the floors below. Then, / it came up the stairs, / and then / it came straight toward his door. It came / right through the heavy door, / and a ghost passed into the room / before his eyes. The face! **He recognized it** / **right away** / **as Marley's**. It was Marley's ghost.

"How now," said Scrooge, / caustic and cold / as ever. "What do you want / with me?"

"Much." Marley's voice, / no doubt about it.

"Who are you?"

"Ask me / who I was."

"Who were you then?" said Scrooge, / raising his voice.

"In life, / I was your partner, / Jacob Marley."

"Mercy! Dreadful apparition, / why do you trouble me? What do you want?" Scrooge's voice trembled / as he spoke.

"I have been traveling / since I died. Though I am dead, / I must walk through / the world of the living. I cannot rest. I cannot stay. I cannot linger anywhere."

"Why?" asked Scrooge.

"Because I'm unhappy. I was very bad to people / when I was alive. If a man stays away from other people / while he is alive, / that man becomes like me," said Marley's ghost.

·**knocker** 門上的門環　·**stare** 盯　·**bang** 砰聲　·**make a fire** 升火　·**fireplace** 壁爐
·**dressing gown** 睡袍　·**nightcap** 睡帽　·**low fire** 微弱的火
·**throw one's head back** 頭向後靠　·**far away** 很遠的　·**drag** 拖
·**cask** 裝酒的木桶　·**wine cellar** 酒窖　·**noise** 聲響　·**pass into** 穿越進入某處
·**recognize** 認出　·**ghost** 鬼魂　·**caustic** 苛刻的　·**as ever** 和以前一樣
·**dreadful** 可怕的　·**apparition** 亡靈　·**linger** 逗留；徘徊
·**stay away from** 離⋯⋯很遠　·**alive** 活著

CLOSE UP

1　**to see if the door was locked** 看看門鎖好了沒
　　〈see if . . .〉是「確認是否⋯⋯」、「看看有沒有⋯⋯」的意思。

2　**He recognized it right away as Marley's.** 他馬上認出是馬里的臉。
　　〈recognize . . . as . . .〉是「認出⋯⋯是⋯⋯」的意思。這裡的 Marley's 是 Marley's face 的意思。

施顧己到了家門口 get to his building，他把鑰匙插進門鎖中 put the key into the lock，但他看著門環 look at the knocker，他看到的不是門環，而是馬里的臉 but Marley's face。施顧己盯 stare 了一會兒 for a moment，然後又變成門環。他說：「呸呸 pooh, pooh！」然後砰一聲 with a bang 關上門 close the door。

施顧己上去他的房間 go up to his room，小心地把門鎖好 lock the door，他檢查了兩次 check twice，看看門鎖好了沒，然後在壁爐裡 in the fireplace 升了一點小火 make a little fire。他換上睡袍 dressing gown、穿上拖鞋 slippers 和戴上睡帽 nightcap，在微火之前 before the very low fire 坐下 sit down。當他把頭靠在椅子上 throw his head back，他聽到屋內有些聲音 hear something，聲音在很遠的地方，但愈來愈近 come closer，聽起來像是某個人 some person 在商人地窖裡的酒桶上 over the casks 拖著很重的鎖鍊 drag a heavy chain。然後，他聽見地板下 on the floors below 發出更大的聲響 the noise much louder，它走上樓梯 come up the stairs，然後走向他的門 come toward his door，它直接穿過很重的門 through the heavy door，一個鬼魂 a ghost 在他眼前 before his eyes 穿進了房間 pass into the room。那張臉 the face！他立刻 right away 認出了是馬里的臉 recognize it as Marley's，那是馬里的鬼魂 Marley's ghost。

「現在如何 how now？」施顧己說，如以往一樣 as ever 苛刻又冷酷 caustic and cold，「你想要我做什麼？」

「很多。」不須懷疑 no doubt about it，是馬里的聲音 Marley's voice。

「你是誰 who are you？」

「問我以前是誰 who I was。」

「你以前是誰 who were you？」施顧己提高了音量。

「活著的時候 in life，我是你的合夥人 your partner 雅各・馬里 Jacob Marley。」

「可憐我 mercy 吧！可怕的鬼魂 dreadful apparition，你為什麼來為難我 trouble me？你想要什麼？」施顧己說話的時候，聲音 voice 顫抖 tremble。

「我死後一直飄蕩 travel，雖然我死了，但我得走遍陽間 the world of the living，不能休息 cannot rest，不能停留 cannot stay，不能在任何地方逗留 cannot linger。」

「為什麼 why？」施顧己問。

「因為我很不快樂 be unhappy，我活著的時候 be alive，對人很差勁 be bad to people，如果一個人活著的時候，與他人保持距離 stay away from other people，那人就會變得跟我一樣 become like me。」馬里的鬼魂說。

as if . . .（假設語氣）：像是……一樣

⇨ 雖然事實並不是那樣，但好像真的發生了一樣。

- It sounded **as if** some person **were dragging** a heavy chain over the casks.
  聽起來像是有人在地窖裡的酒桶上拖著重重的鎖鍊。（過去式）

- -

- They were as happy **as if** they **had eaten** a king's meal.
  他們很快樂，有如吃了一頓國王的大餐。（過去完成式）

"I am here tonight / to warn you / that you have yet a chance / and hope of escaping my fate," said Marley's ghost.

"This is the chain / I made during my lifetime. Every time / I refused to help / those in need, / the chain became longer and heavier. When I died, / our chains were about the same, Scrooge, / but now, / after seven years, / yours is much longer than mine. I want to help you / not to be unhappy / like me / when you die."

"How?" asked Scrooge.

"You will be visited / by three more ghosts," answered Marley's ghost. "Expect the first / tonight / when the bell tolls one. Expect the second / tomorrow night / at the same hour. The third will come / the next night, / when the last stroke of twelve / has rung."

The ghost began floating out the window.

"But wait. Will I see you again? Can't you tell me more?"

"No, Scrooge, / you won't see me again. Remember / what I told you, / for your own sake, / or you will soon / see your own heavy chain."

The ghost disappeared out the window, / which was wide open.

As Scrooge went to the window / to see / where Marley had gone, / he suddenly heard some crying / down below. Again, / Scrooge's heart froze. The voices came / not from people, / but from ghosts. He quickly closed the window. He tried to say, "Humbug," / but he stopped / at the first syllable.

"This couldn't have happened. I will go to sleep, / and tomorrow / everything will be fine," he thought. Then, he went to bed / and fell into a troubled sleep.

When Scrooge awoke, / it was still so dark. "Was it all a dream?" he wondered. Just then, / the clock tolled / a deep, dull, hollow one.

Light flashed up / in the room / in an instant, / and the curtains of his bed / were drawn aside / by a strange figure. The ghost was an old man / with long white hair. He held / a branch of fresh green holly / in his hand. From the top of his head, / a bright clear jet of light / sprang.

"I am / the Ghost of Christmas Past," he said.

"Whose past?" "Your past," answered the ghost.

"What do you want?" "Rise / and walk with me."

· warn 警告　· escape 逃離　· fate 命運　· toll（鐘）敲　· stroke 鐘敲的動作
· ring 響　· float 飄　· for one's own sake 看在……的份上　· disappear 消失
· freeze 呆住；僵住　· syllable 音節　· troubled sleep 睡不安穩　· awake 醒來
· hollow 空洞的　· flash up 閃爍　· in an instant 一剎那　· draw . . . aside 拉到一邊
· figure 身形　· holly 冬青　· a jet of light 一縷光　· spring 光芒出現

CLOSE UP

1　**every time I refused to help those in need** 每次我拒絕幫助那些有需要的人
〈every time . . . 〉意「每次都……」；〈refuse to . . . 〉意「拒絕去……」；〈in need〉意「處於困境中的、窮困的」。

2　**came not from people, but from ghosts** 不是人發出的，而是鬼魂發出的
〈not . . . but . . . 〉是「不是……而是……」的意思。

3　**This couldn't have happened.** 這不可能發生。
〈could have p.p.〉意「可能已經……了」；〈couldn't have p.p.〉意「不可能……的」。

「今晚我是來警告你warn you，你還有機會和希望a chance and hope可以脫離我的命運escape my fate。」馬里的鬼魂說。

「這是我在世時during my lifetime造成的鎖鍊the chain，每次我拒絕幫助refuse to help那些有需要的人those in need，這些鎖鍊就會變得更長、更重become longer and heavier。我死的時候，我們的鎖鍊差不多一樣長be about the same，施顧己，但現在，七年後的現在after seven years，你的比我還要長be much longer，我想幫你help you，等你死的時候不要像我一樣不快樂。」

「怎麼做how？」施顧己問。

「將有三個鬼魂three more ghosts來拜訪你，」馬里的鬼魂回答：「今夜tonight當鐘敲第一下toll one的時候，第一個the first會來。第二個the second明晚tomorrow night同樣的時間at the same hour會來。第三個the third隔天晚上the next night午夜第12聲鐘響the last stroke of twelve的時候會來。」

鬼魂開始飄出窗外float out the window。

「等等wait，我會再見到你嗎？你不能再告訴我多一點tell me more嗎？」

「不，施顧己，你再也見不到我了，記得我跟你說的話。為了你自己好for your own sake，要不然你很快就會看到你沉重的鎖鍊your own heavy chain。」

鬼魂在窗外消失disappear out the window，窗戶大開be wide open。

施顧己走到窗前go to the window看看馬里消失的地方，他突然聽到一些下面down below傳來的叫聲hear some crying，施顧己的心又僵住了freeze，這些聲音不是人發出的，而是鬼魂發出來的come from ghosts。他很快地把窗戶關上close the window。他試著說：「騙人的東西humbug。」但他講了一個音節就停了。

「這不可能發生couldn't have happened，我要去睡覺go to sleep，明天一切都會很好。」他想，然後他上床睡覺go to bed，睡得很不安穩fall into a troubled sleep。

當施顧己醒來awake，外面還是一片漆黑。「是一場夢a dream嗎？」他納悶，此時just then，鐘敲了很深、很鈍、很空洞deep, dull, hollow的一聲。

一瞬間in an instant有光light在房間裡閃爍flash up。床的帷幔the curtains of his bed被一個很奇怪的身形a strange figure拉到旁邊be drawn aside。鬼魂是一個老人an old man，他有長長的白髮with long white hair手裡拿著一枝青翠的冬青枝hold a branch fresh green holly。他的頭頂上from the top of his head散發出spring一縷又白又亮的光芒right clear jet of light。

「我是過去聖誕節的鬼魂Ghost of Christmas Past。」他說。

「誰的過去whose past？」「你的過去your past。」鬼魂回答。

「你想要什麼？」「起身rise和我走吧walk with me。」

---

be + p.p.（被動語態）

⇨ 主詞「承受或接受」動詞的動作時使用的說法，行為者用by標示。

• You will **be visited by** three more ghosts. 還有三個鬼魂會來拜訪你。

• The curtains of his bed **were drawn** aside **by** a strange figure. 床的帷幔被一個奇怪的身形拉到旁邊。

Scrooge got up from his bed. He held the ghost's hand, / and they passed through the wall together. Suddenly, / they were standing in the country / where he had lived / as a boy. It was clear enough / by the decorations in the shops / that there, too, / it was Christmastime.

They saw / many boys and girls / going home across the fields, / happily shouting "Merry Christmas" / to each other. Scrooge remembered / the happiness and joy / when he was a child. He could feel tears / on his cheek.

"Are you sad?" asked the ghost.

"No, no, I am … happy," said Scrooge.

"They are not real. They are only spirits / from Christmas past. They cannot see us."

But Scrooge knew the spirits, / just as he knew / the streets, the houses, and the townspeople. Then, / they saw Scrooge as a boy, / reading on his own / in an empty classroom. Seeing himself / as he had once been, / Scrooge sat down at a desk / next to him / and began to cry.

"It's me. Once / when I was a boy, / I was left alone here / on Christmas. My father and mother / weren't at home. Now, suddenly, / I wish I would … " Scrooge's voice grew quiet.

"What do you wish?" the ghost asked.

"Last night, / a young boy / came to my office window / and sang me a Christmas carol. I just got angry / and told him to leave. I wish / I'd given some money to that poor boy," said Scrooge / with heavy sadness.

The ghost smiled. "Let's see / another Christmas," he said.

This time, / Scrooge saw the office / where he had first worked. He saw Mr. Fezziwig, / the man whom he had worked for. Young Scrooge was helping them / prepare the office / for a Christmas party. Soon, / there were / many young people / there. They were his fellow apprentices. They were enjoying themselves / and dancing. Even he, / Scrooge himself, / was dancing and enjoying himself.

·**rise** 起身　·**get up from** 從……起來　·**hold one's hand** 抓著某人的手
·**pass through** 穿越　·**decoration** 布置　·**tear** 眼淚　·**spirit** 靈魂
·**on one's own** 獨自　·**sit down** 坐下　·**be left alone** 被單獨留下　·**grow quiet** 變小聲
·**get angry** 生氣　·**prepare** 準備　·**fellow** 同伴的　·**apprentice** 學徒

CLOSE UP

1　**seeing himself as he had once been** 看到從前的自己
如果是〈as he is〉的話，是「像他現在的樣子」的意思；〈as he had once been〉則是「像他以前的樣子」。

2　**They were enjoying themselves** 他們玩得很開心
〈enjoy oneself〉是「享樂」、「玩樂」、「度過愉快的時光」的意思。

施顧己從床上起來 **get up from his bed**，他抓著鬼魂的手 **hold the ghost's hand**。他們一起穿牆 **pass through the wall**，突然間他們站在鄉下 **stand in the country**。當他還是小男孩的時候 **as a boy** 曾經住在那裡。商店裡 **in the shops** 的布置 **by the decorations** 清楚地 **be clear enough** 透露出那是聖誕節期 **Christmastime**。

他們看到許多男孩女孩 **many boys and girls** 穿過田野 **across the fields** 回家 **go home**，快樂地 **happily** 互相 **to each other** 叫嚷 **shout**「聖誕快樂」。施顧己記得兒時的幸福、快樂 **the happiness and joy**，他感受到自己臉頰上 **on his cheek** 的淚水 **tears**。

「你很難過嗎？」鬼魂問。

「不，不，我是……快樂。」施顧己說。

「他們不是真的 **be not real**，他們只是過去聖誕節的鬼魂 **spirits from Christmas past**，他們看不見我們 **cannot see us**。」

但是施顧己認識那些鬼魂，正如他認得那些街道、房子和鎮上的人，然後，他們看到施顧己還是個小男孩 **Scrooge as a boy**，獨自一個人 **on his own** 在空蕩蕩的教室裡 **in an empty classroom** 讀書，看到他自己 **see himself** 從前的樣子，施顧己坐在他隔壁的桌上 **sit down at a desk**，開始哭了起來 **begin to cry**。

「那是我 **it's me**，從前當我還是小男孩的時候，聖誕節 **on Christmas** 我一個人被留在這裡 **be left alone here**，我父母不在家 **be not at home**，現在突然間，我希望我可以……」施顧己愈說愈小聲 **grow quiet**。

「你希望怎麼樣？」鬼魂問。

「昨晚 **last night** 有個小男孩 **a young boy** 來我辦公室的窗戶旁邊 **come to my office window**，對我唱一首聖誕頌歌 **sing me a Christmas carol**，我只是很生氣 **get angry**，叫他離開 **tell him to leave**，但願我給了那可憐的男孩 **that poor boy** 一點錢 **give some money**。」施顧己非常悲傷地說 **with heavy sadness**。

鬼魂微笑，「我們來看另一個聖誕節 **see another Christmas**。」他說。

這次 **this time**，施顧己看到他第一次工作的辦公室 **see the office**，他看見費茲威先生 **see Mr. Fezziwig**，他以前為他工作過，年輕的施顧己在幫他們為聖誕舞會 **Christmas party** 布置辦公室 **prepare the office**，不久，許多年輕人 **many young people** 來了。他們跟他一起當學徒 **his fellow apprentices**。他們很快樂 **enjoy themselves** 地跳舞 **dance**，就連他，施顧己自己，也在跳舞和玩樂。

where（關係副詞）

⇨ 放在表場所的名詞後，where 所引導的關係子句，就是用來修飾該名詞的。

• Suddenly, they were standing in *the country* **where** he had lived as a boy.

突然間，他們站在鄉下，他兒時住過的地方。

• This time, Scrooge saw *the* office **where** he had first worked.

這次，施顧己看到他第一次工作的辦公室。

At the end of the party, / Mr. and Mrs. Fezziwig said / "Merry Christmas" / to everybody.

"It's old Mr. Fezziwig's office. He was such a happy, kind boss."

The ghost looked at Scrooge / and asked, "What's the matter?"

"I was thinking of my clerk, / Bob Cratchit. I wish / I'd said something to him / yesterday," said Scrooge.

The ghost smiled again. "Come, / my time grows short," said the ghost. "Another Christmas," he said.

The scene changed. Scrooge again / saw himself. He was older now / –a man in the prime of life. He was sitting / with a young woman. She had once been his girlfriend. She was crying.

"No, it's too late. You have another love now," she said.

"What? What other love?" Scrooge asked.

"Money. / You love only money now, / not me. Goodbye."

"No more! Ghost! Please remove me / from this place," Scrooge cried / in pain.

"No, Scrooge. I told you / that these were shadows / of the things / that have been," said the ghost. "There is / one more scene."

Years had passed / since the last scene. Scrooge saw a beautiful woman / smiling with her children / in a warm house. The door opened, / and the father came in. His arms / were full of Christmas presents. He gave one / to each of his children. The children laughed and shouted / as they opened the presents.

Scrooge looked at the mother. She was the woman / from Scrooge's past. She had left him / because he had been more interested in money / than in her. Looking at the happy family, / Scrooge realized / what he had lost.

"No more! Leave me, ghost," shouted Scrooge.

"This was your life. These things happened / and cannot be changed. Only the future / can be changed," the ghost said.

"Please, ghost, / I cannot bear it. Haunt me / no longer!" Scrooge shouted sadly.

As Scrooge struggled with the spirit, / he suddenly became exhausted. He was overcome by drowsiness / and sank into a heavy sleep.

· boss 老闆　·scene 場景　·the prime of life 人生的黃金時期　·remove 調動
· in pain 很痛苦　·shadow 影子　·be interested in 對……感興趣　·bear 承受
· haunt 被鬼纏住　·struggle with 對抗　·exhausted 精疲力盡的　·overcome by 被……戰勝
· drowsiness 疲倦　·sink into 陷入

CLOSE UP

1 **grows short** 變短 / **became exhausted** 變得精疲力盡
〈grow/become＋形容詞〉是「愈來愈……了」的意思，表狀態的變化；grow表感覺地漸漸地產生變化。

2 **remove me from this place** 把我從這個地方帶走
〈remove ... from ...〉是「把……送出／移出……」的意思。

3 **had been more interested in money than in her** 對錢比對她更感興趣
〈be interested in ...〉是「對……有興趣」的意思。這裡的money和her是兩個相互作比較的對象。

4 **was overcome by drowsiness** 屈服於疲倦
〈be overcome by ...〉是「沒有勝過……」、「被……擊敗」的意思。

舞會結束時，費茲威夫婦向大家說：「聖誕快樂」。

「那是老費茲威先生的辦公室，他真是一個又快樂又善良的老闆 **such a happy, kind boss**。」

鬼魂看著施顧己問：「怎麼回事 **what's the matter**？」

「我想到我的職員鮑伯‧克萊契 **think of my clerk, Bob Cratchit**，但願我昨天和他說點什麼 **say something to him**。」施顧己說。

鬼魂又微笑了。「來吧 **come**，我的時間 **my time** 不多了 **grow shorter**，」鬼魂說。「另一個聖誕節 **another Christmas**。」他說。

場景 **the scene** 變換 **change**，施顧己又看到他自己 **see himself**，現在他年紀大了一點 **be older**，正處於人生的黃金時期 **in the prime of life**。他和一個年輕女子 **with a young woman** 坐在一起，她曾是他的女朋友 **his girlfriend**，她在哭 **cry**。

「不，一切都太遲了，你現在另有所愛了 **have another love**。」她說。

「什麼 **what**？什麼另有所愛 **what other love**？」施顧己問。

「錢，你現在只愛錢 **love only money**，不愛我，再見。」

「不要再繼續 **no more** 了！鬼魂！帶我離開這裡 **remove me from this place**。」施顧己痛苦地 **in pain** 大叫。

「不，施顧己，我跟你說過這只是往事 **the things that have been** 的幻影 **shadows**，」鬼魂說：「還有一個場景 **one more scene**。」

距上一個場景之後，又過了很多年。施顧己看到一個美麗的女人 **a beautiful woman** 在一個溫暖的房子裡 **in a warm house** 對著她的孩子 **with her children** 微笑。門開了，父親 **the father** 走進來 **come in**，他的雙臂裡 **his arms** 都是聖誕禮物 **be full of Christmas presents**，他給每一個孩子 **to each of his children** 一個禮物。當他們拆禮物 **open the presents** 時又笑又叫 **laugh and shout**。

施顧己看著那個母親 **look at the mother**，她是施顧己過去的女朋友 **the woman from Scrooge's past**，因施顧己對錢更有興趣 **be more interested in money**，所以她離開了他 **leave him**。看著幸福的家庭，施顧己明白自己失去了什麼。

「不要再繼續了！放過我吧 **leave me**，鬼魂。」施顧己大叫。

「這是你的人生 **your life**，已經發生的事 **these things happened** 不能改變 **cannot be changed**，只有未來 **only the future** 可以改變 **can be changed**。」鬼魂說。

「求求你，鬼魂，我受不了了 **cannot bear it**，不要再 **no longer** 纏著我 **haunt me** 了！」施顧己傷心地大叫。

施顧己和鬼魂對抗 **struggle with the spirit**，他突然感到精疲力盡 **become exhausted**，他被睡意征服 **be overcome by drowsiness**，沉沉睡去 **sink into a heavy sleep**。

GRAMMAR POINT

I wish . . .（假設語氣）

⇨ I wish 後接的從屬子句，若用「過去完成式」，就表示所期望的事與過去的事實相反。

- **I wish I'd said** something to him yesterday. 但願我昨天和他說點什麼。
- **I wish I'd given** some money to that poor boy. 但願我給了那可憐的男孩一點錢。

Scrooge awoke / in his bedroom. It was one in the morning again / –time for the second ghost. He looked around his bedroom. There was nobody / there. He went to the door of his living room.

"Come in, / Ebenezer Scrooge," said a voice.

He opened the door / and saw something very surprising. The room looked so different. The walls were covered with Christmas trees. Heaped upon the floor / were / turkeys, geese, pigs, sausages, plum puddings, chestnuts, apples, and great bowls of punch. Upon the couch / in the center of the room / sat a happy giant, / holding a glowing torch / which lit the room.

"Come in. Come in. I am / the Ghost of Christmas Present," said the giant.

"Ghost, / I learned a lot / from the ghost / last night. Tonight, / if you have / something to teach me, / take me / anywhere you want," said Scrooge.

"Touch my robe," said the giant.

Scrooge did / as he was told. Scrooge found / they were walking / in a London street / on Christmas morning. The ghost took him / to the Cratchits' house. At the door, / the ghost smiled and stopped / to bless Bob Cratchit's dwelling.

Mrs. Cratchit, Bob's wife, / was preparing their Christmas dinner. Just then / Bob Cratchit was coming back from church / with the youngest son, Tiny Tim. Tiny Tim was ill / and used a crutch / to walk.

The family sat down / to eat their meal. They had only / one goose, some potatoes, and a small Christmas pudding. It seemed very small / for such a large family, / but nobody complained. Though it was a very simple Christmas meal, / they were still as happy / as if they had eaten a king's meal. After dinner, / all the Cratchit family / gathered around the fire. Bob proposed, "A Merry Christmas / to us all, my dears. God bless us!"

· **surprising** 令人驚訝的　· **be covered with** 充滿了　· **be heaped upon** 在……上面堆滿
· **bowl of punch** 一碗雞尾酒　· **couch** 沙發　· **glowing torch** 發光的火把　· **light** 照亮
· **find** 發現　· **the Cratchits** 克萊契一家 (= the Cratchit family)　· **bless** 祝福
· **crutch** 柺杖　· **complain** 抱怨　· **as if** 有如；好像　· **gather** 聚集
· **propose** 提議為……乾杯

CLOSE UP

1　**were covered with Christmas trees** 蓋滿了聖誕樹
〈be covered with . . .〉是「被……覆蓋」的意思。

2　**Heaped upon the floor were turkeys, geese, pigs, . . .** 地上堆滿了火雞、鵝、豬……
正常的語序是〈Turkeys, geese, pigs, . . . were heaped upon the floor.〉，將 heaped upon the floor 拿到句首的話，主詞 (turkeys, geese, pigs, . . .) 和動詞 (were) 就要倒裝。主詞太長或要用新主詞的話，就會像這樣用倒裝法，是在文學或說明文中常出現的結構。

3　**Upon the couch in the center of the room sat a happy giant.** 房間正中央的沙發上坐著一個快樂的巨人。
也是倒裝句，正常的語序是〈A happy giant sat upon the couch in the center of the room.〉。

施顧己在他房間裡 in his bedroom 醒來 awake，現在是凌晨一點 one in the morning，第二個鬼魂出現的時間到了 time for the second ghost。他看看自己的房間 look around his bedroom，沒有人 nobody 在，他走到客廳的門口 go to the door of his living room。

「請進 come in，艾伯納瑟 · 施顧己 Ebenezer Scrooge。」一個聲音說。

他打開門 open the door，看到一個令他非常吃驚的東西 something very surprising，房間看起來很不一樣 look so different。牆上 the walls 蓋滿聖誕樹 be covered with Christmas trees。地板上 upon the floor 堆滿了 be heaped 火雞 turkeys、鵝 geese、豬 pigs、香腸 sausages、梅子布丁 plum puddings、栗子 chestnuts、蘋果 apples、很多好喝的雞尾酒 great bowls of punch。房間正中央 in the center of the room 的沙發上 upon the couch 坐了一個很快樂的巨人 a happy giant，拿著 hold 一個發光的火把 a glowing torch 照亮整個房間 light the room。

「請進，請進，我是現在聖誕節的鬼魂 the Ghost of Christmas Present」巨人說。

「鬼魂，我從昨晚的鬼魂那裡學到很多 learn a lot，今晚如果你有什麼要教我的 something to teach me，帶我 take me 到任何你想帶我去的地方 anywhere you want。」施顧己說。

「摸我的袍子 touch my robe。」巨人說。

施顧己照他所說的 as he is told 去做，施顧己發現他們在聖誕節的早晨 on Christmas morning 走在倫敦的街頭 walk in a London street，鬼魂帶他到克萊契的家 take him to the Cratchits' house，到了門口 at the door，鬼魂微笑並停下 smile and stop 來祝福鮑伯 · 克萊契的住所 bless Bob Cratchit's dwelling。

克萊契太太 Mrs. Cratchit，鮑伯的妻子 Bob's wife 在準備他們的聖誕晚餐 prepare their Christmas dinner。這時候，鮑伯 · 克萊契帶著他最小的兒子 the youngest son 小提姆 Tiny Tim 從教堂回來 come back from church。小提姆生病了 be ill，得靠柺杖 use a crutch 才能走路。

一家人坐下來吃他們的晚餐 eat their meal，他們只有一隻鵝 one goose，一些馬鈴薯 some potatoes，和一個小小的聖誕布丁 a small Christmas pudding，要給這麼大的家庭 for such a large family 吃，它看來非常小 seem very small，但沒有人抱怨。雖然那是一頓很簡樸的聖誕大餐 a very simple Christmas meal，他們仍然很快樂，好像吃了一頓國王的大餐 eat a king's meal。晚餐後 after dinner 克萊契一家人 all the Cratchit family 圍著爐火 gather around the fire，鮑伯提議大家舉杯說：「祝我們大家 to us all 聖誕快樂，我親愛的家人，神祝福我們 bless us！」

GRAMMAR POINT

such a/an + 形容詞 + 名詞：這麼一個……的…… ⇨ 表「程度相當高的」的意思。

- It seemed very small for **such a large family**. 它看來對這麼大的家庭來說非常小。
- Mr. Fezziwig was **such a happy, kind boss**. 費茲威先生是這麼一個又快樂、又善良的老闆。

"God bless us everyone!" said Tiny Tim. Tiny Tim sat / very close to his father's side / upon his little stool. He was very sick. Bob held his withered little hand / in his / as if he loved the child / and wished to keep him by his side, / but he dreaded / that Tiny Tim might be taken from him.

"Will he be here / next Christmas?" Scrooge asked.

"With help," replied the ghost.

Scrooge raised his head / when he heard his name spoken.

"Let's drink / to Mr. Scrooge," said Bob.

"To Scrooge?" Mrs. Cratchit's face reddened, / and she said, "Why should we drink / to that old, stingy, unfeeling man?"

"My dear," was Bob's mild answer, "it's Christmas Day."

"Well, you are right. I'll drink to him. But nothing we do / could make that mean old man / feel happy or merry," said Mrs. Cratchit.

The mention of his name / cast a dark shadow / on the party, / which lasted / for a full five minutes. After some time, / the Cratchits became cheerful again. They were not a handsome family. They were not well dressed. But they were happy, grateful, and pleased with one another.

The ghost took Scrooge away / from the Cratchits' house. The two of them / walked through the streets of London. People were going to parties / with their friends and families. Suddenly, / they were in a cold, dark, empty place. They looked through the window / of a small house. Inside, / there was / a big family / in a very small room. Yet they were happy / and were singing Christmas carols together.

Scrooge asked, "Who are they?"

"They are poor miners," answered the ghost. "They have hard lives / working inside the Earth / to dig up coal."

Slowly, / the scene vanished, / and Scrooge suddenly heard / a hearty laugh. It was his nephew Fred's house. Fred was telling everyone / about his visit to his uncle.

·stool 凳子 ·withered 枯萎的 ·dread 懼怕 ·be taken from 被帶走 ·redden 變紅
·stingy 小氣的 ·unfeeling 無情的 ·mention 提到 ·cast a shadow 蒙上陰影
·last 持續 ·cheerful 歡樂的 ·well dressed 穿著體面 ·grateful 感恩的
·pleased with 滿意的 ·take . . . away from . . . 把……從……帶走
·look through 看穿；看出去 ·Christmas carol 聖誕頌歌 ·miner 礦工 ·dig up 挖
·vanish 消失

CLOSE UP

1 **Let's drink to Mr. Scrooge.** 我們來敬施顧己先生。
〈drink to . . . 〉是「為……而乾杯」的意思。

2 **nothing we do could make that mean old man feel happy or merry**
我們做什麼都不能讓那吝嗇老頭幸福或快樂。
nothing we do是主詞，could make是動詞，that mean old man是受詞，feel happy or merry是受詞補語，也就是〈make＋受詞＋受詞補語〉的結構，翻譯成「讓某人怎麼樣」就可以了。

「神祝福我們每一位 bless us everyone！」小提姆說，他坐在小凳子上 upon his little stool，離他爸爸很近 close to his father's side。他病得很重，鮑伯握著 hold 他衰弱的小手 his withered little hand，好像他很愛這個孩子 love the child，希望把他留在身邊 keep him by his side。他很害怕 dread 小提姆會被帶走 be taken from him。

「下一個聖誕節 next Christmas 他還會在這裡 be here 嗎？」施顧己問。

「有人幫忙的話 with help。」鬼魂回答。

施顧己聽到有人說他的名字 hear his name spoken，便抬起頭來 raise his head。

「我們來敬施顧己先生 drink to Mr. Scrooge」鮑伯說。

「敬施顧己先生？」克萊契太太氣得面紅耳赤，她說：「為什麼我們要敬那個又老又吝嗇又無情 old, stingy, unfeeling 的傢伙？」

「我的親愛的，」鮑伯溫和地回答：「今天是聖誕節。」

「好吧，你是對的，我會敬他，但我們做什麼都不能讓那個吝嗇的老頭 that mean old man 幸福或快樂 feel happy or merry。」克萊契太太說。

一提到他的名字 the mention of his name 派對上 on the party 就蒙上一層陰影 cast a dark shadow，整整持續 last 了五分鐘 for a full five minutes。過了一陣子 after some time，克萊契一家人 the Cratchits 又開始歡樂 become cheerful。他們不是很富裕的一家人 a handsome family，穿得不體面 be not well dressed，但他們很快樂、很感恩 be grateful，而且相處融洽 be pleased with one another。

鬼魂把施顧己帶離 take Scrooge away 克萊契的家 from the Cratchits' house，他們兩個 the two of them 經過倫敦街頭 walk through the streets of London。路上行人帶著他們的朋友和家人 with their friends and families 正要赴宴 go to parties，突然間，他們身處一個又冷又暗又空曠的地方 a cold, dark, empty place，從一間很小的房子 a small house 的窗戶往裡看 look through the window，裡面有一間很小的房間 in a very small room，那裡有一大家子的人 a big family 擠在一間小房間裡，但他們很開心，一起唱聖誕頌歌 sing Christmas carols。

施顧己問：「他們是誰？」

「他們是很窮的礦工 poor miners。」鬼魂回答：「他們在地底下工作 work inside the Earth，挖煤礦 dig up coal，生活過得很艱辛 have hard lives。」

慢慢地，場景 the scene 消失 vanish 了。施顧己突然聽到開懷大笑的聲音 hear a hearty laugh，那是他外甥佛萊德的家 Fred's house，佛萊德告訴大家他去拜訪他舅舅的事 his visit to his uncle。

GRAMMAR POINT

which（關係代名詞） ⇨ 代替前面出現的整個子句。

- The mention of his name cast a dark shadow on the party, **which** lasted for a full five minutes. 一提到他的名字就讓派對蒙上陰影，這種氣氛整整持續了五分鐘。

- He visited Fred's house, **which** pleased everyone there.
他到佛萊德的家，在場的每個人都很高興。

"So when I said 'Merry Christmas' to him, / he replied 'Bah, humbug!'" said Fred. Everyone laughed.

"He's a strange old man," said Fred. "He is rich, / but he doesn't do anything good / with his money. He even lives / like he's poor. I invite him / to have Christmas dinner with us / every year, / but he never comes. Someday, / perhaps / he will change his mind. And someday / perhaps / he will pay poor Bob Cratchit more money / as well."

For the rest of the evening, / Scrooge and the ghost / watched his nephew and friends / enjoy their Christmas party. Then, / the clock struck twelve. Scrooge looked around for the ghost, / but he saw the ghost / no more. Then, / he remembered Marley's prediction, / and he lifted his eyes.

Scrooge saw a solemn phantom coming / like a mist along the ground / toward him. **Unlike the others**, / he could not see / this one's face or body. It was covered / from head to toe / in a long black garment. The only visible part / of the phantom / was one outstretched hand.

The phantom moved / slowly and silently. As it came near him, / Scrooge bent down upon his knee, / for the ghost seemed to scatter / gloom and mystery / as it moved. The ghost did not speak at all.

"**I am in the presence of** / the Ghost of Christmas Yet to Come," said Scrooge. "You are about to show me the things / which have not happened yet, / but will happen / in the time before us," Scrooge said, / looking at the strange ghost. "Is that so, / Spirit?"

The ghost silently moved its head a little / and pointed with its hand. Scrooge suddenly found himself / in the middle of the city. The ghost stopped / beside a group of businessmen. Scrooge could hear / some of them talking.

"I don't know much about it. I only know / he's dead," said one great fat man.

"When did he die?" inquired another.

"Last night, / I believe."

"What has he done / with his money?" asked a red-faced gentleman.

"I haven't heard," responded the first man. "He didn't leave it to me / though. That's / all I know."

"At least / his funeral will be very cheap," said one man.

· **change one's mind** 改變心意　· **strike**（鐘）敲　· **prediction** 預言
· **solemn** 嚴肅的；莊重的· **phantom** 幽靈　· **mist** 薄霧　· **unlike** 不像
· **from head to toe** 從頭到腳　· **garment** 衣服　· **visible** 可見的
· **outstretched** 伸出的　· **bend down upon one's knee** 曲膝　· **scatter** 散布
· **gloom** 黑暗；憂鬱　· **mystery** 神秘　· **point** 指向　· **funeral** 葬禮

CLOSE UP

1　**unlike the others** 不像其他人
介系詞unlike是like（像……）反義字；unlike是「不像……」、「和……不同」的意思。

2　**I am in the presence of the Ghost of Christmas Yet to Come.**
我在未來聖誕節的鬼魂面前。
〈be in the presence of . . .〉是「站在……的面前」的意思。
〈yet to come〉是「還沒出現的」、「即將出現的」的意思。在這裡是「未來（future）」的意思。

「當我跟他說『聖誕快樂』，他回答：『呸，騙人的東西！』」佛萊德說完，大家都笑了。

「他是個怪老頭a strange old man。」佛萊德說：「他很有錢，但他沒有用錢with his money做過什麼好事don't do anything good，甚至自己也過得像窮人一樣。我每年every year邀他invite him跟我們with us一起吃聖誕晚餐have Christmas dinner，他從來不來never come。哪天someday，說不定他會改變心意change his mind，哪天說不定他也會給可憐的鮑伯‧克萊契加薪pay more money。」

接下來的夜晚，施顧己和鬼魂看他的外甥和朋友his nephew and friends享受他們的聖誕派對enjoy their Christmas party，那時鐘敲了12下strike twelve。施顧己四處找鬼魂，但看不見它，他想起馬里的預言remember Marley's prediction，睜開雙眼lift his eyes。

施顧己看到一個莊嚴的幽靈a solemn phantom，像地上的迷霧一樣a mist along the ground朝他走過來，不像其他鬼魂unlike the others，他看不見這個鬼魂的臉或身體。它從頭到腳from head to toe都被一件又長又黑的衣服in a long black garment蓋住be covered，鬼魂身上唯一看得到的部分the only visible part是一隻伸出來的手one outstretched hand。

鬼魂緩慢、安靜地slowly and silently移動，當它靠近他come near him，施顧己曲膝bend down upon his knee，因為那鬼魂移動時似乎散發出scatter陰鬱和神秘的氣息gloom and mystery，他一語不發do not speak。

「未來聖誕節的鬼魂the Ghost of Christmas Yet to Come我在你面前。」施顧己說。「你將要讓我看show me尚未發生但將要發生in the time before us之事，」施顧己看著這個奇怪的鬼魂說：「是這樣嗎，鬼魂？」

鬼魂微微地點了一下頭move its head a little，用手指了一下point with its hand。施顧己突然發現他在市中心in the middle of the city，鬼魂在一群商人a group of businessmen旁邊停了下來，施顧己聽見一些人談話。

「我知道的不多don't know much about it，我只知道他死了。」一個很胖的男人說。

「他什麼時候死的？」另一個人問。

「我相信是昨晚。」

「他的錢他怎麼處置？」一個紅臉的先生問。

「我還沒聽說haven't heard。」第一個男人回答：「他沒有留給我don't leave it to me，那是我所知道的all I know。」

「至少at least，他的葬禮his funeral會草草了事be very cheap。」一個男人說。

GRAMMAR POINT

for + 主詞＋動詞：因為……

⇨ 表話講完後，又附帶地說出理由，這時for引導的子句要放在句尾，前面還要加逗點。

- Scrooge bent down upon his knee, **for** the ghost seemed to scatter gloom and mystery.
  施顧己曲膝，因為鬼魂似乎散發出陰鬱和神秘的氣息。

- I didn't follow them, **for** something dangerous was likely to happen.
  我沒有跟著他們，因為危險的事似乎就要發生。

"That's true. He had no friends. No one liked him, / so nobody will go to his funeral."

Scrooge did not understand / why the ghost wanted him / to listen to this conversation, / but he knew / the ghost would not answer him, / so he did not ask.

They left the busy scene / and went to an obscure part of the town. The streets were dark and small. They visited a dirty shop / full of horrible old things / you can imagine / –iron, old rags, bottles, clothes, and bones. It was a place / where people came to sell their things / when they needed money.

Scrooge watched / as three people brought things / to sell to the shopkeeper. They were from the same dead man's house.

"What have you got / to sell?" asked the shopkeeper.

One woman took out / some towels, silver teaspoons, and other small things, / and said, "He doesn't need these now."

"No indeed, ma'am," answered the shopkeeper.

"Take a look at these," said the other woman. "Bed curtains and blankets. He isn't likely to catch a cold / without them / now."

Scrooge listened to this dialogue / in horror. "Ghost, I see. The case of this unhappy man / might be my own."

The scene had suddenly changed, / and Scrooge found himself / in another terrible room. There was a bare bed / with no blankets / or curtains around it. A pale light from outside / fell straight upon the bed. On it, / unwatched, unwept, and uncared for, / was the dead body / of the unknown man. He was covered by a thin sheet.

The ghost, / as silent as ever, / merely pointed at the body. Scrooge realized / that the ghost wanted him / to look at the face of the dead man, / but he could not do it.

"I cannot look at his face," cried Scrooge. "Let me see some tenderness / connected with this death, / or this dark chamber / will be forever in my memory."

The scene changed to another home. A woman stood up / as her husband entered the room. "Have you gotten any news?" she asked.

· obscure 默默無名的　· horrible 可怕的　· bone 骨頭　· shopkeeper 店主
· take out 拿出　· indeed 確實　· catch a cold 感冒　· in horror 在恐懼之中
· case 案例　· terrible 可怕的　· bare 光的；空的　· pale light 暗淡的光
· unwatched 無人看守的　· unwept 無人哭泣的　· uncared for 無人關切的
· dead body 死屍　· be covered by 覆蓋著　· sheet 床單　· point at 指著某物
· tenderness 良善　· connected with 有關於　· chamber 房間　· stand up 站起來

CLOSE UP

1　**On it, . . . , was the dead body of the unknown man.** 上面……是一個不明人士的屍體。
副詞片語 on it 出現在句子前的話，主詞（the dead body of the unknown man）和動詞（was）要倒置，變成倒裝句。

2　**as silent as ever** 如以往一樣安靜
〈as . . . as ever〉是「像以前一樣」的意思。例 He is as greedy as ever.（他如以往一樣貪心。）

「這倒是真的，他沒有朋友 **have no friends**，沒有人 **no one** 喜歡他 **like him**，所以沒有人 **nobody** 會參加他的葬禮 **go to his funeral**。」

施顧己不懂為什麼鬼魂要讓他聽這一段談話 **listen to this conversation**，但他知道鬼魂不會回答他，所以他沒問。

他們離開這個忙碌的場景 **leave the busy scene**，到鎮上某個不知名的地區 **an obscure part of the town**。街道又黑又小 **be dark and small**，他們造訪了一間髒髒的小店 **visit a dirty shop**，裡面充滿你可以想像到的可怕古物 **horrible old things**——有鐵 **iron**、舊破布 **old rags**、瓶子 **bottles**、衣服 **clothes** 和骨頭 **bones**，這是人需要錢 **need money** 可以賣東西 **sell their things** 的地方。

施顧己看著三個人 **three people** 帶了東西 **bring things** 來賣給店主 **sell to the shopkeeper**。

「妳有什麼要賣？」店主問。

一個女人拿出 **take out** 了一些毛巾 **some towels**、銀茶匙 **silver teaspoons** 和其他小東西 **other small things**，然後說：「他現在不需要這些了。」

「確實不需要了，女士。」店主回答。

「看看這些 **take a look at these**，」另一個女人說：「床簾 **bed curtains**、毯子 **blankets**，他現在沒有它們 **without them** 也不會感冒 **catch a cold** 了。」

施顧己很驚恐地 **in horror** 聽這段對話 **listen to this dialogue**。「鬼魂，我懂了，這個不幸的男人的案例 **the case of this unhappy man** 可能就是我自己的。」

場景突然變了，施顧己發現他自己在另一個恐怖的房間 **in another terrible room**。那裡有一張空床 **a bare bed** 沒有毯子或床簾，暗淡的光線 **a pale light** 從外面直接照射在床上 **fall upon the bed**。沒有人看守 **unwatched**、沒有人哭 **unwept**、沒有人關心 **uncared for**，一個不明人士 **the unknown man** 的死屍 **the dead body** 躺在那張床上。屍身上蓋了 **be covered** 一層薄薄的床單 **by a thin sheet**。

鬼魂一如以往地安靜 **as silent as ever**，只是指向那個屍體 **point at the body**。施顧己明白鬼魂要他看一下 **look at** 死人 **the dead man** 的臉 **the face**，但他辦不到。

「我不敢看他的臉，」施顧己大叫，「讓我看 **let me see** 一些有關他死亡 **connected with this death** 好的一面 **some tenderness**，不然 **or** 這黑暗的房間 **this dark chamber** 會永遠 **forever** 存在我的記憶裡 **in my memory**。」

場景換到另一個家 **change to another home**。一個女人在她丈夫進來 **enter the room** 的時候站了起來 **stand up**。「你有沒有什麼消息 **any news** 呢？」她問。

be likely to . . . ：可能會……　　**it is likely that . . .** ：可能會……

⇨〈be likely to . . .〉可以換成〈it is likely that . . .〉。
　　如果是〈be not likely to . . .〉的話，則是「可能不會……」的意思。

- He **isn't likely to** catch a cold without them now.
  = It **isn't likely that** he will catch a cold without them now.
  他現在沒有它們也不可能感冒了。

"When I visited him / to find out / if we could pay the money / one week later," he answered, "an old woman told me / he was dead."

"That's great news," she said. "I'm sorry for saying that. I mean / that now we have time to get the money / that we have to pay."

"No, ghost! Show me someone / who's sorry about a death, / not someone / who's happy because of a death," shouted Scrooge.

The ghost took him / to poor Bob Cratchit's house. Scrooge saw the family / sitting quietly around the fire. They were talking about Tiny Tim.

"I met Fred, / Mr. Scrooge's nephew," said Bob. "And he said / that he was very sorry / to hear about Tiny Tim."

Bob turned to his family / and said, "We must never forget / what a good boy Tiny Tim was."

"No, never father," shouted all the children.

Then, / Bob Cratchit broke down / all at once. He couldn't help it / as the tears flowed down his face.

"Ghost," said Scrooge, "something informs me / that our parting moment / is at hand. Tell me. Who was the dead man / we saw?"

The Ghost of Christmas Yet to Come / took Scrooge to a churchyard. The ghost stood among the graves / and pointed down to one. Scrooge crept toward it, / trembling as he went, / and followed the finger / to read the name on the neglected grave: EBENEZER SCROOGE.

"Am I that man / who lay upon the bed? No, ghost! Oh no, no. I am not / the man I was. I will not be / the man I must have been / but for this evening. Why show me this / if I am past all hope? Assure me / that I may yet change these shadows."

· be sorry about 很遺憾　· break down 崩潰　· all at once 突然
· cannot help it 忍不住　· inform 告知　· parting moment 離別時刻
· at hand 即將到來　· churchyard 教堂的墓地　· grave 墳墓　· creep 緩慢行進
· neglected 棄置的　· lie 躺　· be past all hope 絲毫沒有希望　· assure 確保

CLOSE UP

1　**to find out if we could pay the money one week later** 看看我們能不能一週之後再還錢
這裡的 if 是「是否」的意思，要依據上下文，選出最合適的意思來用。

2　**he was very sorry to hear about Tiny Tim** 他聽說小提姆的事，感到很遺憾
sorry 除「對不起」的意思外，「遺憾」、「可惜」、「可憐」等意思也常被使用。

3　**our parting moment is at hand** 我們分開的時刻即將到來
〈 . . . be at hand〉是「……即將到來」的意思。

4　**the man I was** 從前的我　/　**the man I must have been** 那個我可能變成的人
因 was 是 be 動詞的過去式，所以前者是「過去是怎樣的人」的意思。been 是 be 動詞的過去分詞，因為〈must have p.p.〉是「（強烈的推測）一定會是……準沒錯」，所以後者是表推測「一定會成為那樣的人」的意思。

5　**but for this evening** 若非今晚
〈but for . . .〉是「要不是……的話」的意思。
例 I would have failed but for your help.（若非你的幫助，我一定會失敗。）

「我去找他 **visit him** 看看 **find out** 我們是不是可以一個星期以後 **one week later** 再還錢 **pay the money** 的時候，」他回答，「一個老婦人告訴他死了 **be dead**。」

「那真是好消息 **great news**，」她說：「我很遺憾這麼說，我的意思 **mean** 是現在我們有時間 **have time** 湊出我們該還 **we have to pay** 的錢 **get the money**。」

「不，鬼魂！讓我看看 **show me** 為死亡感到難過 **be sorry about a death** 的人，而不是為死亡感到高興 **be happy** 的人。」施顧己大叫。

鬼魂帶他 **take him** 到可憐的鮑伯‧克萊契的家 **to poor Bob Cratchit's house**。施顧己看到那家人靜靜地坐在火堆旁 **sit around the fire**，他們在談論小提姆 **talk about Tiny Tim**。

「我遇見佛萊德 **meet Fred**，施顧己先生的外甥 **Mr. Scrooge's nephew**，」鮑伯說：「他說他很難過 **be very sorry** 聽到小提姆的事 **hear about Tiny Tim**。」

鮑伯轉向他的家人 **turn to his family**，說：「我們永遠不要忘記 **never forget** 小提姆是個多麼好的小男孩 **what a good boy**。」

「不，永遠不會，父親。」所有的孩子大叫。

然後，鮑伯‧克萊契突然 **all at once** 崩潰了 **break down**，淚水 **the tears** 從臉上滑落時 **flow down his face**，他再也忍不住了 **cannot help it**。

「鬼魂，」施顧己說：「某些事告訴我 **inform me** 我們分開的時刻 **our parting moment** 就要到了 **be at hand**，告訴我 **tell me**，我們看到的死人是誰？」

未來聖誕節的鬼魂帶他到教堂的墓地 **a churchyard**，鬼魂站在墳墓之間 **stand among the graves**，指向其中一座墳墓 **point down to one**。施顧己慢慢地走向它 **creep toward it**，邊走邊顫抖 **tremble**，跟著手指 **follow the finger** 看到被棄置的墳墓 **the neglected grave** 上面寫著名字 **read the name**：艾伯納瑟‧施顧己。

「我是那個躺在床上的人 **lie upon the bed** 嗎？不，鬼魂！喔，不，不，我不是從前的我 **the man I was**，若非今晚 **but for this evening** 我一定還是從前的我 **the man I must have been**。如果我完全無望 **be past all hope**，為什麼給我看這個 **show me this**？向我保證 **assure me** 我還能改變這些幻影 **change these shadows**。」

GRAMMAR POINT

關係代名詞 ⇨ 代替前面出現的名詞（先行詞），關係代名詞引導的子句，用來修飾先行詞。

• Now we have time to get *the money* **that** we have to pay.
現在我們有時間去湊我們該還的錢。

• Show me *someone* **who**'s sorry about a death, not *someone* **who**'s happy because of a death.
讓我看看為死亡感到難過的人，而不是為死亡感到高興的人。

• Who was *the dead man* **(whom)** we saw? 我們看到的死人是誰？

• Am I *that man* **who** lay upon the bed? 我是那個躺在床上的人嗎？

Scrooge continued, "I will honor Christmas / in my heart / and try to keep it / all the year. I will live / in the past, present, and future. I will never forget the lessons / that I have been taught."

Then, / the phantom began to disappear, / and Scrooge realized / that he was back in his own bedroom. Best and happiest of all, / time was before him. He had time / to make amends.

Scrooge heard the church bells / ringing loudly. Running to the window, / he opened it / and put out his head. It was a clear, bright, stirring, golden day.

"What day is it today?" cried Scrooge / to a boy down on the street.

"Today? It's Christmas Day, sir," answered the boy.

"Christmas!" Scrooge was surprised. All of the visits from the ghosts / had taken place / in one night.

"Do you know / the butcher's shop down the street?" Scrooge asked. "Please go / and tell the butcher / I'll buy a big goose. Come back with the man, / and I'll give you a nice tip." The boy ran off quickly.

"I'll send it to Bob Cratchit's. He won't know / who is sending it. It's twice the size of Tiny Tim," Scrooge thought to himself.

Scrooge then dressed himself / in his Sunday best / and went out onto the streets. Many people were on the streets, / and Scrooge gave each of them / a delighted smile. He said, "Good morning, sir," or "A Merry Christmas to you," to everyone he passed.

Later in the afternoon, / he walked toward his nephew's house. He passed the door / a dozen times / before he had the courage / to go up and knock. But he finally did.

Fred was very surprised / to see his uncle. "Uncle, why are you here?" he asked.

"I have come to dinner. Will you let me in, Fred?" Scrooge asked.

"Of course you may!" cried out Fred.

Fred was very happy, / and so were his wife and all their friends. They had a wonderful party together.

· honor 紀念　·lesson 教訓　·make amends 彌補　·stirring 令人興奮的
·take place 發生　·butcher's shop 肉舖　·butcher 肉販　·tip 小費
·think to oneself 心中想著　·dress oneself 打扮　·one's Sunday best 一個人最好的衣服
·delighted 愉快的　·a dozen times 很多次　·courage 勇氣　·uncle 舅舅

CLOSE UP

1　**It's twice the size of Tiny Tim.** 它是小提姆的兩倍大。
〈倍數＋名詞〉是「幾倍的……」的意思。「兩倍」是twice，從四倍開始用〈數字＋times〉的形式來表現，例如：four times（四倍）。

2　**Scrooge then dressed himself in his Sunday best** 施顧己穿上他最好的衣服。
〈dress oneself in . . .〉是「穿上……（服裝）」的意思。

施顧己繼續說：「我會在心裡 in my heart 紀念聖誕節 honor Christmas，一年到頭 all the year 都會試著記住 keep it，我會活在活去、現在和未來 in the past, present, and future，永遠不會忘記我學到的教訓 never forget the lessons。」

幽靈消失了 disappear，施顧己明白他回到 be back 自己的房間裡 in his own bedroom。最棒也最快樂的 best and happiest of all 是時間在他面前，他還有時間 have time 挽救一切 make amends。

施顧己聽到了教堂的鐘聲 the church bells 響得很大聲 ring loudly，跑到窗邊 run to the window，打開窗戶 open it，探出頭來 put out his head，外面是晴朗 clear、明亮 bright、令人興奮 stirring、珍貴的 golden 一天。

「今天是哪一天 what day？」施顧己對著街上的一個男孩大叫。

「今天？今天是聖誕節 Christmas Day 啊，先生。」男孩回答。

「聖誕節！」施顧己很驚訝 be surprised，所有鬼魂的來訪 the visits from the ghosts 都發生 take place 於一夜之間 in one night。

「你知道街上 down the street 肉販的店 the butcher's shop 嗎？」施顧己問，「請幫我去告訴肉販，我要買一隻肥鵝 buy a big goose，跟著肉販 with the man 回來 come back，我會給你豐厚的小費 a nice tip。」男孩很快地跑去 run off。

「我要把它送到鮑伯‧克萊契的家，他不會知道是誰送給他的，這比小提姆還大兩倍 twice the size of Tiny Tim。」施顧己心裡想。

施顧己穿上他最好的衣服 dress himself in his Sunday best，走到街上去 go out onto the streets。街上有許多人 many people，施顧己給他們每一個人 each of them 親切的微笑 give a delighted smile。他對每個經過的人說：「早安 good morning，先生。」或「祝你聖誕快樂 Merry Christmas to you。」。

傍晚時 later in the afternoon，他朝他外甥的家 toward his nephew's house 走去，他走過他家門 pass the door 很多次 a dozen times，才有上前 go up 敲門 knock 的勇氣 have the courage，最後他做到了。

佛萊德見到自己的舅舅 see his uncle 非常驚訝。「舅舅，你為什麼在這裡 why are you here？」他問。

「我來吃晚餐 come to dinner，佛萊德，你願意讓我進來 let me in 嗎？」施顧己問。

「當然願意！」佛萊德大聲說。

佛萊德非常高興，他太太和他們的朋友也一樣，他們一起過了一個很美妙的 wonderful 聖誕節。

So am I.：我也是。

- You are happy. **So am I.** (= I **am also happy.**) 你很快樂。我也是。
- Fred was very happy, and **so were** his wife and all their friends.
  = Fred was very happy, and **his wife and all their friends** were also very happy.
  佛萊德很高興，他太太和他們的朋友也都一樣。

The next day, / Scrooge went to the office / early in the morning. He wanted to be there / before Bob got there. Bob was eighteen minutes late. As Bob walked in, / Scrooge said, "Hello. What do you mean / by coming here at this time of day?"

"I'm very sorry, sir. I'm late," replied Bob.

"Yes, I think you are," said Scrooge.

"Now, I'll tell you what, / my friend," said Scrooge. "I'm not going to stand this sort of thing / any longer. And therefore . . . therefore, / I am going to pay you more money!"

Scrooge continued, "I'll raise your salary / and assist your struggling family. We will discuss your affairs / this very afternoon," Scrooge said / with a nice smile.

That afternoon, / Scrooge took Bob out for a drink / and explained / how he was going to help him.

Scrooge was better than his word. He did everything / he said he was going to do / and more. He became a friend of the Cratchit family, / and to Tiny Tim, / who did not die, / he was like a second father. He became as good a friend, / as good a master, / and as good a man / as the city ever knew.

Some people laughed at him / because he had changed. Scrooge did not mind. Scrooge's own heart laughed, / and that was quite enough for him. He had no further dealings with ghosts, / but he lived happily ever afterward.

·**stand** 忍受　·**this sort of thing** 這種事　·**raise salary** 加薪　·**assist** 幫助
·**struggling** 生存困難的　·**affairs** 事情　·**this very afternoon** 今天下午
·**second father** 像父親一樣的人　·**laugh at** 嘲笑某人　·**do not mind** 不在意
·**dealings with** 跟誰打交道　·**ever afterward** 從此以後

CLOSE UP

1　**What do you mean by coming here at this time of day?**
你這個時間才來上班是什麼意思？
〈What do you mean by + V-ing . . . ?〉是「……到底是什麼意思呢？」。

2　**I'm not going to stand this sort of thing.** 我不會再繼續忍受這種事。/
I am going to pay you more money. 我將要付你更多錢。/
explained how he was going to help him 解釋他將要如何幫他 /
he said he was going to do 他說他將要做
〈be going to . . .〉是「將會去……」的意思，提到「已經計畫好或決定好未來要去做的事」，或是「看到現在的狀況，決定未來一定要去做的事」時使用。這裡用 was going to，因為主要子句的動詞 explained 和 said 是過去式，因時式要一致，所以要用過去式。

隔天 **the next day** 施顧己一大早 **early in the morning** 就進了辦公室 **go to the office**，他希望在鮑伯到達之前 **get there** 先到那裡 **be there**。鮑伯遲到了 18 分鐘 **eighteen minutes late**。當鮑伯走進來 **walk in**，施顧己說：「哈囉 **hello**，你這個時間 **at this time of day** 才來上班 **come here** 是什麼意思？」。

　　「非常抱歉，先生，我遲到了 **be late**。」鮑伯回答。

　　「是的，我想你是。」施顧己說。

　　「現在，我的朋友，我要跟你說 **tell you what**，」施顧己說：「我不打算再忍受這種事 **this sort of thing**，因此 **therefore**……，我要幫你加薪 **pay you more money**。」

　　施顧己繼續說：「我要加你的薪水 **raise your salary**，幫助 **assist** 你艱困的家庭 **your struggling family**，我們今天下午 **this very afternoon** 來談談你的事 **discuss your affairs**。」施顧己微笑地說 **with a nice smile**。

　　那天下午 **that afternoon**，施顧己帶鮑伯出去 **take Bob out**，喝杯飲料 **for a drink**，解釋 **explain** 他要如何幫助鮑伯 **help him**。

　　施顧己比他說的還要更好 **be better than his word**，他說到做到，而且還要有過之而無不及 **everything and more**。他成了克萊契一家人的朋友 **become a friend**，對還活著的小提姆來說，他就像第二個父親一樣 **like a second father**。他成了眾所皆知的好朋友、好老闆和大善人。

　　有些人為他的改變而嘲笑他 **laugh at him**，施顧己並不在意 **do not mind**，他內心 **Scrooge's own heart** 在笑 **laugh**，這對他來說已然足夠 **be quite enough**。他沒有繼續和鬼魂打交道 **dealings with ghosts**，從此以後 **ever afterward** 過著幸福快樂的日子 **live happily**。

Super
Reading
Story
Training
Book

6

The Last Leaf

— O. Henry

The Last Leaf

In a little district / west of Washington Square, / the streets have run crazy / and broken themselves into small strips / called "places." These "places" / make strange angles and curves. One street crosses itself / a time or two. An artist once discovered / a valuable possibility / on this street. Suppose / a collector with a bill / for paints, paper, and canvas / should, / **in taking this route,** / suddenly meet himself coming back, / **without a cent having been paid on account.**

So, / to quaint old Greenwich Village, / the art people soon came prowling, / hunting for north windows and eighteenth-century gables and Dutch attics and low rents. Then, / they imported pewter mugs and a dish or two / from Sixth Avenue / and became a "colony."

At the top of / an ugly, three-story brick house, / Sue and Johnsy had their studio. "Johnsy" was a nickname for Joanna. One was from Maine; / the other from California. They had met at the restaurant Delmonico's / on Eighth Street / and **had found** / **that their tastes in art, food, and clothes** / **were so similar** / **that the joint studio resulted.**

That was in May. In November, / a cold, unseen stranger, / whom the doctors called Pneumonia, / visited the colony, / touching one here and there / with his icy fingers. Over on the east side, / this ravager strode boldly, / claiming scores of victims, / but his feet trod slowly / through the maze of the narrow and moss-grown "places."

Mr. Pneumonia was not / what you would call a gentleman. A small woman / with blood thinned by the warm California zephyrs / was no match for the tough and deadly illness.

·**district** 地區 ·**run crazy** 錯綜複雜 ·**strip** 條狀物 ·**valuable** 可貴的
·**possibility** 機會 ·**suppose** 假如 ·**collector** 討債者 ·**take a route** 沿著路走
·**on account** 賒帳 ·**quaint** 奇怪的 ·**prowl** 摸索 ·**gable** 三角牆
·**attic** 閣樓 ·**rent** 房租 ·**import** 引進 ·**colony** 藝術區 ·**three–story** 三層樓
·**studio** 工作室 ·**nickname** 暱稱 ·**result** 導致 ·**pneumonia** 肺炎
·**ravager** 掠奪者 ·**stride** 邁步 ·**boldly** 大膽地 ·**scores of** 許多 ·**victim** 受害者
·**tread** 踏 ·**maze** 迷宮 ·**moss–grown** 長滿青苔的 ·**zephyr** 微風；西風
·**deadly** 致命的 ·**be no match for** 不是某人的對手

CLOSE UP

1 **in taking this route** 沿著這條路走 / **without a cent having been paid** 沒有收到半分錢
〈in + V–ing〉是「在做……中」的意思。〈without + V–ing〉是「不用做……」的意思。
這裡的 a cent 是動名詞片語 having been paid 的主詞。

2 **had found that their tastes in art, food, and clothes were so similar that the joint studio resulted** 發現她們對藝術、飲食、衣著的品味十分相似，於是聯合工作室誕生了
〈that their tastes in art, food, and clothes were so similar〉這部分是 had found 的受詞。
整句是〈so…that…〉（如此……以致……）的結構。

最後一葉

華盛頓廣場Washington Square西邊的一個小區in a little district，街道the streets縱橫交錯run crazy，將這一帶分割成一小條一小條break themselves into small strips稱為「街道」called "places"。這些「街道」形成了奇特的角度和曲線make strange angles and curves，一條街one street自己本身就交叉cross itself一次或兩次a time or two。曾經once有一個藝術家an artist在這條街上發現了它的可貴之處a valuable possibility，如果一個討債者帶著顏料、紙和畫布的帳單a collector with a bill，走這條路take this route收帳，他會突然suddenly發現他遇到沒有收到半毛錢的自己meet himself coming back。

於是藝術家the art people很快地摸索到come prowling這個奇特有趣、古老的quaint old格林威治村Greenwich Village。他們尋找面北的窗戶north windows，18世紀的三角牆eighteenth-century gables、荷蘭式的閣樓Dutch attics，以及低廉的房租low rents，然後，他們又從第六街from Sixth Avenue買進import了一些白鑞杯子pewter mugs和一兩個盤子a dish or two，組成了一個「藝術區」become a "colony"。

在一棟醜陋的三層樓磚屋an ugly, three-story brick house的頂樓at the top，蘇和瓊西Sue and Johnsy設立了他們的工作室have their studio。瓊西是喬安娜的暱稱a nickname for Joanna，她倆一個one來自緬因州from Maine，另一個the other來自加州from California。她們是在第八大道的德爾蒙尼戈飯館相遇的，彼此一談，發現她們對藝術、飲食、衣著in art, food, and clothes的品味tastes十分相似be so similar，於是聯合工作室the joint studio誕生了result。

那是五月的事in May，到了十一月in November，一個冷酷、隱形的陌生人a cold, unseen stranger，醫生稱之為「肺炎」Pneumonia造訪了「藝術區」visit the colony。用他冰冷的手指with his icy fingers這裡碰一下，那裡碰一下touch one here and there。在廣場東側over on the east side，這個掠奪者this ravager明目張膽地邁步stride boldly，奪去了許多受害者的性命claim scores of victims，但他步伐在經過如迷宮maze般，窄小又長滿青苔的「藝術區」時，慢了下來tread slowly。

肺炎先生Mr. Pneumonia可不是一個你會稱之為紳士的人，一個被加州溫暖的西風the warm California zephyrs吹得面無血色with blood thinned的弱女子a small woman更不是這個難纏、可怕疾病the tough and deadly illness的對手match。

one / the other ⇨ 兩個中一個用one來表示，剩下的一個則用the other來表示。

- **One** was from Maine; **the other** from California.
  一個來自緬因州，另一個來自加州。

- Two artists lived in the building. **One** lived on the first floor; **the other** lived at the top.
  兩個藝術家住在這棟建築物，一個住一樓，另一個住頂樓。

But he attacked Johnsy, / and she lay, / scarcely moving, / on her painted iron bedstead, / looking through the small Dutch windowpanes / at the blank side of the next brick house.

One morning, / the busy doctor invited Sue into the hallway.

"She has one chance in– / let us say, ten," he said, / as he shook down the mercury / in his clinical thermometer.

"And that chance is / for her to want to live. Sometimes / when people give up trying to live, / it doesn't matter / what medicines I give. Your friend has made up her mind / that she's not going to get well. Has she anything on her mind?"

"She . . . she wanted to paint the Bay of Naples / some day," said Sue.

"Paint? Bosh! Does she have anything on her mind / worth thinking about twice, / like a man, for instance?"

"A man?" said Sue, / with a hard sound in her voice. "Is a man worth– / but, no, Doctor. There is nothing of the kind."

"Well, it is the weakness then," said the doctor. "I will do all / that science, / so far as it may be employed by me, / can accomplish. But whenever my patient / begins to count the carriages / in her funeral procession, / I subtract fifty percent / from the power of medicine to cure. If you can get her to ask one question / about the new winter styles in cloak sleeves, / I will promise you / a one-in-five chance for her / instead of one in ten."

After the doctor left, / Sue went into the workroom / and cried a napkin to a pulp. Then, / she swaggered into Johnsy's room / with her drawing board, / whistling a popular tune.

Johnsy lay, / scarcely making a move under the bedclothes, / with her face toward the window. Sue stopped whistling, / thinking she was asleep.

- **scarcely** 幾乎不　・**bedstead** 床架　・**windowpane** 窗戶玻璃　・**blank** 空白的
- **shake down** 搖下；甩下　・**mercury** 水銀　・**clinical thermometer** 體溫計
- **give up** 放棄　・**it doesn't matter** 無所謂　・**make up one's mind** 下定決心
- **get well** 好起來　・**weakness** 缺點　・**accomplish** 完成；做到
- **funeral procession** 喪禮隊伍　・**subtract** 扣除　・**cure** 治療
- **get . . . to . . .** 讓某人達到　・**cloak** 披風　・**cry a napkin to a pulp** 把毛巾哭得一團濕
- **swagger** 精神抖擻　・**whistle** 吹口哨　・**popular tune** 流行曲調

CLOSE UP

1　**Has she anything on her mind? / Does she have anything on her mind?**
她有什麼心事嗎？
〈have . . . on one's mind〉是「有……的念頭」、「有……在心裡」、「擔心……」的意思

2　**so far as it may be employed by me** 盡我所知地治病
這是 so far as I may employ it 的被動語態，it 是指 science。這裡的 employ 是「使用、駕馭」的意思，science 是「知識」。〈so far as . . .〉（到目前為止）。

可是，他攻擊了瓊西 **attack Johnsy**。她躺 **lie** 在漆過的鐵床架上幾乎一動不動 **scarcely move**，只能透過小小的荷蘭式玻璃窗凝視 **look at** 隔壁磚屋 **the next brick house** 的空牆 **the blank side**。

　　　　有一天早晨，忙碌的醫生 **the busy doctor** 請蘇和他一起到走廊去 **invite Sue into the hallway**。

　　　　「讓我們這麼説吧 **let us say**，她只有十分之一的機會 **one chance in ten**。」他一邊説，一邊把診療用溫度計裡 **in his clinical thermometer** 的水銀 **the mercury** 甩下去 **shake down**。

　　　　「這一成希望 **that chance** 在於她求生的意志 **want to live**。有時候，人不想活 **give up trying to live**，不管我給什麼藥 **what medicines I give** 都沒有用 **it doesn't matter**。妳的朋友已經下定決心 **make up her mind**，她不想要康復 **get well**，她有什麼心事 **anything on her mind** 嗎？」

　　　　「她……她希望有一天 **some day** 能畫那不勒斯的海灣 **paint the Bay of Naples**。」蘇説。

　　　　「畫畫？胡説 **bosh**！她還有其他值得再次回味的事 **worth thinking about** 嗎？例如 **for instance**，男人 **like a man**？」

　　　　「男人？」蘇扯著嗓子説：「有男人值得……，不，醫生，沒有這種人 **nothing of the kind**。」

　　　　「好吧，這是不利之處 **the weakness**，」醫生説：「我會盡我所知地 **do all that science** 治好她，盡我所能地 **so far as it may be employed by me** 治好她，可是當我的病人 **my patient** 開始算 **count** 她出殯 **in her funeral procession** 時會有多少馬車 **the carriages** 送葬，治療效果 **the power of medicine to cure** 就降低一半了 **subtract fifty percent**。如果妳能讓她問一個有關冬季大衣袖子新樣式 **styles in cloak sleeves** 的問題 **ask one question**，我保證能讓她痊癒機率從一成 **one in ten** 提升為兩成 **one in five**。」

　　　　醫生走後，蘇走進工作室 **go into the workroom**，把小毛巾哭得一團濕 **cry a napkin to a pulp**，然後她拿著畫板 **with her drawing board** 精神抖擻地走進瓊西的房間 **swagger into Johnsy's room**，口裡吹了一首流行曲 **whistle a popular tune**。

　　　　瓊西躺著，被子底下 **under the bedclothes** 的身體幾乎完全不動 **scarcely make a move**，臉向著窗戶。蘇以為瓊西在睡覺 **be asleep**，就不再吹口哨 **stop whistling**。

GRAMMAR POINT

分詞片語 ⇨ 省略連接詞和主詞，以分詞引導的子句，就叫作「分詞片語」。

- she lay, <u>scarcely **moving**</u>, . . . **looking** through the small Dutch windowpanes . . .
她躺著幾乎不動，……透過小小的荷蘭式玻璃窗凝視……

- Johnsy lay, <u>scarcely **making** a move under the bedclothes</u>, . . .
瓊西躺著，在被子下幾乎完全不動，……

- Sue stopped whistling, <u>**thinking** she was asleep</u>. 蘇以為瓊西在睡覺，就不再吹口哨了。

She arranged her board / and began a pen-and-ink drawing / to illustrate a magazine story. Young artists must **pave their way to art** / by drawing pictures / for the magazine stories / that young authors must write / to **pave their way to literature.**

As Sue was sketching / a pair of elegant horseshow riding trousers and a monocle / on the figure of the hero, / an Idaho cowboy, / she heard a low sound, / several times repeated. She quickly went to the bedside.

Johnsy's eyes were open wide. She was looking out the window / and counting backwards. "Twelve," she said, / and a little later, "eleven"; / and then "ten," and "nine"; / and then "eight" and "seven" almost together.

Sue looked out the window. What was there / to count? There was only a bare, dreary yard / to be seen, / and the blank side of the brick house / twenty feet away. An old, old ivy vine, / twisted and decayed at the roots, / climbed halfway up the brick wall. The cold breath of autumn / had taken most of its leaves from the vine / until its skeleton branches clung, / almost bare, / to the bricks.

"What is it, / dear?" asked Sue.

"Six," said Johnsy, / in almost a whisper. "They're falling faster now. Three days ago, / there were almost a hundred. **It made my head ache** / **to count them.** But now it's easy. **There goes another one.** There are only five left now."

"Five what, / dear? Tell your Sudie."

"Leaves. On the ivy vine. When the last one falls, / I must go, too. I've known that / for three days. Didn't the doctor tell you?"

"Oh, I have never heard of such nonsense," complained Sue, / with magnificent scorn. "What have old ivy leaves to do with your getting well? And you used to love that vine so, / you naughty girl. Don't be like that. Why, / the doctor told me this morning / that your chances for getting well real soon / were / —let's see exactly what he said— / he said / the chances were ten to one. Why, / that's almost as good a chance as we have in New York / when we ride on the streetcars / or walk past a new building."

· arrange 架好　·pen-and-ink drawing 鋼筆畫　·illustrate 畫　·literature 文學界
· horseshow 馬術表演　·riding trousers 馬褲　·monocle 單片眼鏡
· count backward 倒數　·bare 荒蕪的　·dreary 陰暗的　·yard 院子
· ivy vine 常春藤　·twisted 盤繞的　·decayed 枯萎的　·skeleton branches 骨幹枝條
· cling to 纏附；抓住　·nonsense 荒唐的話　·with magnificent scorn 非常輕蔑
· have to do with 與……有何關連　·ten to one 九成；百分之九十
· as good a chance as 和……機會一樣大

1　**pave their way to art** 為通往藝術界而舖路 / **pave their way to literature** 為通往文學界而舖路
〈pave one's way to . . .〉是「為某人朝……發展作準備」的意思。

2　**It made my head ache to count them.** 讓我數得頭都疼了。
〈make 受詞＋原形動詞〉是「使某人怎麼樣」的意思，這裡的 It 是虛主詞，to count them 是真主詞。

3　**There goes another one.** 又掉了一個。
〈there goes . . .〉是「走了」、「沒有了」、「（機會等）溜走了」的意思。

她架好畫板 arrange her board，開始為雜誌裡的故事 illustrate a magazine story 畫鋼筆插畫 a pen–and–ink drawing，年輕畫家 young artists 不得不為雜誌裡的故事畫插畫，為通往藝術界而舖路 pave their way to art，而年輕作家 young authors 不得不為雜誌寫故事，為通往文學界而舖路 pave their way to literature。

蘇正在幫故事中的英雄 the hero，一個愛達荷州牛仔 an Idaho cowboy 的身上描繪 sketch 一件馬術表演穿的精緻馬褲和一片單片眼鏡時，她聽見了一個低沉的聲音 a low sound，重複了好幾次 several times repeated，她趕忙走到床邊 go to the bedside。

瓊西眼睛睜得大大的 be open wide，望著窗外 look out the window，倒數 count backward，「十二 twelve」她說，過了一會兒 a little later，「十一 eleven」，然後 and then「十 ten」、「九 nine」，接著幾乎同時 almost together 數「八 eight」、「七 seven」。

蘇看看窗外，窗戶外面有什麼可以數呢？只看見 to be seen 一片荒蕪陰暗的院子 a bare, dreary yard，20 英呎外 twenty feet away 還有一面磚屋的空牆 the blank side。一棵很老很老的常春藤 an old, old ivy vine，枯萎 decayed 的根盤繞 twisted 在一塊，蔓延至磚牆的半腰處 climb halfway up the brick wall。秋天的寒風 the cold breath of autumn 將藤葉幾乎全數吹落 take most of its leaves from the vine，只有光禿的 bare 枝條 its skeleton branches 還纏附在磚塊上 cling to the bricks。

「什麼，親愛的？」蘇問道。

「六 six」瓊西低聲說：「現在它們掉得更快 fall faster 了。三天前 three days ago，還有將近一百個 almost a hundred，讓我數 count 得頭都疼 make my head ache 了，但現在很好數。又掉了一個 another one，只剩下五個了 only five left。」

「五個什麼 five what，親愛的？告訴妳的小蘇。」

「葉子 leaves，那棵常春藤上的 on the ivy vine，等最後一葉 the last one 落下 fall，我也要走了 must go。我三天前就已經知道了，難道醫生沒告訴妳嗎？」

「喔，我從來沒聽過這麼荒唐的話 such nonsense，」蘇輕蔑地 with magnificent scorn 抱怨 complain 道，「老常春藤的葉子 old ivy leaves 跟妳康復 your getting well 有什麼關係？妳這個淘氣的女孩 you naughty girl，妳以前很喜歡那棵常春藤 love that vine so。別這樣嘛 don't be like that，醫生今天早上告訴我，妳康復的機會 your chances for getting well，讓我想想他怎麼說的 what he said，他說機會有九成 ten to one，那就跟我們在紐約 in New York 搭電車 ride on the streetcars 或走過一棟新建築 walk past a new building 的機會一樣大。」

GRAMMAR POINT

動名詞意思上的主詞 ⇨ 用所有格或受格來表示。

- What have old ivy leaves to do with **your/you** getting well?
  老常春藤的葉子跟妳的康復有什麼關係？

- She was upset about **Johnsy's/Johnsy** giving up trying to live.
  她很擔心瓊西放棄努力活下去的念頭。

"Try to have some broth now, / and let Sudie go back to her drawing, / so she can sell it to the editor. Then, / I'll buy port wine for her sick child / and pork chops for her greedy self."

"You don't need to get / any more wine," said Johnsy, / keeping her eyes fixed out the window.

"There goes another. No, I don't want any broth. That leaves just four. I want to see the last one fall / before it gets dark. Then, I'll go, too."

"Johnsy, dear," said Sue, / bending over her, "will you promise / to keep your eyes closed / and not to look out the window / until I am done working? I must hand my drawings in / by tomorrow. I need the light, / or I would pull the shade down."

"Couldn't you draw / in the other room?" Johnsy asked coldly.

"I'd rather be here / beside you," said Sue. "Besides, / I don't want you / to keep looking at those silly ivy leaves."

"Tell me / as soon as you have finished," said Johnsy, / closing her eyes, / and lying white and still / as a fallen statue, "because I want to see the last one fall. I'm tired of waiting. I'm tired of thinking. I want to turn loose my hold on everything / and go sailing down, down, / just like one of those poor, tired leaves."

"Try to sleep," said Sue. "I must call Behrman up / to be my model for the old hermit-miner. I'll just be gone / for a minute. Don't try to move / until I come back."

Old Behrman was a painter / who lived on the ground floor / beneath them. He was past sixty / and had a long beard / like Michelangelo's Moses / curling down from his wide head. Behrman was a failure in art. He had been painting / for forty years, / but he had never produced anything noteworthy. He had always been about to paint a masterpiece, / but he had never yet begun it. For several years, / he had painted nothing / except for minor advertisements here and there.

- **broth** 湯　· **port wine** 紅葡萄酒　· **fixed** 不動的　· **bend over** 彎腰
- **hand in** 交出　· **shade** 窗簾　· **I'd rather** 我最好　· **fallen** 倒下的
- **statue** 雕像　· **turn loose** 鬆開　· **call up** 聯絡　· **hermit−miner** 隱居的礦工
- **beard** 大鬍子　· **Moses** 摩西　· **failure** 失敗　· **noteworthy** 值得注意的
- **masterpiece** 傑作　· **minor** 較小的；不重要的　· **advertisement** 廣告

1　**here beside you** 陪在妳身邊 / **Besides, I don't want you to . . .** 而且，我不希望妳
〈beside〉當介系詞，意「在……旁邊」。〈besides〉當副詞時，是「此外」的意思。

2　**I'm tired of waiting. I'm tired of thinking.** 我懶得等待。我懶得思考。
〈be tired of . . . 〉是「厭倦／懶得……」的意思。

3　**except for minor advertisements** 除了小廣告
〈except for . . . 〉和〈except . . . 〉意思一樣，是「除了……之外」的意思。

「現在喝點湯吧 have some broth，讓小蘇回去畫畫 go back to her drawing，這樣才能賣給編輯 sell it to the editor，然後我會買一點紅葡萄酒 port wine 給她生病的孩子 her sick child（指瓊西），還會買一點豬排 pork chops 給貪吃的她自己（指蘇）her greedy self。」

「妳不用再買酒了。」瓊西眼睛繼續盯著 keeping her eyes fixed 窗外說。

「又掉了一片 another，不，我不想喝湯。只剩下四片葉子 just four 了，我想在天黑前看最後一葉掉落 see the last one fall，然後我也要走了 will go。」

「瓊西，親愛的，」蘇彎下腰 bend over her 對她說：「妳可以答應我在我完成工作前，閉上眼 keep your eyes closed，不要往窗外看嗎？我明天 by tomorrow 一定要交插畫 hand my drawings in，我需要光線 need the light，要不然我就把窗簾拉下來了 pull the shade down。」

「妳不能到另一間房間畫 draw in the other room 嗎？」瓊西冷冷地問道。

「我要在這 here 陪妳 beside you。」蘇說：「而且 besides，我不希望妳一直看著 keep looking at 那些蠢藤葉 those silly ivy leaves。」

「妳一畫完 finish，就告訴我 tell me。」瓊西閉著眼說 close her eyes，臉色蒼白、一動也不動地躺在床上 lie white and still，像一座倒下的雕像 as a fallen statue，「因為我想看最後一葉凋零，我不想等待 be tired of waiting，不想思考 be tired of thinking，我想要鬆開 turn loose 抓住每件事 my hold on everything 的手，飄下去，飄下去 go sailing down, down，像那些可憐、疲倦的葉子一樣。」

「試著睡覺 try to sleep，」蘇說：「我得和貝爾曼聯絡 call Behrman up，請他當隱居的老礦工模特兒 be my model。我只是離開 will be gone 一會兒 for a minute。我回來前 come back，妳別亂動。」

老貝爾曼 Old Behrman 是住在她們樓下 beneath them 一樓 on the ground floor 的畫家 a painter，年過60 be past sixty，留著一把長鬍子 have a long beard，看起來像是米開朗基羅的摩西雕像，寬寬的頭 from his wide head 蓄著卷卷的 curl 鬍子。貝爾曼是個失敗的畫家 a failure in art，畫了40年 paint for forty years，卻沒有創作出 never produce 半點值得注意的作品 anything noteworthy。他一直想要畫一幅曠世傑作 paint a masterpiece，但他卻從未動過筆 never begin it。幾年下來 for several years，他除了到處 here and there 畫些小廣告 minor advertisements，什麼也沒畫過 paint nothing。

He earned a little / by serving as a model / for those young artists in the colony / who could not pay for a professional. He drank gin to excess / and still talked about his coming masterpiece. For the rest, / he was a fierce little old man, / who made fun of anyone who was soft / and who regarded himself as a bulldog / ready to protect the two young artists / living in the studio above him.

Sue found Behrman / smelling strongly of juniper berries / in his dimly lit den below. In one corner / was a blank canvas on an easel / that had been waiting there / for twenty-five years / to receive the first line of the masterpiece. She told him about Johnsy's fancy / and how she feared / she would, / indeed, light and fragile as a leaf herself, / float away / when her slight hold upon the world / grew weaker.

Old Behrman, / with his red eyes plainly streaming, / shouted about / how silly Johnsy's idea was.

"What!" he cried. "Are there people in this world / so foolish to believe / that they will die / when a leaf falls off a vine? I have never heard of such a thing. No, I will not pose as a model / for you. Why did you allow such a silly thought / to enter her head? Oh, that poor little Miss Johnsy."

"She is very ill and weak," said Sue, "and the fever has left her mind / filled with thoughts of death and other horrible things. Very well, Mr. Behrman, / if you do not care to pose for me, / you don't have to. But I think / you are a horrid old man."

"You are just like a woman!" yelled Behrman. "Who said / I will not pose? Go on. I will go with you. For half an hour, / I have been trying to say / that I am ready to pose. God, this is not a place / in which someone / as pretty as Miss Johnsy / should lie sick. Someday, / I will paint a masterpiece, / and we shall all go away. God, yes."

· **pay for** 付錢給　· **professional** 專業的　· **to excess** 太多　· **for the rest** 此外
· **fierce** 火爆的　· **make fun of** 嘲笑　· **dimly lit** 昏暗的　· **den** 小房間　· **fancy** 胡思亂想
· **fear** 害怕　· **fragile** 脆弱的　· **float away** 飄走
· **slight hold upon the world** 對世界的留戀　· **plainly** 顯然　· **stream** 流淌
· **pose (as a model)**（身為模特兒）擺姿勢　· **horrid** 糟的　· **lie sick** 躺著生病

CLOSE UP

1 **regarded himself as a bulldog** 自認為是鬥牛犬
〈regard ... as ...〉是「認為……是……」、「把……看作是……」的意思。這裡的bulldog看作是「警衛」的意思也可以。

2 **with his red eyes plainly streaming** 紅紅的眼睛顯然在流淚
〈with＋受詞＋補語〉這片語，是表同時發生的狀況。受詞是his red eyes，補語是plainly streaming。

3 **allow such a silly thought to enter her head** 容許這麼蠢的念頭進入她的腦中
〈allow ... to ...〉是「允許……去做……」的意思。

4 **has left her mind filled with thoughts** 讓她心裡充滿念頭
〈leave＋受詞＋補語〉是「讓……成為／保持……狀況」的意思。

在藝術區 **in the colony** 那些年輕畫家負擔不起請專業模特兒的費用 **cannot pay for a professional**，於是他靠當模特兒 **serve as a model** 賺一點錢 **earn a little**。他毫無節制地喝酒 **drink gin to excess**，仍然一直提起他要畫的大作 **his coming masterpiece**。除此以外 **for the rest**，他是個火爆的小老頭 **a fierce little old man**，嘲笑 **make fun of** 那些軟弱的人 **anyone who is soft**，他卻認為自己 **regard himself as** 是保護 **protect** 樓上工作室兩位年輕畫家的鬥牛犬 **a bulldog**。

蘇在樓下他那間昏暗的小房間裡 **in his dimly lit den** 找到了渾身酒味的貝爾曼 **smell strongly**。在房間一個角落裡 **in one corner** 的畫架上 **on an easel** 一張空白的畫布 **a blank canvas** 在那裡等了 25 年 **for twenty-five years**，等待畫下傑作的第一條線 **receive the first line**。她告訴貝爾曼瓊西的胡思亂想 **Johnsy's fancy**，還說她怕瓊西真的像葉子一樣 **as a leaf** 又輕又脆弱 **light and fragile**。當她對世界的留戀 **her slight hold upon the world** 愈來愈少 **grow weaker**，她可能真的會飄走 **float away**。

老貝爾曼紅紅的眼睛 **his red eyes** 顯然在流淚 **plainly stream**，他大聲說道瓊西的胡思亂想 **Johnsy's idea** 有多愚蠢 **how silly**。

「什麼 **what**！」他大聲說道：「這世上有人笨到 **so foolish** 會相信一片葉子 **a leaf** 從藤上掉落 **fall off a vine** 時，人就會死去 **will die** 嗎？我從來沒聽說過這怪事，不，我不會為妳當模特兒擺姿勢 **will not pose as a model**。妳竟容許這麼蠢的念頭 **such a silly thought** 進入她的腦海裡 **enter her head**？喔，可憐的瓊西小姐。」

「她病得很重且很虛弱 **be ill and weak**。」蘇說：「發燒 **the fever** 讓她滿腦子都是死亡和其他恐怖的念頭 **death and other horrible things**。好吧 **very well**，貝爾曼先生，如果你不願意當我的模特兒 **do not care to pose**，那就算了 **don't have to**，但我覺得你真是一個糟老頭 **a horrid old man**。」

「女人就是女人 **just like a woman**！」貝爾曼大叫，「誰說我不擺姿勢了？走吧，我跟妳去 **go with you**，我不是已經說我準備好要給妳擺姿勢 **be ready to pose** 說了半小時了嗎？天啊 **god**，像瓊西小姐這麼漂亮的小姐 **as pretty as Miss Johnsy** 在這裡生病真是不應該，總有一天，我會畫出一幅曠世傑作，我們都可以離開 **go away** 這裡。老天啊，是的。」

GRAMMAR POINT

關係代名詞 ⇨ 一般來說，關係代名詞直接放在先行詞之後，不過有時候，在先行詞和關係代名詞之間會插入修飾片語等。

- . . . for *those young artists* in the colony **who** could not pay for a professional

  ……那些藝術區的年輕畫家負擔不起請專業模特兒的錢

- . . . *a blank canvas* on an easel **that** had been waiting there for twenty-five years . . .

  ……畫架上空白的畫布擺在那裡等了25年

Johnsy was sleeping / when they went upstairs. Sue pulled the shade down to the windowsill / and motioned Behrman to go into the other room. In there, / they fearfully peered out the window / at the ivy vine. Then, / they looked at each other / for a moment / without speaking. A persistent, cold rain / was falling / along with some snow. Behrman, / in his old blue shirt, / took his seat / as the hermit-miner / on an upturned kettle for a rock.

When Sue awoke from an hour's sleep / the next morning, / she found Johnsy / with dull, wide-open eyes / staring at the drawn green shade.

"Pull it up. I want to see," she ordered in a whisper.

Wearily, Sue obeyed.

But, incredibly, / despite the beating rain and fierce gusts of wind / that had lasted throughout the entire night, / there still remained one ivy leaf / against the wall. It was the last one / on the vine. Still dark green near its stem, / but, with its serrated edges tinted yellow / as it was beginning to decay, / it hung bravely from a branch / some twenty feet above the ground.

"It is the last one," said Johnsy. "I thought / it would surely fall during the night. I heard the wind. It will fall today, / and I shall die / at the same time."

"Dear, dear!" said Sue, / leaning her worn face down to the pillow. "Think of me, / if you won't think of yourself. What would I do?"

· **windowsill** 窗臺　· **motion** 示意　· **fearfully** 恐懼地　· **peer out** 向外看
· **persistent** 不停的　· **take one's seat** 坐下　· **upturned** 翻過來　· **wearily** 無力疲倦地
· **incredibly** 不可思議地　· **despite** 儘管　· **gusts of wind** 一陣強風　· **remain** 留著
· **serrated** 鋸齒狀的　· **tinted** 染上顏色　· **decay** 枯萎　· **worn face** 倦容

CLOSE UP

1 **motioned Behrman to go into the other room** 示意貝爾曼到另一間房間
〈motion . . . to . . .〉是「示意……去做……」的意思。

2 **A persistent, cold rain was falling along with some snow.**
一陣寒冷的雨伴隨著雪花不停地下著。
〈along with . . .〉是「伴隨著……地」、「和……一起地」的意思。

3 **with its serrated edges tinted yellow** 鋸齒狀的邊緣染上了黃色
以〈with＋受詞＋補語〉組成的片語，表同時發生的狀況；受詞是 its serrated edges，補語是 tinted yellow。

他們上樓 **go upstairs** 以後，瓊西正在睡覺，蘇把窗簾拉至窗臺 **pull the shade down to the windowsill**，示意貝爾曼到另一間房間 **go into the other room**。在那裡 **in there**，他們膽顫心驚地凝視 **fearfully peer** 窗外那棵常春藤，後來他們一語不發地 **without speaking** 彼此對望了一會兒 **for a moment**。一陣寒冷的雨 **a cold rain** 伴隨著雪花 **along with some snow** 不停地下著 **persistent**。貝爾曼穿著他老舊的藍襯衫 **in his old blue shirt** 坐 **take his seat** 在充當岩石 **for a rock** 被翻過來的鐵壺上 **on an upturned kettle**，扮成隱居的礦工 **as the hermit–miner**。

第二天早晨 **the next morning**，蘇只睡了一小時 **an hour's sleep** 就醒來 **awake**。她看到瓊西無神的雙眼睜得大大的 **with dull, wide–open eyes** 盯著拉下來的綠窗簾 **stare at the drawn green shade**。

「把窗簾拉起來 **pull it up**，我想看。」她低聲命令。

蘇無力地 **wearily** 照做了 **obey**。

神奇地 **incredibly**，儘管整夜 **throughout the entire night** 不停地風吹 **fierce gusts of wind** 雨打 **the beating rain**，牆上 **against the wall** 還有一片常春藤的葉子 **one ivy leaf**。這是藤上最後一葉 **the last one on the vine**，靠近根部 **near its stem** 還是深綠色 **dark green**，但是鋸齒狀的邊緣 **its serrated edges** 已經枯萎 **begin to decay** 染上了黃色 **tinted yellow**。它勇敢地掛在 **hang bravely** 離地20呎高 **some twenty feet above the ground** 的枝條上 **from a branch**。

「這是最後一葉了，」瓊西說：「我聽到風聲 **hear the wind**，以為它昨晚 **during the night** 一定會掉 **surely fall**，它今天一定會掉 **fall today**，同時我也會死 **die at the same time**。」

「唉唷，唉唷 **dear, dear**！」蘇滿臉倦容地靠著枕頭，「如果妳不肯為自己想想，那為我想一想 **think of me** 吧！我該怎麼辦呢 **what would I do**？」

> **despite**：不管……、不顧…… (= in spite of) ⇨ 注意不要錯誤地寫成了 despite of。

- **Despite** the beating rain and fierce gusts of wind, . . . there still remained one ivy leaf against the wall. 不管風吹雨打，……牆上還留著一片常春藤的葉子。

- **Despite** my effort to keep her alive, she died. 不管我多努力讓她活下來，她還是死了。

But Johnsy did not answer. The most lonesome thing / in the entire world / is a soul / when it is making ready / to go on its mysterious, far journey. The fancy seemed to possess her / more strongly / as, / one by one, / **the ties that bound her to friendship and to Earth** / were loosed.

The day passed, / and even in the twilight, / they could see the lone ivy leaf / clinging to its stem against the wall. And then, / with the coming of the night, / the north wind again began to blow / while the rain still beat against the windows / and ran down the eaves.

When it was light enough, / Johnsy, the merciless, / commanded that the shade be raised.

The ivy leaf was still there.

Johnsy lay for a long time / looking at it. And then she called to Sue, / who was stirring her chicken broth / over the gas stove.

"I've been a bad girl, Sudie," said Johnsy. "Something has made / that last leaf stay there / to show me / how wicked I was. It is a sin / to want to die. You may bring me a little broth now / and some milk with a little port in it, / and . . . No, bring me a hand-mirror first, / and then pack some pillows about me, / and I will sit up / and watch you cook."

An hour later, / she said, "Sudie, / someday I hope to paint the Bay of Naples."

The doctor came in the afternoon, / and Sue had an excuse / to go into the hallway / as he left.

"**Even chances**," said the doctor, / taking Sue's thin, shaking hand / in his. "With good nursing, / you'll win. And now **I must see another case** / I have downstairs. Behrman, his name is / —some kind of an artist, / I believe. Pneumonia, too. He is an old, weak man, / and the attack is acute. There is no hope for him, / but he goes to the hospital today / to be made more comfortable."

· make ready to 準備好 · possess 佔據 · tie 連結 · be loosed 鬆脫 · twilight 星光
· beat 打 · eave 荷蘭式的屋簷 · merciless 無情地 · command 吩咐 · stir 攪拌
· wicked 壞的 · sin 罪 · pack 疊 · sit up 坐起來 · have an excuse to 有藉口去……
· even chances 五成機會 · acute（病情）嚴重的

CLOSE UP

1 **the ties that bound her to friendship and to Earth** 她與友誼和世上一切事物的連結
〈bind . . . to . . .〉是「把……和……綁在一起」的意思。〈that . . . Earth〉這部分是修飾the ties的關係子句。

2 **Even chances 五成機會**
even一般當副詞，是「甚至」或「連」的意思，也可以當形容詞，意「同一個的」、「平均的」、「對等的」、「偶數的」。
形容詞：例 They are even in length.（他們一樣長。）/ an even number（偶數）

3 **I must see another case 我得去看另一個病患**
case的基本意思是「（特殊的）情況、案例」的意思，它也有「患者」的意思，把它想成是「罹患疾病或受傷的案例」也可以。

可是瓊西沒回答，世上 in the entire world 最孤寂的人 the most lonesome thing 就是準備好 make ready 要赴上神秘、遙遠旅途 go on its mysterious, far journey 的靈魂 a soul 了，胡思亂想 the fancy 愈來愈強烈地 more strongly 佔據她全部的心思 possess her，且一個接一個 one by one，讓她與友誼及世上一切事物 bind her to friendship and to Earth 的連結 the ties 鬆脫 be loosed 了。

白天過去了，甚至到了黃昏 in the twilight，他們也能看見那孤單的常春藤葉 the lone ivy leaf 仍然緊抓著牆上的根 cling to its stem，然後，夜晚來臨 with the coming of the night，北風 the north wind 又開始呼嘯 blow，雨 the rain 不停拍打著窗戶上的玻璃 beat against the windows。雨水沿著荷蘭式的屋簷流下來 run down the eaves。

天色濛濛 be light enough 時，瓊西，毫不留情地 Johnsy, the merciless 吩咐 command 人拉起窗簾 the shade be raised。

那片常春藤葉依然在那裡 still there。

瓊西躺著看它 look at it 看了很久 for a long time，然後她叫了 call to 在瓦斯爐邊攪拌雞湯 stir her chicken broth 的蘇。

「我真是一個壞女孩 a bad girl，」瓊西說：「那最後一葉 that last leaf 留在那裡 stay there 是為了證明我 show me 之前多壞 how wicked。想死 want to die 是一種罪過 a sin，妳現在可以給我一點湯了 bring me a little broth，再給我一點加紅酒的牛奶 some milk，然後……不，先給我一面小鏡子 a hand–mirror first，幫我把枕頭墊高一點 pack some pillows about me，我就可以坐起來 sit up 看妳煮飯 watch you cook。」

過了一個鐘頭 an hour later，她說：「小蘇，我希望有一天 someday 能去畫那不勒斯的海灣 paint the Bay of Naples。」

下午 in the afternoon 醫生來了，他離開時，蘇找藉口 have an excuse 到走廊上 go into the hallway。

「有五成希望 even chances，」醫生握著蘇瘦弱、顫抖的手說：「好好地照料 with good nursing，妳會成功的 win，現在我得下樓去看另一個病患 see another case 了。他名字叫貝爾曼，好像也是畫家 some kind of an artist，應該也是肺炎 pneumonia, too。他又老又虛弱 an old, weak man，病情嚴重 the attack is acute。他沒有希望 no hope 了，但今天要把他送到醫院去 go to the hospital，讓他更舒服一點 be made more comfortable。」

GRAMMAR POINT

command that + 主詞 (+ should) + 原形動詞

⇨ 在和建議、請求、主張、命令等有關的一般動詞(suggest, demand, insist, command, etc.)後，在當作受詞的 that 子句中，動詞形態必須是〈should ＋原形動詞〉或沒有 should 只留下〈原形動詞〉。

• Johnsy, the merciless, **commanded** that the shade **(should) be raised**.
  瓊西，無情地吩咐人拉起窗簾。

• The doctor **insisted** that he **(should) go** to the hospital.　醫生堅持他應該要就醫。

The next day, / the doctor said to Sue, "She's out of danger. You've won. Nutrition and care now / —that's all she needs."

That afternoon, / Sue went to the bed / where Johnsy lay, / contentedly knitting / a very blue and very useless woolen shoulder scarf, / and she put one arm around her, pillows and all.

"I have something to tell you, / my dear," she said. "Mr. Behrman died of pneumonia / in the hospital today. He was ill / for only two days. The janitor found him / on the morning of the first day / in his room downstairs / helpless with pain. His shoes and clothing / were soaked and icy cold. They couldn't imagine / where he had been / on such a dreadful night. And then they found / a lantern, still lit, / a ladder that had been dragged from its place, / some scattered brushes, / and a palette with green and yellow colors mixed on it, / and—look out the window, dear, / at the last ivy leaf on the wall. Didn't you wonder / why it never fluttered or moved / when the wind blew? Ah, darling, / it's Behrman's masterpiece. He painted it there / the night that the last leaf fell."

·out of danger 脫離險境　·nutrition 營養　·contentedly 安心地　·die of 死於
·janitor 工友　·helpless 無助的　·be soaked 濕透　·dreadful 可怕的　·drag 拖
·scattered 散落的　·flutter 飄動

CLOSE UP

1　**on such a dreadful night** 在這麼可怕的夜晚
　〈such a/an＋形容詞＋名詞〉such 是強調程度的「如此……的」的意思。

2　**a palette with green and yellow colors mixed on it** 還有一塊混著綠色和黃色的調色盤
　〈with＋受詞＋補語〉的片語，是表同時發生的狀況，受詞是 green and yellow colors，補語是 mixed on it。

隔天**the next day**，醫生跟蘇說：「她已脫離險境**be out of danger**，妳成功了，現在她只需要**all she needs**營養和照料**nutrition and care**了。」

　　那天下午**that afternoon**，蘇到瓊西躺著的床邊，瓊西愉快地在編織**knit**一條深藍色**very blue**，且毫無用處的**very useless**羊毛披肩**a woolen shoulder scarf**，蘇用一隻胳臂抱住瓊西和枕頭。

　　「我有件事要告訴妳**have something to tell you**，親愛的，」她說：「貝爾曼先生**Mr. Behrman**今天在醫院**in the hospital**因肺炎過世了**die of pneumonia**，他只病**be ill**了兩天**for only two days**。頭一天早上**on the morning of the first day**工友**the janitor**發現他在他樓下的房間裡**in his room**痛苦又無助**helpless with pain**。他的鞋子和衣物**his shoes and clothing**都濕透**be soaked**了，且覆蓋著冷冷的薄冰**and icy cold**。他們無法想像**can't imagine**這麼凄風苦雨的夜晚**on such a dreadful night**他還能上哪兒去**where he has been**。後來，他們找到一盞提燈**a lantern**，燈還亮著**still lit**，一把被拖來的**be dragged**梯子**a ladder**，一些散落的畫筆**some scattered brushes**，還有一塊混著綠色和黃色顏料**with green and yellow colors mixed on it**的調色盤**a palette**。妳看看窗外**look out the window**牆上那最後一葉**the last ivy leaf**。妳難道沒好奇過為什麼風吹的時候它從來不飄動**never flutter or move**嗎？啊，親愛的，那是貝爾曼的傑作**Behrman's masterpiece**，他在最後一葉**the last leaf**落下的那一晚，畫上去的**paint it there**。」

GRAMMAR POINT

die of / die from：因……而死

⇨ 一般來說，因疾病而去世，用of；因受傷或意外而死，用from。

- Mr. Behrman **died of** pneumonia in the hospital today. 貝爾曼先生今天在醫院因肺炎過世了。
- She **died from** injuries after the car accident. 她因車禍重傷不治。

Answers
and
Translations

What Men Live By

pp. 2–3

Stop & Think

- Why couldn't Simon pay for the sheepskins? 為什麼西門付不出買羊毛皮的錢？
  ⇨ His customers did not give him any money. 他的顧客沒還他半毛錢。

- What did Simon see behind the church? 西門在教堂後面看到什麼？
  ⇨ He saw a naked man. 他看到一個赤身露體的男人。

CHECK UP

1 Simon had five rubles.   F
2 Simon wanted to buy some sheepskins.   T
3 There was a robber next to the church.   F
4 Simon was afraid of the naked man.   T

1 西門有五個盧布。
2 西門想要買一些羊皮。
3 教堂旁邊有強盜。
4 西門很怕那個赤身露體的男人。

pp. 4–5

Stop & Think

- What did Simon give the man? 西門給那男人什麼？
  ⇨ He gave the man his coat, boots, and a stick. 他給那男人他的大衣、靴子和一根枴杖。

- What did Simon's wife think about her husband? 西門的妻子怎麼看她的丈夫？
  ⇨ She thought he had been out drinking. 她以為他出門喝酒了。

CHECK UP

1 The man said that   a. very disappointed with Simon.
2 Simon felt glad   b. to help another person.
3 Matryna was   c. was a drunkard.
4 Matryna thought that Simon   d. God had punished him.

1 那人說神懲罰他。
2 西門很高興能幫助別人。
3 瑪琪娜對西門很失望。
4 瑪琪娜以為西門喝醉了。

Stop & Think

• **What did Simon say to make Matryna calm down?** 西門說了什麼讓瑪琪娜冷靜下來？
  ⇨ He said that anger is a sin. 他說生氣是罪惡。

CHECK UP

1 What did Matryna feel for the stranger? (c)
   a. concern   **b.** love   **c.** pity

2 What happened after the man smiled? (a)
   a. A light came from his face.   **b.** Simon felt pity for him.   **c.** Matryna's heart softened.

1 瑪琪娜對陌生人的感覺是什麼？
   a. 關心   **b.** 愛   **c.** 憐憫
2 那人笑了以後發生了什麼事？
   a. 他的臉上發出光芒。   **b.** 西門憐憫他。   **c.** 瑪琪娜的心軟了下來。

Stop & Think

• **What work did Michael know?** 麥可會做什麼工作？
  ⇨ He did not know anything. 他什麼也不會。

• **Who was in the carriage?** 誰在馬車上？
  ⇨ A gentleman in a fur coat was in the carriage. 穿著毛皮大衣的紳士在馬車上。

CHECK UP

1 Simon and Matryna had no more of bread.
2 The stranger's name was Michael.
3 Simon offered Michael food and shelter in return for work.
4 Michael became a very skilled bootmaker.

1 西門和瑪琪娜沒有麵包了。
2 陌生人的名字是麥可。
3 西門給麥可食物和住的地方，作為工作的報酬。
4 麥可變成了一個手藝很好的靴匠。

Stop & Think

• **What did Michael do when he looked behind the gentleman?** 麥可看到紳士後面的時候，他做了什麼？
  ⇨ He smiled. 他微笑了。

CHECK UP

1 The gentleman showed Simon some expensive leather.
2 The gentleman terrified Simon.
3 The gentleman wanted his boots in two days.
4 Michael made slippers for the gentleman.

1 紳士給西門看了一些昂貴的皮革。
2 紳士讓西門很害怕。

3 紳士希望在兩天內拿到他訂製的靴子。

4 麥可為紳士做了拖鞋。

pp. 12–13

Stop & Think

• **What happened to the gentleman?** 紳士怎麼了？

⇨ He died in the carriage. 他死在馬車上。

CHECK UP

1 Michael smiled two times in six years.　　　　　T

2 A woman with two girls came to Simon's hut.　　T

3 The two girls were cousins.　　　　　　　　　　F

4 The woman was the girls' mother.　　　　　　　F

1 麥可在六年之中笑了兩次。

2 有個帶著兩個女孩的婦人來到西門的木屋。

3 兩個女孩是表姊妹。

4 婦人是女孩的媽媽。

pp. 14–15

Stop & Think

• **How did the girl's leg get injured?** 女孩的腿是怎麼受傷的？

⇨ Her mother rolled on it and crushed it when she died.
她母親臨死前翻身壓到她身上，把她的腿壓壞了。

• **What happened as everyone was talking?** 大家說話的時候發生了什麼事？

⇨ A bright light filled the room. 強光充滿了房間。

CHECK UP

1 The woman said the girls　　　　　　　　a. was not an ordinary man.

2 Michael asked Simon and Matryna　　　　b. were precious to her.

3 Simon realized that Michael　　　　　　　c. to forgive him.

1 婦人說女孩對她而言很寶貴。

2 麥可求西門和瑪琪娜原諒他。

3 西門知道麥可不是凡人。

pp. 16–17

Stop & Think

• **Why did God punish Michael?** 神為何懲罰麥可？

⇨ He disobeyed God. 他違背神的旨意。

• **What did God order Michael to learn about?** 神命令麥可學習什麼？

⇨ To learn three truths: Learn what dwells in man. Learn what is not given to man.
And learn what men live by.
認識三項真理：認識什麼住在人裡面，認識神沒有賜給人什麼，認識人靠什麼活著。

1 Why did Michael smile three times? (a)
   a. He learned three truths.   **b.** He saw God.   **c.** He knew the little girls.

2 Whose soul was Michael supposed to take? (b)
   a. Simon's soul   **b.** the mother's soul   **c.** the girls' souls

1 為什麼麥可微笑了三次？
   a. 他學會了三項真理。   **b.** 他看見神。   **c.** 他認識小女孩。
2 麥可應該帶走誰的靈魂？
   a. 西門的靈魂   **b.** 母親的靈魂   **c.** 女孩的靈魂

pp. 18−19

Stop & Think

• **What did Michael do when he returned to Earth?** 麥可回到人間以後，做了什麼？
   ⇨ He took the mother's soul. 他把母親的靈魂帶走了。

• **What was the second truth?** 第二項真理是什麼？
   ⇨ Men are not given the knowledge to know what they need.
      人沒有知道自己需要什麼的能力。

CHECK UP

1 Michael could return to Heaven after he learned all three truths.
2 Michael learned the first truth from Matryna.
3 Michael learned another truth from the rich man.

1 麥可學會三項真理以後才能回到天堂。
2 麥可從瑪琪娜身上學會第一項真理。
3 麥可從富人身上學會第二項真理。

pp. 20−21

Stop & Think

• **What was the third truth?** 第三項真理是什麼？
   ⇨ All men live because love is in them. 人活著是因愛在他們裡面。
      All men live by love. 人靠愛而活。

CHECK UP

1 Michael learned the third truth from the woman.
2 A bright light surrounded Michael's body.
3 Did Michael fly away from Simon's house? (Yes)

1 麥可從婦人身上學會了第三項真理。
2 有道亮光包圍著麥可的身體。
3 麥可從西門家飛走嗎？（是）

How Much Land Does a Man Need?

pp. 22−23

Stop & Think

- **Why was the younger sister annoyed?** 為什麼妹妹覺得很煩？
  ⇨ The elder sister was boasting about the advantages of town life. 姊姊誇口鎮上的生活有多好。

- **How would Pahom feel if he had plenty of land?** 如果帕霍姆有很多土地，他會覺得怎麼樣？
  ⇨ He would not fear the Devil himself. 他就不怕撒旦。

CHECK UP

1 How did the younger sister feel about her way of life? (b)
   a. She felt anxious.   **b.** She liked it.   **c.** She wanted to change it.

2 Where was the Devil sitting? (b)
   a. on the stove   **b.** behind the stove   **c.** under the stove

1 妹妹覺得自己的生活方式怎麼樣？
   a. 她覺得很焦慮。   b. 她很喜歡。   c. 她想要改變。

2 撒旦坐在哪裡？
   a. 爐子上面   b. 爐子後面   c. 爐子下面

pp. 24−25

Stop & Think

- **Why did Pahom fine his neighbors?** 為什麼帕霍姆要罰鄰居錢？
  ⇨ They were trespassing on his land. 他們非法入侵他的土地。

CHECK UP

1 The Devil decided to   **a.** and became a landowner.
2 Pahom bought a farm   **b.** trespass on his land on purpose.
3 Pahom's neighbors began to   **c.** have a contest with Pahom.
4 Pahom took Simon   **d.** to court for trespassing.

1 撒旦決定要和帕霍姆比賽。
2 帕霍姆買下一塊地，成為地主。
3 帕霍姆的鄰居開始故意穿越他的地。
4 帕霍姆把西門帶到法庭，告西門非法入侵他的土地。

pp. 26−27

Stop & Think

- **What did the stranger tell Pahom about the village?** 關於村莊，陌生人跟帕霍說了什麼？
  ⇨ Anyone who moved there was given twenty-five acres of land for free.
     任何搬到那裡的人都可以免費得到25畝地。

- **Why was Pahom not happy in the village?** 為什麼帕霍姆在村裡不開心？
  ⇨ He had to rent other people's land every year. 他每年都要跟別人租地。

1 The peasant came from a land beyond the Volga River.   T
2 The village beyond the Volga gave everyone 250 acres of land for free.   F
3 Pahom visited the village to find out about the land.   T
4 Pahom was ten times better off than before.   T

1 農夫來自伏爾加河的另一邊。
2 伏爾加另一邊的村莊免費送250畝地給每個人。
3 為了解那塊地帕霍姆造訪了那座村莊。
4 帕霍姆比以前富裕10倍。

---

pp. 28–29

Stop & Think

• **How much land did the peddler buy?** 小販買了多少地？
 ⇨ He bought thirteen thousand acres of land. 他買了13,000畝地。

CHECK UP

1 The peddler said that the Bashkirs sold their land for cheap prices.
2 Pahom decided to visit the land of the Bashkirs.
3 The Bashkirs pitched their tents beside a river.
4 Pahom told the interpreter that he had come about some land.

1 小販說巴什基爾人用很低的價錢賣土地。
2 帕霍姆決定要去參觀巴什基爾人的地。
3 巴什基爾人在河邊紮營。
4 帕霍姆跟通譯員說，他為了土地而來。

---

pp. 30–31

Stop & Think

• **What did Pahom say about the Bashkirs' land?** 帕霍姆覺得巴什基爾人的土地怎麼樣？
 ⇨ They had plenty of it, and it was good land. 他們有很多地，而且都很肥沃。

• **What did Pahom give to the chief?** 帕霍姆給首領什麼東西？
 ⇨ He gave the chief the best dressing gown and five pounds of tea.
   他給首領最好的袍子和五磅茶葉。

CHECK UP

1 The Bashkirs wanted to repay Pahom for his gifts.
2 The Bashkirs told Pahom to point out the land he wanted.
3 The chief arrived while the Bashkirs were arguing.
4 Did the chief speak to Pahom in Russian? (Yes)

1 巴什基爾人想要答謝帕霍姆送的禮物。
2 巴什基爾人叫帕霍姆指出他想要的地。
3 巴什基爾人在吵架的時候，首領來了。
4 首領跟帕霍姆用俄文交談嗎？（是）

pp. 32–33

Stop & Think

• **How much was the land Pahom wanted to buy?** 帕霍姆想買的地要多少錢？

  ⇨ It was one thousand rubles a day. 一天1,000盧布。

• **What was the condition the chief gave Pahom?** 首領給帕霍姆什麼條件？

  ⇨ He had to return to the spot where he started on the same day, or he would lose his money.
  他必須在一天內回到起點，不然他就會失去他的錢。

CHECK UP

1 What did Pahom want the chief to give him with the land? (a)
  a. a deed   **b.** some money   **c.** some servants

2 How far did Pahom think he could walk in one day? (b)
  a. 20 miles   **b.** 35 miles   **c.** 50 miles

1 帕霍姆希望首領給他土地跟什麼？
  a. 一份契約   **b.** 一些錢   **c.** 一些僕人

2 帕霍姆覺得自己一天可以走多遠？
  a. 20哩   **b.** 35哩   **c.** 50哩

pp. 34–35

Stop & Think

• **What happened to Pahom in his dream?** 在夢裡帕霍姆發生了什麼事？

  ⇨ He was lying dead in front of the Devil. 他橫屍在撒旦面前。

• **What did the chief put down to mark the starting spot?** 首領在起點放了什麼東西當作記號？

  ⇨ He put down his fox-fur cap on the ground. 他把狐皮帽放在地上。

CHECK UP

1 Pahom had a dream   **a.** on the fox-fur cap.
2 The Devil was   **b.** the night before the contest.
3 Pahom put his money   **c.** laughing in Pahom's dream.

1 比賽前一夜帕霍姆做了一個夢。
2 在帕霍姆的夢裡撒旦在笑。
3 帕霍姆把他的錢放在狐皮帽上。

pp. 36–37

Stop & Think

• **Why did Pahom not lie down at lunch?** 為什麼帕霍姆午餐的時候不躺下來休息？

  ⇨ He did not want to fall asleep. 他不想睡著。

CHECK UP

1 Pahom walked for 100 yards on the first side of the square.   F

2 Pahom did not stop to have lunch.   F

3 Pahom made the first side and the second side of the square too long.   T

1 帕霍姆走正方形的第一邊時走了100碼的距離。
2 帕霍姆沒有停下來吃午餐。
3 帕霍姆走正方形的第一邊和第二邊走得太長了。

pp. 38–39

Stop & Think

• **What did Pahom throw away while he was returning to the hill?** 回山丘的路上，帕霍姆把什麼丟掉？
  ⇨ He threw away his coat, boots, flask, and cap. 他把大衣、靴子、水壺、帽子都丟了。

• **What was Pahom afraid of as he returned to the hill?** 帕霍姆回山丘的時候害怕什麼？
  ⇨ He was afraid of death. 他怕死。

CHECK UP

1 Pahom thought he had tried for too much land.
2 Pahom kept his spade and used it as a support.
3 Pahom's heart was beating like a hammer.

1 帕霍姆認為他謀求太多土地了。
2 帕霍姆留下鏟子，用來當支撐的枴杖。
3 帕霍姆的心跳動得像鐵鎚在敲打一樣。

pp. 40–41

Stop & Think

• **How much land did Pahom need?** 帕霍姆需要多少土地？
  ⇨ He needed six feet from his head to his heels. 他從頭到腳只需要六呎地。

CHECK UP

1 The sun set at the bottom of the hill faster than at the top.
2 The chief said that Pahom had gained much land.
3 Pahom's servant saw that he was dead.
4 Did the Devil win his contest with Pahom? (Yes)

1 山丘下的日落比山丘上的還快。
2 首領說帕霍姆得到很多土地。
3 帕霍姆的僕人看到他死了。
4 撒旦贏了帕霍姆嗎？（是）

A Christmas Carol

pp. 44–45

Stop & Think

• **How did people feel about Scrooge?** 大家對施顧己有什麼看法？

⇨ They avoided him. 他們躲著他。 / They didn't like him. 他們不喜歡他。

CHECK UP

1	Scrooge was a greedy man.	T
2	Scrooge and Marley still worked together.	F
3	Bob Cratchit was Scrooge's boss.	F

1 施顧己是一個貪心的人。
2 施顧己和馬里仍然一起工作。
3 鮑伯・克萊契是施顧己的老闆。

pp. 46–47

Stop & Think

• **What did Scrooge's nephew ask him to do?** 施顧己的外甥要他做什麼？

⇨ To go to Christmas dinner. 去吃聖誕晚餐。 /
To have dinner with his family. 跟他的家人一起吃晚餐。

• **What did Scrooge give Bob Cratchit for Christmas?** 聖誕節，施顧己給鮑伯・克萊契什麼東西？

⇨ He gave Bob Cratchit the day off. 他給鮑伯・克萊契一天的假。

CHECK UP

1 Scrooge said that Marley <u>died</u> seven years ago.
2 The men asked Scrooge to give them some <u>money</u>.
3 Scrooge paid Bob Cratchit his day's <u>wages</u> for Christmas.
4 Bob Cratchit promised to arrive <u>early</u> the day after Christmas.

1 施顧己說馬里七年前過世了。
2 那些男人要施顧己給他們一些錢。
3 施顧己付了一天薪水給鮑伯・克萊契過聖誕節。
4 鮑伯・克萊契答應聖誕節隔天早點上班。

pp. 48–49

Stop & Think

• **What went into Scrooge's room?** 什麼東西進到施顧己的房間？

⇨ Marley's ghost went into Scrooge's room. 馬里的鬼魂進到施顧己的房間。

CHECK UP

1 What kind of noise did Scrooge hear? (b)
   a. a screaming man   **b.** a dragging chain   **c.** a laughing woman

2 What could Marley not do? (a)
   a. rest   **b.** speak   **c.** move

1 施顧己聽到什麼聲響？
   a. 男人的尖叫聲   **b.** 鎖鍊拖行的聲音   **c.** 女人的笑聲
2 馬里不能做什麼？
   a. 休息   **b.** 說話   **c.** 移動

---

pp. 50−51

Stop & Think

- **How many ghosts will visit Scrooge?** 多少鬼魂會來拜訪施顧己。
  ⇨ Three ghosts will visit him. 三個鬼魂會來拜訪他。

- **What was the first ghost to visit Scrooge?** 第一個來拜訪施顧己的鬼魂是什麼？
  ⇨ The first ghost was the Ghost of Christmas Past. 第一個鬼魂是過去聖誕節的鬼魂。

CHECK UP

1 Marley said that Scrooge's chain was longer than his own.
2 The first ghost was going to come at one in the morning.
3 The first ghost looked like an old man.

1 馬里說施顧己的鎖鍊比自己的還長。
2 第一個鬼魂會在凌晨一點來。
3 第一個鬼魂看起來像一個老頭。

---

pp. 52−53

Stop & Think

- **What time of year did the ghost take Scrooge to?** 鬼魂帶施顧己到一年當中的什麼時候？
  ⇨ The ghost took Scrooge to Christmastime. 鬼魂帶施顧己到聖誕節期。

CHECK UP

1 Scrooge and the ghost   **a.** were not real.
2 The images Scrooge saw   **b.** in an office for Mr. Fezziwig.
3 Scrooge once worked   **c.** passed through the wall together.

1 施顧己和鬼魂一起穿牆。
2 施顧己看到的畫面不是真的。
3 施顧己曾經在費茲威先生的辦公室裡工作過。

---

pp. 54−55

Stop & Think

- **Who did Scrooge see with himself?** 施顧己看到誰跟他在一起？
  ⇨ He saw his old girlfriend. 他看到他以前的女朋友。

- **What did Scrooge tell the ghost?** 施顧己跟鬼魂說什麼？
  ⇨ Scrooge told the ghost to leave him. 施顧己請鬼魂放過他。

1 Scrooge never had a girlfriend in his entire life.   <u>F</u>
2 Scrooge loved money more than people.   <u>T</u>
3 The beautiful woman Scrooge saw was his mother.   <u>F</u>
4 Scrooge asked the ghost to show him some more scenes.   <u>F</u>

1 施顧己這輩子從來沒交過女朋友。
2 比起人，施顧己更愛錢。
3 施顧己看到的美麗女人是他媽媽。
4 施顧己請鬼魂讓他看更多場景。

pp. 56–57

Stop & Think

• **Who was the second ghost?** 第二個鬼魂是誰？
⇨ It was the Ghost of Christmas Present. 是現在聖誕節的鬼魂。

• **What did Bob Cratchit's family have to eat?** 鮑伯・克萊契家人有什麼可以吃？
⇨ They had a goose, some potatoes, and a small Christmas pudding.
他們只有一隻鵝，一些馬鈴薯，和一個小小的聖誕布丁。

CHECK UP

1 There was a <u>giant</u> sitting in the middle of Scrooge's living room.
2 The ghost told Scrooge to <u>touch</u> his robe.
3 <u>Tiny Tim</u> needed to use a crutch to walk.
4 The Cratchits had a simple meal, but they <u>enjoyed</u> it.

1 有一個巨人坐在施顧己客廳的正中央。
2 鬼魂叫施顧己摸他的袍子。
3 小提姆需要用枴杖走路。
4 克萊契一家吃了一頓很簡單的晚餐，但他們得很高興。

pp. 58–59

Stop & Think

• **Who did Bob Cratchit propose a toast to?** 鮑伯・克萊契提議為誰乾杯？
⇨ He proposed a toast to Scrooge. 他提議為施顧己乾杯。

CHECK UP

1 How did Mrs. Cratchit feel about drinking to Scrooge? (c)
   a. pleased   **b.** nervous   **c.** unhappy

1 克萊契太太覺得為施顧己乾杯怎麼樣？
   a. 高興   **b.** 緊張   **c.** 不高興

pp. 60–61

Stop & Think

• **Who was the third ghost?** 第三個鬼魂是誰？
⇨ It was the Ghost of Christmas Yet to Come. 是未來聖誕節的鬼魂。

1 Fred wanted Scrooge to give Bob Cratchit more money.
2 The third ghost wore black clothes.
3 The third ghost said nothing.
4 Were the people the ghost showed Scrooge talking about a marriage? (No)

1 佛萊德希望施顧己給鮑伯・克萊契更多錢。
2 第三個鬼魂穿黑衣服。
3 第三個鬼魂一語不發。
4 鬼魂給施顧己看的人在談論一個婚禮？（不）

pp. 62–63

Stop & Think

• **Where did the three people get the items they were selling?** 這三個人是從哪裡拿到他們要賣的東西？
   ⇨ They got them from the dead man's house. 他們從死人的家裡拿的。

CHECK UP

1 The shopkeeper asked the women ————— a. what they had to sell.
2 One woman was selling   b. bed curtains and blankets.
3 The ghost pointed at   c. a dead body covered by a sheet.

1 店主問女人，她們有什麼要賣。
2 一個女人在賣床簾和毯子。
3 鬼魂指著一具蓋著床單的死屍。

pp. 64–65

Stop & Think

• **Why was the Cratchit family sad?** 為什麼克萊契一家人很傷心？
   ⇨ Tiny Tim died. 小提姆死了。

CHECK UP

1 The Ghost of Christmas Yet to Come took Scrooge to a churchyard.   T
2 Scrooge wanted to know who the dead man was.   T
3 The name on the grave was Scrooge's.   T

1 未來聖誕節的鬼魂帶施顧己去教堂的墓地。
2 施顧己想知道那死人是誰。
3 墳墓刻了施顧己的名字。

pp. 66–67

Stop & Think

• **What did Scrooge tell the boy to do?** 施顧己叫男孩做什麼？
   ⇨ Go to the butcher's shop and bring the butcher back. 去肉販的店，把肉販帶來。

1 Scrooge realized that all three ghosts had visited him in <u>one night</u>.
2 Scrooge sent <u>the goose</u> to Bob Cratchit's house.
3 Scrooge went to his nephew's house to <u>have dinner</u>.

1 施顧己知道三個鬼魂的來訪只發生於一夜之內。
2 施顧己把鵝送到鮑伯・克萊契的家。
3 施顧己到外甥家吃晚餐。

pp. 68–69

Stop & Think

• **What did Scrooge tell Bob Cratchit he was going to do?**
施顧己跟鮑伯・克萊契說他要做什麼？

⇨ Scrooge said that he would raise his salary and assist his family.
施顧己說他要幫他加薪及幫助他的家庭。

• **How did Scrooge act toward Tiny Tim?** 施顧己怎麼對小提姆？

⇨ He became a second father to Tiny Tim. 他變成小提姆的第二個父親。

CHECK UP

1 What did Scrooge promise Bob Cratchit? (c)
 a. a bigger house   **b.** a healthy family   **c.** a higher salary

2 What kind of man did Scrooge become? (b)
 a. a greedy man   **b.** a good man   **c.** a silly man

1 施顧己答應鮑伯・克萊契什麼？
 a. 一棟更大的房子   **b.** 一個健康的家庭   **c.** 更高的薪水
2 施顧己變成什麼樣的人？
 a. 貪心的人   **b.** 好人   **c.** 傻瓜

Step 6

The Last Leaf

pp. 72–73

Stop & Think

• **What kind of people went to old Greenwich Village?** 什麼樣的人會去老格林威治村？
 ⇨ Art people went there. 藝術家會到那邊去。

• **What happened in the colony in November?** 十一月的時候藝術區發生了什麼事？
 ⇨ Many people caught pneumonia. 很多人得了肺炎。

1 There were "<u>places</u>" in Washington Square.
2 People went to old Greenwich Village looking for low <u>rents</u>.
3 Sue and <u>Johnsy</u> lived together.
4 Did many people get pneumonia in May? (No)

1 在華盛頓廣場有「街道」。
2 人們到老格林威治村尋找低廉的房子。
3 蘇和瓊西住在一起。
4 很多人在五月得了肺炎嗎？（不）

pp. 74–75

Stop & Think

• **What did the doctor say Johnsy needed to do?** 醫生說瓊西該怎麼做？
  ⇨ She needed to want to live. 她需要求生意志。

• **What did the doctor want Sue to do?** 醫生要蘇做什麼？
  ⇨ Get Johnsy to think of something valuable to her. 讓瓊西去想對她有意義的事。

CHECK UP

1 The doctor said Johnsy had one chance in ten to <u>live</u>.
2 <u>Medicine</u> is less effective when patients think about death.
3 Sue <u>cried</u> very hard after the doctor left.

1 醫生說瓊西有一成機會可以存活。
2 病人不想活的時候，藥效會減弱。
3 醫生走了以後，蘇哭得很傷心。

pp. 76–77

Stop & Think

• **What was Johnsy counting?** 瓊西在數什麼？
  ⇨ She was counting the leaves on the ivy vine. 她在數常春藤上的葉子。

CHECK UP

1 Johnsy was counting backward.   T
2 Johnsy said she would die when the last leaf fell.   T
3 Sue said Johnsy's chances of living were ten to one.   T

1 瓊西在倒數。
2 瓊西說最後一葉掉的時候，她也會死。
3 蘇說瓊西存活的機會有九成。

pp. 78–79

Stop & Think

• **What did Sue ask Johnsy to do?** 蘇要瓊西做什麼？
  ⇨ Close her eyes and not look out the window. 閉上眼，不要看窗外。

• **Who was Behrman?** 貝爾曼是誰？
  ⇨ He was a painter who lived downstairs from Sue and Johnsy. 他是住在蘇和瓊西樓下的畫家。

1 What did Johnsy ask Sue to do? (a)
   a. draw in another room   **b.** give her some broth   **c.** pull the shade down

2 What kind of an artist was Behrman? (c)
   a. a successful one   **b.** an average one   **c.** a failed one

1 瓊西要蘇做什麼？
   a. 到別的房間畫畫   **b.** 給她一點湯   **c.** 把窗簾拉下來
2 貝爾曼是什麼樣的畫家？
   a. 很成功的   **b.** 一般的   **c.** 失敗的

---

pp. 80–81

Stop & Think

• **What did Behrman drink _too much of_?** 貝爾曼喝了太多什麼？
  ⇨ He drank too much gin. 他喝了太多酒。

CHECK UP

1 Behrman worked as   **a.** in one corner of Berhman's den.
2 There was a blank canvas   **b.** pose as a model for Sue.
3 Behrman thought Johnsy's idea   **c.** a model for artists in the colony.
4 Behrman decided to   **d.** was silly.

1 貝爾曼在藝術區當畫家的模特兒。
2 在貝爾曼小房間的一個角落有一張空白的畫布。
3 貝爾曼認為瓊西的念頭很愚蠢。
4 貝爾曼決定為蘇當模特兒擺姿勢。

---

pp. 82–83

Stop & Think

• **What did Johnsy tell Sue to do when she woke up?** 瓊西醒了以後，要蘇做什麼？
  ⇨ She told Sue to pull up the shade. 她叫蘇把窗簾拉起來。

• **What did Johnsy and Sue see outside?** 瓊西和蘇看到外面有什麼？
  ⇨ They saw one ivy leaf against the wall. 他們看到牆上有一片常春藤葉。

CHECK UP

1 Sue and Behrman looked out the window at the ivy vine.
2 There was still one leaf left on the vine.
3 Johnsy thought the last leaf would fall during the night.
4 Was Johnsy ready to die? (Yes)

1 蘇和貝爾曼看著窗外的常春藤。
2 藤上還留著一片葉子。
3 瓊西認為最後一葉晚間就會掉落。
4 瓊西在等死嗎？（是）

pp. 84–85

Stop & Think

• What did Sue and Johnsy see the next morning? 隔天早上蘇和瓊西看到什麼？

⇨ The ivy leaf was still on the vine. 常春藤葉還在藤上。

CHECK UP

1 Johnsy looked at the last leaf for a long time.
2 Johnsy said it was wicked for her to want to die.
3 The doctor told Sue that Behrman had pneumonia.
4 The doctor said that Johnsy needed nutrition and care.

1 瓊西看著最後一葉看了很久。
2 瓊西說她一心求死很不應該。
3 醫生跟蘇說貝爾曼得了肺炎。
4 醫生說瓊西需要營養和照料。

pp. 86–87

Stop & Think

• What happened to Behrman? 貝爾曼怎麼了？

⇨ He died of pneumonia. 他死於肺炎。

CHECK UP

1 The janitor saw Behrman painting outside.   F
2 Behrman was found with his shoes and clothes soaking wet.   T
3 Behrman painted the last leaf.   T
4 The last leaf was Behrman's masterpiece.   T

1 工人看到貝爾曼在外面畫畫。
2 貝爾曼被發現的時候，他的鞋子、衣服全都濕透了。
3 貝爾曼畫了最後一葉。
4 最後一葉是貝爾曼的傑作。

英文閱讀素養訓練課

Super Reading Story Training Book

經典文學故事

作　　　者	Michael A. Putlack & e-Creative Contents
譯　　　者	陳怡靜／彭尊聖
校　　　對	黃詩韻
編　　　輯	陳怡靜
封 面 設 計	林書玉
內 文 排 版	郭瀞暄／執筆者
製 程 管 理	洪巧玲
出 版 者	寂天文化事業股份有限公司
發 行 人	黃朝萍
電　　　話	+886-(0)2-2365-9739
傳　　　真	+886-(0)2-2365-9835
網　　　址	www.icosmos.com.tw
讀 者 服 務	onlineservice@icosmos.com.tw
出 版 日 期	2022 年 05 月 初版一刷（寂天雲隨身聽 APP 版）

英文閱讀素養訓練課：經典文學故事（寂天雲隨身聽
APP版） / Michael A. Putlack, e-Creative Contents著；
陳怡靜、彭尊聖譯. -- 初版. -- [臺北市]：
寂天文化, 2022.05-印刷
　　冊；　公分
ISBN 978-626-300-128-2 (16K平裝)

1.CST: 英語 2.CST: 讀本

805.18　　　　　　　　　　　　　111005830

劃 撥 帳 號	1998620-0 寂天文化事業股份有限公司
	訂購金額 600（含）元以上郵資免費
	訂購金額 600 元以下者，請外加郵資 65 元
	【若有破損，請寄回更換，謝謝】